TARNISHED GOLD

What Reviewers Say About Ann Aptaker's Work

"This is a brilliantly written book which makes every lover of historical fiction swoon with bliss. And for all who like to have a glimpse back into what organized crime was like in NYC after WW II and living as a dyke, this is an illuminating read. Ann Aptaker easily takes us back in time to NYC of 1949 with dirty cops, gunslinging gangsters, beautiful ladies and impressive cars. Kudos to Ann Aptaker for this gem of a book which will delight lovers of historical fiction and noir."—*Curve Magazine*

"An author can make a time and place come alive and this was certainly true of Ann Aptaker's book *Criminal Gold*. We're plunged into the heart of 1940s criminal New York with a thrilling tale of murder and deception. …Aptaker has set herself up for a cracking series not only because of the character of Cantor Gold but for choosing a period of time that is fascinating to read about." —*Crimepieces.com*

"…a noir novel with a sexual twist. I did not find the novel to be so much about crime as it was about being oneself. Cantor insists on living openly; she is a free woman because she has taken her freedom and this is much unlike those of us who had to fight to live openly as we do. …This is author Aptaker's first novel and if this is an indication of what she can do, we need to welcome her to the canon of gay literature."—*Reviews by Amos Lassen*

Visit us at www.boldstrokesbooks.com

By the Author

Criminal Gold

Tarnished Gold

TARNISHED GOLD

by

Ann Aptaker

2015

Credits
Editor: Ruth Sternglantz
Production Design: Susan Ramundo
Cover Design By Sheri (graphicartist2020@hotmail.com)

Acknowledgments

Thank you to everyone at Bold Strokes Books for their support, and especially to my editor, Ruth Sternglantz, for her patience with me, her willingness to understand my vision and tolerate my orneriness.

Special thanks to my sister Yren Berry, who's smarter and more talented than I am, and who stands by me in all things.

Dedication

The memory lingers on.

Chapter One

On a freighter sailing into New York Harbor, 1950

The first killer to come at me tonight is the wind. The cold October wind smacks me in the face, claws at my flesh right through my raincoat, and tries to toss me overboard as I swing myself over the ship's rail and down the rope ladder. The ladder's wild in the wind, shimmying like a hopped-up stripper, slamming me against the hull of the freighter, a French bucket hauling a cargo of sweet perfumes and smelly cheeses. I'm not the type of dame who wears perfume, though I'm happy to wallow in the scented skin of the ladies in my life. Too bad the freighter's only carrying the dollar-ninety-eight a bottle variety, the kind whose aroma lingers in a headache; not worth pilfering any bottles to give to the ladies.

If I want to live long enough to enjoy a classier variety of perfumed nights, I'd better get a better handle on this rope ladder. The wind wants to smash me to pieces as I climb down the bone-twisting fifty-foot descent to Red Drogan's tugboat. And now there's a second killer snapping at my ankles: spray from the churning river soaks the rope, makes it slippery. I might as well be trying to get a foothold on slithering eels. Even my crepe-soled shoes can't always hold the rungs. My heart's lurching up my throat and my stomach nearly plummets out my ass as I'm thrown on a wild slide down the rope ladder, a death ride that burns my palms until my hands finally—finally!—get a grip.

My heart and my stomach crawl back to where they belong.

After a few deep breaths, trying not to choke on the sea spray flying down my throat, steadying myself as best I can, I climb down the rungs again only to face one more killer, the one waiting for me at the bottom of the rope ladder, the killer who wants to crush me to death. If I misjudge the jump to Drogan's tug, I'll land between the tug and the freighter, crushed to a pulp and bony splinters.

This is a helluva way to slip a priceless piece of art through New York Harbor, but I'm in a dangerous racket, a smuggler of fine art and other treasure. The harbor is the front door to my business, and business is booming. The American engine's gone into overdrive since the Second World War ended five years ago, cranking out prosperity as fast as the mint can print money. Everyone's rushing to spend their new dough on their share of the American Dream: a house with a patch of lawn in front, a barbecue grill in the backyard, and a living room tricked out with matching furniture and a console television set.

But some people have more highfalutin dreams. They use their new dough to buy class, a ticket out of low-rentsville and into high society. Nothing says you're a class act more than old art on your new walls. And if the art you crave isn't always available, that's where I come in. In exchange for swinging in the wind on nights like this to satisfy the cravings of private collectors and curators at big museums, I earn fistfuls of cash, the kind it takes to have my silk suits custom tailored, buy a new car every year, and enjoy the amusements of my outlaw life.

Sure, my racket's a crime, but in the sneering eyes of the Law my *life* is a crime just because I romance women. I can't figure why the Law even gives a damn, but it gives enough of a damn to want to throw people like me in jail for it.

So if the Law's got nothing better to do than be a bedroom bully, then the hell with 'em. I'll go right on romancing pretty women and earning my dough by sticking my finger in the Law's eye, something I've been doing since I was a rough kid growing up in Coney Island, though if I'm careless in the next few seconds, get chewed up by the wind, and miss the jump to Drogan's tug, there won't be enough of me left to enjoy women or money or anything else.

It's only a few feet now from the bottom of the rope ladder to the deck of the tug, but the river is making a grab for my ankles and the wind won't let go of me, hurls me in all the wrong directions. Drogan's keeping the prow of his tug against the starboard hip of the freighter, but it's tough for me to figure the angle of my jump because the freighter's heaving on the swells of the river while the half dozen other tugs working the ship turn her into its berth. Drogan's tug is rolling like a rubber ducky in a splash pool. If I come in too sharp or too shallow, I'll meet that third killer, the one whose sea-drooling mouth is waiting to crush me.

Dammit! The wind is really piling it on now, whipping me high over the river and blowing black smoke in my face from the tug's funnel. The smoke stings my eyes, blurs my vision. I can barely see the tug's deck, and glare off the river blots my view of the deck even more. The glare's from a light, a light I'm not happy about. It's the mast light of a cop cruiser.

Why the hell are the harbor police here now? Tonight's operation's been set up tight as a drum, the freighter's captain and any other wagging tongues paid into silence. Maybe the cops are just cruising by. Maybe they want some perfume for their wives. Maybe they don't even see the speck that's me swinging against this huge freighter.

I can't linger in this wind any longer. I'm jangling on the swaying ladder like a skeleton, my teeth rattling from the cold and my bones vibrating from the grinding engines of the freighter, but I've got to make the jump!

❖

"*Aaayyah!*" explodes from my throat when the sting of ice-cold water evidently rouses me from the dead.

I hear what sounds like splintering wood, then realize its Drogan's familiar voice. "You missed," he says, standing over me with a bucket, grinning, which is not a soothing sight. Sure, Drogan's got all his teeth, but they're on a face that could be mistaken for tree bark. And that croaky voice of his coming through that brittle grin doesn't do anything to smooth the impression. "Caught your foot on the gunwale and went tumblin' over yourself on the deck," he says. "Landed headfirst. Even caught your chin on the capstan along the way. You're a helluva sight." Now he's laughing, a raw cackle that could strip the scales from fish. "The suave act Cantor Gold with dirty duds an' a bloody chin!"

My hand goes to the burning pain on my chin. Yeah, it's slick with blood. The cut's not big but the pain feels deep. It'll leave a scar. Well, it'll have company. I've got quite a collection of souvenirs, heartwarming reminders of my wrestling matches with the Grim Reaper.

Standing up is tough enough with my legs all banged up and my head spinning from my crash landing, but the roll of the tugboat on the choppy river makes it even tougher. Drogan finally gives me a hand, pulls me to my feet. "Get inside the cabin," he says. "Clean yourself up and take care of that chin. First-aid kit's where it always is."

"That cop cruiser," I say. "They spot us?"

"I doubt it. And anyways, soon as you was on deck, I wove around through the other boats and made like I was pushin' the freighter. Then I took off and lost 'em for good."

"I suppose the other tugmen won't talk."

"Course not."

"And you brought the stuff I wanted from my apartment?"

"Yeah. The briefcase, a pack of smokes, blue suit and the trimmin's." When Drogan's sure I won't topple over from my bruises, he climbs back up into the wheelhouse. Somebody's got to drive this tub.

It feels good to get out of the wet wind and into the cabin where it's warm and dry. I find the pack of Chesterfields among the stuff Drogan brought from my apartment, light up a smoke, and take a deep drag to smooth out my knotted innards and tangled joints.

Drogan must've done his bob and weave separating us from the freighter while I was sleeping off my crash landing on the deck, and now we're steaming up the East River to the next rendezvous spot in tonight's job.

The object of that job is in a small folio sewn into the lining of my raincoat. I'm anxious to have a look at it, check its condition before I deliver it to the client tonight, but in my present state I might drip blood on it or smear it with my grimy hands. Checking the goods will have to wait until I've cleaned my bloodied chin, washed the sea and the soot off the rest of me, and changed out of my dirty clothes and into my dark blue pinstripe double-breasted silk suit and trimmin's, as Drogan called them: a pale yellow shirt with ruby cabochon cufflinks, blue and gray striped tie with red highlights, pale yellow socks, oxblood cordovan wing tips, and a dark green wool overcoat and brown tweed cap I'll put on when I go ashore. By the time I finish off with a red silk pocket handkerchief and more or less comb my hair—a short brown mop that's as untamable as I am—I feel tip-top again, even laugh a little about Drogan tagging me a suave act, then I settle down to business and slice open the seam of the raincoat with my pocket knife.

Some people's mouths water when they get excited about something. Other people's hearts beat faster. But my breathing slows and quiets even though I'm excited as a little kid unwrapping a birthday present when I pull the folio from the lining of the raincoat and unwrap the rubber sheathing protecting it against the damp. It's always like this when I come to this part of the job; next to the thrill of cash crossing my palm, this is my favorite part of my racket, when it's just me and a knockout work of art.

I'm a dyed-in-the-wool city dog. All the nature I need is in Central Park. But what I'm looking at when I open the folio—a small sixteenth-century watercolor of plants and grasses in a marshy patch—takes my breath away. It's the work of the

German Renaissance master Albrecht Dürer, a guy better known for nightmarish etchings of Death, engravings of melancholy Philosophy, and scary pictures of the Apocalypse. But if ecstasy has a hidden soul, Dürer found it and laid it bare in this little clump of everyday weeds. It's not just his skill with a brush that gets me, the drawing so precise that all the greenery in the picture has been identified by people who know their grass. No, what really gets to me is what's in the bend and sway of these marshy weeds. Dürer got inside their ecstasy, inside their pure pleasure in being alive.

The history of this little watercolor, though, is a different story. Its life has been more knock-around than pleasurable, surviving nearly four hundred and fifty years of royal murders, dynastic overthrows, political treachery, and religious wars. It's been sold for cash, stolen for greed, kept hostage for revenge, and passed hand to hand through centuries of scholars and rogues. Its most recent adventure—at least, before its wild ride out of Europe with me— was when it was looted by the Nazis back in 1938, stolen from the Jacobson family of Berlin by Hermann Goering's jackboots. But its wanderings might finally be coming to an end. Tonight's job is one of those rare times in my line of work when I'll be delivering stolen goods back to the rightful owner; well, the most recent rightful owner, in any case, the widow Mrs. Hannah Jacobson.

Sure, the justice in tonight's job feels great, but I don't kid myself. I'm no saint. I'm not in the business of rescuing works of art for the betterment of humanity. I don't worship motherhood or babies either. I don't think much of the American Dream. And I don't risk my life for free.

❖

First it was wind and water. Now it's filth and fumes. I may be the master of a high-class racket, but I pay for it by risking my life and having my senses molested.

This latest sensory irritant, an assault of muck, noise, and stink, is courtesy of Newtown Creek, a meandering sludge separating the boroughs of Brooklyn and Queens. Sooty factories and gassy refineries glowing red along its banks spew out everything from chemicals to copper to fertilizer, and even the fat of butchered animals, turning the creek into a putrid waterway slimy as a swamp and smelly as a toilet. Barges lumber along carrying factory goods and waste, a chunk of it human. Newtown Creek's dark water is one of the New York Mob's favorite dumping sites. Sometimes the water-bloated corpses float to the surface, but not often. Cement boots don't float.

But this dingy wasteland and its miserable slop of water has its own charm: a terrific view of the city. Back across the East River, Manhattan Island rises into the night sky like an electric dream, its millions of lights challenging the stars. It's no contest. The city wins. The city always wins because it's powered by money and dreams. Nothing burns brighter than money or hotter than dreams.

But Drogan didn't ferry me into Newtown Creek for the view. I'm here for a rendezvous with the beautiful Rosie Bliss, a cabbie with daredevil driving skills and a taste for my outlaw life. Her talents and tastes make Rosie the perfect driver for my racket: reliable on the pickup, fast on the getaway. She also has a fondness for the knifelike scar above my lip, which she likes to explore regularly, and while she's at it, she explores the rest of me. I like exploring Rosie, too. She has a number of scenic peaks and valleys where I enjoy spending time.

Our rendezvous tonight is in a backwater along the last branch of the creek. Assuming Rosie's on time—and she always is; Rosie never lets me down—she's already parked her cab on the abandoned pier. Rosie drives a big Checker that looks like every other Checker Cab in New York, which is exactly why I'll be traveling in the backseat when Rosie drives me to Hannah Jacobson's apartment. I'd rather not use my own car when I carry goods. The cops know my Buick and if they're in the mood they'll sure as hell pull me over. If I'm caught holding goods, the Law will throw me into the women's joint up in Bedford Hills, and I'm not a fan of long-term confinement no matter how many dames are around to keep me company—well, not yet, anyway. It might be okay in my golden years, my needs seen to by a few hundred pretty little murderesses and thieves.

But tonight I'm counting on the cops passing me by. I'll be riding in one of thousands of cabs in New York. Cops don't pay attention to a cab with a passenger in the darkened backseat. They won't know I'm on the move.

We're coming up on the pier. Drogan's cut his lamps and his mast light. He's running slow, dark, and quiet as he lines up the tug against the old wharf. Rosie's cab is barely visible in the shadows, her headlights off and the engine idling. Only the windshield reflects a stray glow of furnace fire from the copper refinery farther down the creek.

I put on my overcoat and cap, pick up the briefcase where I stowed the folio, and walk out onto the deck, ready to disembark the tug. Tonight's work is almost done. A wad of cash is almost in my hands.

Before I step off the tug, I nod up to Drogan in the wheelhouse. He nods back at me. Our nods confirm our next moves. He'll pilot the tug to an even more out-of-the-way spot, maybe even out to sea, and sink my raincoat and my other clothes where they'll never be found. Tomorrow morning, I'll meet him at his berth and give him his cut of tonight's payoff.

Drogan shoves off as soon as I'm on the pier. There's nobody around now except Rosie, but I step lightly anyway. Call it a habit of my trade. In just a few strides I'm at Rosie's cab and getting into the backseat.

That trace of fiery glow from the copper refinery drifts into the cab, highlights Rosie's blond hair, turns it into an aura of pink mist. The light slides along her cheek as she looks over her shoulder to greet me. Even in this thin light, Rosie is a peaches-and-cream temptation whipped up by the Heavenly Angels of Lust. She says, "Welcome home. I missed you. What's that?" in a whisper as erotic as it is tender.

"What's what? My briefcase? You know the one. I've put the goods in it." The words are barely out of my mouth before Rosie's out of the cab and sliding next to me in the backseat.

"No," she says, "not that. *This*." She takes my chin between her fingers and says, "Jesus, Cantor, what the hell was it this time?" scolding me like a schoolmarm chastising her most troublesome child. "You gambled with your life again just for the thrill of it? Or did you step in front of some guy's brass knuckles?"

"The wind pimped me out to the capstan on Drogan's tug. Damn thing was rough trade."

"Sure, go ahead, make jokes, but that gash looks nasty."

"I thought I cleaned all the blood off."

"Yeah, well, looks like you got most of it, but even in this lousy light that gash is red as a stop sign. You're gonna have a new scar."

"In that case," I say, sliding my arm around her waist and pulling her to me—even in her cabbie's rough duds of jacket, work shirt, and slacks, Rosie's body is all curves and softness, inviting as a favorite pillow—"I hope you'll like playing with the new scar as much as you like fooling around with the old ones."

Supple and warm against me, she whispers, "Sure, Cantor, you know I—" But she stops saying what she knows I don't want her to say and does what she knows I want her to do. Her kiss goes down better than words. She's delicious, a perfect welcome-home treat.

I wouldn't mind taking the kiss further, all the way to fucking her right here in the backseat of the cab, but there's a bundle of cash calling me across the river. So all I do is mumble between tastes of Rosie's juice. "Listen, I told Mrs. Jacobson…I'd be at her place…before ten o'clock. I'll finish up tonight's business as quick as I can, then how about you and I go to my place, open a bottle of scotch—"

"Then you'll open me."

"Yeah…" Welcome home.

CHAPTER TWO

Drive out of the Midtown Tunnel and Manhattan hits you like an explosion. Light comes straight at you, then rushes skyward, lifted on the tumult of the city's noise. But explosions have fissures of darkness, too, and the explosion that's New York has plenty of darkness coiled inside its bursting light.

I know something about those dark fissures. Some of them I know intimately, enjoy the sins and pleasures that lure me there. Some I know to stay clear of, where things happen that are none of my business. And some I've stumbled into and almost didn't make it out alive.

But the crimes and dangers inside the city's darkness are nothing compared to the horrors that Hannah Jacobson survived, an orgy of monsters with gluttonous appetites for torture and murder. After devouring millions, the monsters simply vomited them into mass graves, emptying their bellies to devour millions more.

The Dürer watercolor in the briefcase next to me in the backseat of Rosie's cab doesn't seem like much of a trophy for surviving the monsters' teeth and claws, but maybe having this small piece of her life back will give Mrs. J some comfort, a way to feel the breath of the family she lost to the ovens of the Nazi feeding frenzy.

Anyway, that's the feeling I got when she hired me to find the watercolor and recapture it. She'd been petitioning the US government and the Allies' art retrieval offices to seize and return her family's looted artwork, a first-rate collection of German masters from the Middle Ages through the nineteenth-century Romantics, but all she got was the usual bureaucratic runaround. Bureaucracies move as slow as clogged sewers, and Hannah Jacobson, a woman in her seventies, doesn't have time to wait for the crap to clear the pipes. So she asked a curator she'd been working with if there was another way to restore her family's artwork, and the curator, a discreet dame I've done business with, introduced Mrs. Jacobson to me.

Compared to the criminals who murdered her family and savaged a continent, Mrs. J, a grandmotherly little woman with alert blue eyes and a comforting-as-chicken-soup smile, considers my smuggling racket a reasonable customer-service operation. After we were introduced, and after she looked me over and said I'd have fit right into the nightlife of pre-war Berlin, she wasted no time in hiring me to retrieve her family's collection piece by piece and by any means necessary. We see eye to eye on that last point.

I'm looking forward to making the old lady happy as Rosie turns the corner onto West End Avenue and parks in front of Mrs. J's building. It's a good-looking spot built during the apartment house boom of the '20s. An awning running all the way to the curb introduces twenty-two stories of limestone and light-colored brick gussied up to resemble palaces in Europe where a lot of New York's teeming masses originally came from. Not the palaces; just Europe.

Rosie's in a teasing mood. After she kills the engine, she says, "Don't be long," in a way that's equal parts invitation and scolding.

"Keep your lovely fires burning," I say. "I'll be back before you know it."

"Oh, I'll know it," she says, her voice a carnal moan and a wise laugh in equal measure. Perfect Rosie.

Like a kid lured by available candy, I reach across the front seat to stroke her a little bit right now, put some of her luscious warmth in my hand, but the building's doorman is already approaching the cab. I haven't seen this guy before, but then again, I've only been here one other time, during the day shift. Anyway, this guy's a short-stack with a pinched face, an elf in a green uniform. The doorman-elf opens the cab before my fingers can reach anything more than the shoulder of Rosie's jacket.

My quick thrill washed up, I get out of the cab. The doorman asks, "Are you expected?" His greeting is friendly enough, but as he gets a better look at me, his face folds up like he's suddenly caught a bad smell. He examines me up and down, making sure I really am what he thinks I am: an oddity he's heard about but never expected he'd see a real live one. And judging by his awkward fascination with the scars on my face and the gash on my chin, I guess he figures I'm gutter trade to boot.

At times like this I like to pull out my slickest smile. It amuses me, and this uniformed elf doesn't look like the kind who'll ram his fist in my nose, so I let my words ooze through my smile. "Kindly tell Mrs. Hannah Jacobson that Cantor Gold is here."

The guy walks ahead of me to the building, relieved of the temptation to either stare or sneer. As he picks up the intercom at the front entrance, I walk past him and into the lobby. I'm halfway to the elevator when I hear him say with that oily friendliness of someone angling to be remembered with a big tip at Christmastime, "Yes, of course, Mrs. Jacobson. I'll send her right up."

By the time I step into the elevator, my grin's not slick anymore. It's just big and wide and it sure feels good and it's not meant for anyone's enjoyment but mine.

❖

The floral carpeting along the twelfth-floor hallway is the extra-thick variety that doesn't just muffle your footsteps, it swallows them. A gorilla in hobnail boots could be stomping to your door and you'd never hear it.

It's nearly ten o'clock when I press the door buzzer at apartment 12A. I hope I haven't stomped all over old lady Jacobson's bedtime.

But when the door opens, she greets me with that comforting smile of hers, as if she has a nice pot of soup simmering in the kitchen. That Home Sweet Home aura glows from the flush of her face, pinkish from the light against her fluffy salmon-colored robe.

"Ah, Cantor. Do come in," she says. Her Old World accent makes my name sound swanky, like it has lineage, makes me glad I'm tricked out in one of my best suits.

As I step into the vestibule, she asks, "May I take your coat and cap?" With Rosie waiting downstairs I wasn't planning on lingering, but my gut's telling me that doing fast business would be a vulgar breach of the old dear's etiquette, so I take my coat and cap off and let her put them in the closet. When she's done, she motions me into the living room.

I don't know much about Mrs. Jacobson, about how she grew up or what her life was like before Hitler gutted it, but somewhere along the line she soaked up a lot of dignity and the know-how to spread it around. Most of my other clients would be grabbing for the goods by now, quick to pay me off and happy to be rid of the likes of me until their next greedy need of my services. But Hannah Jacobson hasn't said a word about the briefcase I'm carrying and what we both know is in it.

I know she's excited about it. I see it in the glint in her eyes, a flicker of desire she's too well mannered to flaunt. As she leads me to the living room, her robe wrapped around her like a cozy blanket, she's not a client preparing to do business; she's a gracious hostess seeing to the comfort of her guest.

Her living room is as comforting and gracious as she is but there's nothing Old World about it. There's nothing especially up to date about it either, though it has the pretty colors of Central Park in springtime. There's a sofa upholstered in pale green damask, matching green damask chairs, and simple but good quality mahogany furniture whose polished surfaces reflect soft pools of light from table lamps around the room. For a woman of cultured taste, there's a surprising absence of art on the pale blue walls, just a few unimportant but otherwise cheerful landscape and floral prints in carved wood frames, all of it looking like they're just taking up space. Most of the wall space is bare, waiting.

"Please, you will sit down, Cantor?" She motions me to one end of the sofa while she seats herself at the other. Lamps on side tables provide good light for viewing the watercolor, which I'm anxious to take from the briefcase and conclude the night's business. But I guess the lamps also throw light on me, because Mrs. J is suddenly paying a lot of attention to my face. She lifts my chin with her fingers, which are stronger than I'd expect and give off a motherly scent of cold cream. "You have been injured," she says. "I hope I haven't caused you—"

I interrupt her by carefully sliding her hand from my chin, treating her hand as something precious: the sleeve of her robe had slid back when she reached for me, the lamplight revealing six jagged numerals tattooed on her arm, numbers that brand Hannah Jacobson as a survivor of the Auschwitz death camp. Those numbers kick aside any possibility that I'd allow this woman who survived hell, to blame herself for my scraped face or for anything, ever, at all. "You haven't caused me a thing I didn't earn," I say. "Cuts and bruises and getting swatted around are the currency of my life."

Nobody's ever looked at me the way Mrs. J is looking at me, as if seeing inside me and finding whatever human feeling survives the brutality that stalks me. No one has ever looked at me with so much pain, or with so much encouragement, the latter riding on a small smile that quivers at the corners, as if the smile's fighting to keep life's threats from breaking through.

I lay her hand back in her lap, let the sleeve of her robe slide along her arm and cover the grotesque arithmetic on her flesh. "C'mon," I say, lightening the mood as I open the briefcase, "you've waited long enough for this. Don't you want to see your prize?"

The wise eyes that shared a survivor's secret with me a moment ago now crinkle with an anticipation that's waited too long and suffered too much. As much as Hannah Jacobson wants this beautiful piece of her life back, she knows it will bring memories: warm memories of love and family, and wretched memories of their torture and death.

Her hands are clenched in her lap, her face has gone stiff, a shield protecting her from unbearably painful thoughts, as I take the folio out of the briefcase and open it. And then a miracle happens, a miracle that a great work of art has the power to pull off. It can heal the wounds of evil. It can drain fear and replace it with joy. It can make Hannah Jacobson smile.

"*Ach, ja…*" comes whispered in the German of her old life, words she utters as if through the memory of a lost dream. "*Ja,* this…this is the right one. This is the one that will start to build again my Theo's legacy. He so loved this picture."

"Theo?"

"My husband, Theodor. The collection of pictures, it was his. And mine, too, yes, but it was Theo's vision, it was his passion. He was a true collector, you understand, a man in love with the great drama of German art. But he loved this little Dürer watercolor more than all the others, more than all the big, important paintings with their religious scenes and their battles. He loved this watercolor because it celebrates *life*. Yes? You can see it, Cantor? You see the life in these stems and leaves?" Her excitement is warm as the sun. I could swear it's actually nourishing those stems and leaves. "Oh, how my Theo loved life!" she says. "He knew such joy in his days, in his work, but especially in his family, in our dear children…" She stumbles now, tripped up by the horror of children murdered, but she keeps staring at the watercolor, sees something in it, and is finally able to speak again—"Gisela, Artur"—whispering their names. "You know, I was a very lucky woman, Cantor. My husband loved me very much."

"He sounds like a wise man."

"Wise? Well, you might say love is a kind of wisdom, yes. Have you ever been in love, Cantor?"

Her question comes at me through a romantic, nostalgia-sweet smile that might as well be a fanged leer taking a bite out of my heart, or what's left of my heart. It's been chewed up bit by bit since that March night two years ago when Sophie disappeared. Sophie de la Luna y Sol…the love of my life…the woman I might've given up my outlaw ways for, if she'd asked me to. But she was snagged right off the street, fell into one of the city's dark fissures, one I've never found. But I keep looking, and in the meantime the pulpy little slug that's left of my heart waits for her. No one else will ever have it.

I'm slowly aware of warmth on my right hand. It's Mrs. Jacobson's hand on mine, and she's talking to me. "I am sorry, Cantor. I did not mean to pry. Please, let me offer you a coffee, or perhaps some tea?"

"What? Oh no, I—thanks, but I really can't stay." I feel like a heel telling her that, but lingering here suddenly has booby traps I didn't count on.

"Of course," she says with the dignity of her instinctive kindness. "Well then, let me pay you and conclude our business. You have certainly earned it. I am very grateful to you, Cantor." She reaches into a pocket of her robe and slides out a thick envelope. "Ten thousand dollars, yes? As we agreed?" Her sleeve has slipped a little again, revealing the last digits of those grisly numbers seared into her flesh.

And then I hear myself saying something unbelievable, something so wacko that if Rosie or Drogan or anyone else in my racket heard me say it they'd cart me off to the loony bin. "I can't take your money."

Mrs. J's caught me looking at her arm because she's suddenly lifting my chin with a no-nonsense push, forcing me to face her. "Of course you will take this money," she says. "We have made a contract that must be honored. I understand that finding the picture and bringing it here must have cost you considerable expense. And I also understand—understand too well, Cantor—that you need money to live in the dignity you are entitled to. Money is part of your armor, yes?" She glances at my expensively tailored suit, then back at me. "It is your armor against a world that wants you demeaned, imprisoned, or dead."

This old woman is teaching me a thing or two about spirit. My hand seems to take the envelope of cash and slide it into my inside pocket not by my will but by Mrs. Jacobson's.

I say, "But it takes money for you to live, too. New York is an expensive town."

"Yes, it is, but I have what I need. And you are right, my husband was a wise man. Before the Nazis stole his money and his business, he was wise enough to invest in my younger brother's business here in America. My brother was a professor of chemistry in Berlin and then in New York. Dr. Marcus Stern. Maybe you've heard of him?"

"I don't keep up much with the academic crowd."

"I see. Well, Marcus was invited to America to give a program of lectures at one of your universities here in New York. That was in 1930. But when Hitler and his hooligans started making serious trouble in Germany, the university let Marcus stay. They gave him sanctuary and a teaching position. It is why he escaped the Nazis." Her relief at her brother's escape and her pride in his American success are real, but there's a hint of resentment under it, resentment that he lived to start a new life while her husband and children were tortured and killed. But she catches herself, and with a small sad but restorative smile, she continues. "So after his classes at the university during the day, at night he developed a formula for one of those new plastics all the industrial men are excited about. He made a fortune from his formula, and he built a good business. He married, and they have a child, a daughter who's a teenager now. It was Marcus who brought me here after the War. And he kept track of the money that would have been Theo's. Marcus signed my husband's stock in the business and his share of the profits over to me. So you see, Cantor? You needn't worry. I am not a millionaire but I will be fine." She pinches my cheek and adds with a laugh, "And I will be a good customer!"

"You will be a treasured customer."

"Thank you. Please, are you sure you won't stay for a coffee?"

"No, someone's waiting."

"Ah, yes, of course. For me, it is time to relax, but for you the night is young." She rises from the sofa with the dignity of an aristocrat and the good cheer of an imp and leads me back to the vestibule where she takes my coat and cap from the closet. "Thank you, Cantor. You've returned my husband's joy to me. You have done something very important. And now, good night."

❖

Rosie's body, supple and warm in my bed, is delicious as fruit in summer. I could spend the rest of the night letting my mouth roam around her breasts, flicking her nipples with my tongue, biting and sucking and coaxing them, but my need to take her again is too powerful, too urgent. Lifting myself, I spread her knees, position my equipment. She takes me in.

My moans mingle with Rosie's. My back arches, my breath rolls through me and out of my mouth in a growl, loud and raspy, grating and insistent, over and over again in a rhythm that's greedy with need but a noise now out of sync with my body because it's not the rasp of my breath but the unrelenting noise of the buzzer at my apartment door.

"Just a...! Just a damn...! *Jee-zuss* fucking Christ!" roars out of me because the door buzzer doesn't stop, its noise an invader that thrusts itself between me and Rosie and pushes us apart. I almost fall off the bed but manage to land on my feet.

I grab my robe and start to storm out of the bedroom with all the grace of an angry gorilla, but Rosie calls me back. "Cantor, you forgot something!" She's pointing at my groin.

Oh yeah, the equipment. I yank the equipment out of the harness, tie my robe, then stomp through the living room, nearly knocking over a table lamp before I turn the light on. All I want is to rip out that goddamn door buzzer, which is still buzzing.

Whoever's pounding that buzzer in the middle of the night, one a.m. by the credenza clock, they'd better be someone who really needs me, needs me so bad its life or death—

—or Sophie? *Sophie? Did you get away from whoever grabbed you? Oh God, Sophie, did you find your way home?*

My clenched hands fumble stupidly with the lock until I turn the doorknob and open the door, ready to pull Sophie to me, hold her, finally hold her again.

"Did we get you outta bed, Gold?" comes from the buzz-saw voice of a guy with a matching buzz-saw personality. His hat, complete with grease stains at the pinches, is pulled low on his ugly, skinny face. The voice, the personality, the hat, and the face belong to Lieutenant Norm Huber, homicide cop.

I don't know which I'll be able to calm first—my aching groin or my aching heart—and keep the pain hidden from Huber's nosy cop instincts. I try pushing the aches down with a deep breath which I hope passes for a groggy yawn and then mumble through the yawn-breath, "What are you doing here, Huber? I didn't kill anybody."

"Not saying you did. Can we come in?" It's not a question, just an offhand remark as Huber and another cop stroll into my apartment. The other cop is less skinny but just as dead eyed and dry faced. Night-shift homicide cops all get that look after a few years of ripe corpses and stale coffee.

The other cop, a guy I don't know, makes himself comfortable in one of my club chairs. The dark red upholstery makes his gray overcoat look even dingier and his misshapen fedora more misshapen. He looks around the room like he's never seen furniture or window drapes before. Then he looks at me like he's never seen a striped robe before.

I wish he'd stop staring. The equipment's gone but I'm still wearing the harness, and if the leather rig peeks out from the robe, and if the moron asks what it is, and Huber—who, I'm dead sure, will know what it is—gets a good look at it, I'll be dragged downtown and tossed in the tank on a morals charge. After that, maybe prison or maybe the Law's other favorite torture for folks of my persuasion, the psycho ward, but either way it's good-bye, Cantor Gold.

The guy finally looks away.

Lieutenant Huber doesn't sit down. He's the tense type, his tweedy brown overcoat hanging in sharp folds along his bony body. "I've got some sad news, Gold. A dame you know is dead." He didn't really say it, he sneered it.

It's like he's holding an ax over my head. If he says her name—if he says Sophie's name, if they finally found her and she's dead—that ax will come down and split my skull.

"It's a shame"—he tsks—"the way the killer cut her up. The woman barely had any face left. You wouldn't have recognized her, Gold. You'd never know the dead pile of pulp on the floor was Hannah Jacobson."

CHAPTER THREE

Huber's announcement cuts me in two. Half of me stunned, the other half wild with relief. I'm punched-in-the-gut staggered that Hannah Jacobson, the sweet, smart, great lady I saw just a few hours ago, survived the hell of Auschwitz only to be murdered in her own apartment in what was supposed to be the safe haven of America, but I could dance with joy that the death Huber dropped in my lap isn't Sophie's. I can keep searching for her.

My dizzying lurch between grief and relief is made worse by Huber's pushy questioning. "Your name came up tonight, Gold. The doorman at the Jacobson place said you visited around ten o'clock. What was your business with the old lady?"

"I didn't kill her, if that's what you're implying."

Huber's grin is tight and ugly, his disapproval of me oozing through his cigar-yellowed teeth. He says, "You know, I almost wish you did kill her. I'd love to be the cop who puts you away for good. You're a prize catch, Gold."

"Spare me the honor. Just tell me why you're here."

His grin shrinks. His disapproval doesn't. "Okay, maybe you didn't kill her, but you're in a dangerous racket. Maybe your business caused her death."

"And how do you figure that?"

"You might've been the last person to see Hannah Jacobson alive. The doorman says you left around ten thirty, says he didn't see anyone else go up to her place until my boys arrived around midnight. Seems a neighbor called after hearing noises and maybe a scream in the Jacobson apartment."

"The neighbor see anything? See anyone leaving?"

"Nope, said she was too scared to look in the hall. Just kept herself to herself until I questioned her. Same story with the rest of the neighbors on the floor. Nobody saw a thing, nobody heard a thing. Nobody ever does." His annoyance at this common denominator of every crime scene is so chewed over you'd think he'd get rid of it by now. But cops can be like a dog with a bone, never letting go even after it's chewed to dust. "Look, what was your business with her, Gold? I didn't see any fancy antiques or snooty artwork around her place, and believe me, once we knew you were involved, I had my boys give the apartment a good going over."

I have to fight to keep my face steady, my eyes level, and my eyebrows from rising like kites in a sudden wind. Huber doesn't know it but he's just told me that the Dürer watercolor's gone.

Someone stole everything from Hannah Jacobson. They stole her life and stole her legacy. And if her face was cut up as bad as Huber says it was, then whoever killed her must've hated her, too. Only someone who hates you wants to obliterate your identity.

"Well, Gold? You gonna tell me what you were doing at the Jacobson place? How'd you know her? Was she hiring you to steal something?"

"Stealing is against the law, Lieutenant."

"Don't toy with me, Gold, or I'll have Tommy put the cuffs on you." Tommy being the quiet cop in my club chair, I assume. "Tommy likes cuffing people," Huber says. "It's his favorite activity. Makes it easy to drag them downtown."

"You want to question me downtown? Okay by me. You won't get any different answers there than you're getting from me here, but sure, I'll play along." And it'll get the cops out of my apartment. The longer they're here, the longer Rosie's trapped in my bedroom. She can't come out, she can't even make a sound; if Huber figures I've got a woman in my bedroom, if he hears Rosie or catches sight of her, he'll toss us both in the tank on a morals charge. So I keep the mood light, keep things focused on getting Huber and his Tommy-boy outta here. "Give me five minutes to get some clothes on and then we can take a nice ride in your nice squad car to your nice precinct."

I start back to the bedroom but Huber grabs the sleeve of my robe. The touch of his cop fingers turns my stomach. He sees me recoil, relishes his spiteful little victory. "I don't trust you, Gold. You might slip out the bedroom window and down the fire escape. So I'm gonna send Tommy into the bedroom with you while you get your clothes. You can bring 'em to the bathroom and change in there. There's no fire escape in your bathroom and you're not about to jump out the window from the tenth floor. Don't worry," Huber adds with an offhand sneer, "Tommy will wait outside."

I'm usually pretty good at getting around cops who want to pin me for my racket, but the woman-love issue is a bigger problem. If Tommy the Cop goes into my bedroom and sees Rosie, Huber will haul us both to the hoosegow. It'll be even worse than the night I spent locked up after a raid on the Green Door Club, where a lot of us were caught dancing too close for the Law's comfort. Get arrested for dancing, and the Law beats you up and gives you a night in jail. Get arrested on a sex rap, and if you're lucky the Law gives you a prison sentence; if you're not so lucky, you get the needles and tubes of the psycho ward.

I think fast but talk slow. I can't let Huber catch on that he worries me. "First of all, Lieutenant, get your talons off my sleeve. You're damaging the silk. And second of all, Tommy isn't going to invade my bedroom, not unless you want my lawyer—You've heard of my lawyer? The one with all the connections to the politicians in City Hall?—well, unless you want him to look into some of your, um, activities, I suggest you keep Tommy right where he is, asleep in my chair." I'm banking on the idea that Huber, like a lot of cops of my acquaintance, has at least a fingertip in some not-so-savory pies, maybe even illegal ones, certainly embarrassing ones. If stuff like that became public it could get him busted back to a traffic beat, maybe even end his career if it touches too many higher-ups.

But he's not flinching. Either the only skeleton Huber's got is the one inside his skin or he's playing me a bare-knuckled game of chicken. He's pushed his hat back to give me the full force of his heavy-lidded leer. "Why do you want to keep us out of your bedroom, Gold?"

"Oh, get off it, Huber. No one likes cops rummaging in their sheets," I say, giving him my own pushback.

"Just answer the question, Gold, and don't throw me threats about your high-priced lawyer. He can look in my bedroom anytime he likes, but right now I want to know why you don't want us looking in yours."

"Look, Lieutenant, you're here on a murder investigation. Stick to it and stop wasting everybody's time."

His leer twists into a cold grin. "Watching you squirm is never a waste of time, Gold."

I don't like being an amusement, not for the cops or for anyone else, and particularly not for this smarmy lieutenant who thinks he's found a way to hang my hide on his trophy wall and get his name in the paper and a round of drinks from his precinct buddies. But I like it even less when he barks a laugh as he pushes past me, rapping the dozing Tommy on the back of the head as he moves toward my bedroom.

I'm a goner and I know it. I can handle it. I can take whatever they'll dish out at the city lockup and in Bedford Hills women's prison, but it's Rosie I'm scared for. Rosie, my beautiful soldier, who stood by me when I walked the floor over losing Sophie, who comes through during every job, no matter the danger. Rosie doesn't deserve the humiliation and brutality that's coming her way.

Huber says, "Open the door, Tommy. Grab anyone who's in there, understand?"

"Even if it's a guy?"

Huber snorts. "Don't make me laugh."

When Tommy opens the door, I feel my gut tighten and my soul weep. I've always been able to avoid this, always been careful to keep the Law out of my pants, been careful to shield any woman who shares my bed. But my luck's run out.

At least Rosie won't be hauled off alone. I'll be right there beside—

"It's empty, Lieutenant. There's nobody there."

Huber pushes into the bedroom, leaving me dumbfounded in the doorway. I catch my breath while the two angry cops rush to the window. It's open.

I feel a smile curl along my lips. Rosie's done it, she's eluded the Law, saved her hide and mine. She must've heard the cops in the living room and made a break for it out the window and down the fire escape. Huber worried about the wrong escapee.

But my smile shrivels up when I remember Huber bragging that anyone could look in his bedroom anytime. Sure, neither Huber nor whoever's in his bed will ever have to gather up their dignity with their clothes and slink away on a fire escape.

❖

I put on a pale apricot shirt, a pale blue and dark green chevron-pattern tie, the same dark blue silk pinstripe suit I wore to Mrs. J's, finish it off with an apricot pocket handkerchief, and throw on the same overcoat and cap I wore earlier. After I get through with the cops, there's someone else I want to look good for.

I head out with Huber and sidekick Tommy.

Their squad car is the usual black-and-green with a chrome grille that looks like a mouth ready to spit. The car hugs the curb in front of my building like a rat claiming territory. Frankly, rats would find a warmer welcome in my neighborhood, a few blocks north of Times Square and just east of Broadway. A lot of theater and nightclub folk live along my street—some whose names you'd know—and jazz musicians who work the local clubs. More than a few of my neighbors are people like me, if you catch my drift, and those who aren't don't mind sharing the sidewalk. Some are even my clients. After mink, diamonds, and lovers, famous actresses like classy art. All in all, the show folk and horn players in my neighborhood live interesting lives, the kind of lives we don't want the vice or narco squads to poke around in.

Which may be why Lieutenant Huber gives the eye to passing pedestrians and they pointedly ignore him.

Tommy gets into the driver's seat of the squad car while Huber hustles me into the backseat. He slams the driver's seat back to make his point, then gets in beside Tommy.

Huber doesn't talk to me during the drive, making this the only time in my life I've enjoyed his company. But we're not headed downtown, we're headed crosstown. "I thought we're going to the precinct house," I say. "What's the angle, Huber?" It wouldn't be the first time the cops have taken someone, me for instance, to an out-of-the-way spot—like one of those dark fissures I mentioned—and beat the crap or a confession out of them. I've never confessed to anything and only gave the cops silence or chitchat. Maybe Huber figures tonight's his night to try again. Maybe he's mad he couldn't hang me with a morals rap.

Or maybe he's just being efficient, actually doing his job, because we've just parked in front of Hannah Jacobson's apartment building.

The same elf of a doorman I dealt with earlier is still on duty. The three people in the world he least wants to see have just gotten out of the squad car.

Huber starts the conversation. "Hello again, Doyle," he says to the doorman. Then, pointing to me, he says, "Is this who you announced to Mrs. Jacobson tonight?"

Doorman Doyle looks me over with even more discomfort than when he saw me a few hours ago. Earlier I was just a freak, as far as he was concerned; now I'm a freak tying him up in a murder. He looks scared, and like he's wishing I'd simply drop dead. "Yeah. Yeah, that's her. Said her name's Cantor Gold. She the one you think killed that sweet old lady?"

"Let's not get ahead of ourselves, Doyle," Huber says. "And now that you've seen her again, do you remember if she was carrying anything? Look her over, try to remember. Take your time."

There's nothing more annoying, or nerve-racking, than a cop with brains. Right now I'd like to knock them out of Huber's skull, but my own smarts tell me to keep cool and don't do anything that might jog the doorman's memory.

"Like what?" he asks.

"Like a box or a package." Huber says it like he wants to add *you dummy*, but his cop discipline kicks in before he can blurt out an insult that could make doorman Doyle clam up. "Maybe something like a jewelry box or something square and flat?"

Like a painting.

"Lemme think," Doyle says, making a show of it. "Nah, I didn't see anything like that."

Before the guy can remember anything he *did* see, like my briefcase, and before Huber can keep pumping the guy, I grab hold of the questioning. "Mr. Doyle," I say with a courtesy I don't feel, "you recognize me as the person who went up to see Hannah Jacobson, right?"

"Yeah, didn't I just say so? It was you, all right."

"And how do you know it was me?"

"'Cause I know," he says. "I recognize you 'cause you're... you're..."

"Come on, Mr. Doyle, you can say it. We're all friends here."

Even in just the light of the building it's easy to see he's blushing like a schoolboy. "'Cause you're...'cause you're wearing the same coat and hat."

I have to hand it to the guy; he wiggled out of that one damn well and wiggled himself exactly where I need him to be. "And you saw me again—what, about a half hour later? That's at least an hour and a half until the police came around midnight, yes?"

The guy gives me an uneasy nod.

"Okay then." I press him. "When I came out of the building and got into the cab waiting for me at the curb, did I seem different? Did I have any blood on my coat? Do you see any blood on it now? Or on my suit," I say, opening the coat. "I'm wearing the same suit. See any blood?"

"No, but—"

"And what about later, after the neighbor heard noises and a scream in Mrs. Jacobson's apartment and called the police. Did you see anyone leave the building? Maybe you saw the killer escape and you didn't even know it."

"I didn't see anybody," he says, chafing and resentful at my constant questions. "And if whoever killed her used the tradesmen's entrance in the back of the building, I wouldn't see them at all. So for all I know, you came back!"

"No, Mr. Doyle, I didn't. Believe me," I say through a slow smile, "I had better things to do."

Huber, no doubt feeling trumped by a criminal taking charge of his investigation, cuts off the conversation with a showy wave of authority. "All right, Doyle," he says, "that's all." Cocking his head toward the door of the building, he says, "Let's go, Gold."

But it isn't *all* as far as I'm concerned. There's more I want from Doorman Doyle, because as every New Yorker knows, no one knows a building's dirty little secrets better than the staff, particularly the super and the doorman. "Listen, Doyle, was there anyone among Mrs. Jacobson's visitors that you didn't like? Anyone ever visit who gave you the jitters? Besides me, I mean," I add with another smile.

"I shouldn't tell tales outta school—"

"School's out," I say.

Fingering his cap as if trying to figure a way he could hide inside the brim and avoid the question, he finally says, "Well, that niece of hers, Miss Stern. Pushy lass, if you ask me."

"Pushy how?"

"You know, just pushy. As if being pretty and young and rich gives her the right to look down her nose."

"Oh," is all I say. Maybe the niece's only pushiness was to push away the advances of Doorman Doyle.

"Let's go, Gold," Huber says again, making his point by prodding me along.

Across the lobby, on our way to the elevator, Huber walks behind me, making sure, I guess, that I don't bolt. He doesn't lay a hand on me but I feel his presence anyway, like bad breath wafting from a sour mouth.

In the elevator, during the ride up, he takes the opposite approach and stands in front of me, nearly pressing me to the wall, making sure he'll be first out of the elevator. Sidekick Tommy is beside him. Huber says, "Stay outside when we're in the apartment, Tommy. Understand? Stay in the hall. I don't want you underfoot."

What's Huber's beef? First he slaps Tommy on the head to wake him from my chair. Now Huber's cutting the guy on the job. I wonder how soon Tommy is going to put in for a transfer.

The uniformed cop posted at the door of Mrs. J's apartment looks bored until he sees me. Then his big pink-and-blond face goes through the usual series of permutations from bafflement to disgust to recognition—secondhand recognition, really, maybe from hearing about me from Huber or the other badge boys who've bandied my name around the precincts over the years.

I have to admit, I take a certain amount of pleasure in my dubious fame with the Law. Knowing that the mere fact of me annoys them gives me joy.

But the joy is gone when I walk into Hannah Jacobson's apartment. The cozy living room with its pools of lamplight where Mrs. J and I shared a bit of life has turned into a charnel house. Where empty walls once seemed to be waiting for rescued artwork, now they're canvases for wild sprays of blood. The sight makes me feel weak in the knees, not from all the blood but from the raging hate that splashed itself across the walls. Hate killed Hannah Jacobson's family, and it finally came for her.

Huber evidently doesn't share my revulsion. Walking around the living room, his coat hanging on his skinny body like bark around a tree, he moves through the death room as if he's the most comfortable man in the world, sidestepping the chalk outline and blood on the rug next to the sofa and the coffee table, where Mrs. J fell dead. The pool of blood looks so large next to the outline of a body so small.

"Well, Gold? Anything to say for yourself? You going to tell me what you were doing here?"

I don't answer him. Instead I walk around the room, looking for anything that's changed since I was here, maybe a clue to what happened to the Dürer, though I know that's just wishful thinking. I'm really just playing for time, running ideas through my head that will keep Huber out of my business with Mrs. J.

Huber may be an obnoxious lout, but he's a perceptive lout. He's caught me looking at the side table at the end of the sofa where Mrs. J sat when I gave her the Dürer. "What is it, Gold?"

"That side table. It's damaged. There's a chip at the corner. I'm pretty sure the table was in good shape earlier."

We're both looking at the floor near the little table. Huber's pulled a handkerchief from his pants pocket. He bends to the floor, uses the handkerchief to retrieve a fragment of mahogany from the rug. "Maybe the fingerprint boys can do something with this," he says. "Maybe you left a little bit of yourself behind."

"Still trying to tie me into something, Lieutenant? Stop wasting the taxpayers' time. There's nothing more for me here, so if you'll excuse me, I'm leaving."

"Not so fast. You still haven't told me what you were doing here."

"And I don't have to. You know I didn't kill her, so my social calls are none of your business."

"Your whole life is police business, Gold. You being the last person to see Hannah Jacobson alive is my business."

"Then you'll have to talk to my lawyer," I say as I walk to the door. "You remember? The high-priced one you're so anxious to let into your bedroom? Good night, Lieutenant."

"Whatever you were doing here, Gold, I'll find out," he calls after me. "I'll find out your connection to the dead woman."

"Do what you have to do, Lieutenant." I'm just about out the door.

"And you, Gold? What are you gonna do about it?"

Good question.

CHAPTER FOUR

The first thing I do about it is find a phone booth and call Judson Zane.

Judson is a young man of many talents. The smartest thing I ever did was hire those talents to work for me. Judson's brain is organized with the precision of a Swiss watch. He's sharp with details, like keeping track of clients and their money, and he has deep contacts among the sort of people who provide services you might need but who'll never ask why you need them. He's also very good at finding out people's secrets, though he's silent as stone when it comes to secrets I need kept. He spends a lot of time on the telephone, which in Judson's hands is a chisel probing for information. Judson is over twenty-one but not by much, is thin and wiry as a clothes hanger, favors shirts without a tie—but more often a white T-shirt tucked into his dungarees—and wears wire-rimmed eyeglasses, which give him the appearance of being shy, but he isn't. Young women from Park Avenue to Delancey Street think Judson's adorable. He's never alone when he doesn't want to be.

After his groggy hello, I say, "It's me, Judson."

"Welcome back Stateside. How'd everything go? You made the delivery?"

"Yeah, I made the delivery, but the job's gone sour."

"Huh? What are you talking about, gone sour? Don't tell me the old lady stiffed us for the ten grand. She didn't sound like the type."

"Hannah Jacobson paid us every dime. But now she's dead and the goods are gone. Stolen."

Judson handles this news the way he always handles tricky news: silently. He's not the type to blurt cheap responses but efficiently sorts out the information and its possible consequences. After he's sorted the bad news I just gave him he says, "How'd it happen?"

"She was murdered, cut up, according to the cops."

"You spoke to the *cops*?"

"Couldn't help it. Huber showed up at my door."

"And he thinks you killed her?"

"Uh-uh. But he knows I was at the Jacobson place tonight because her doorman spilled it. I was able to sidestep Huber about what I was doing there, at least for now, so he still doesn't know about the goods. He doesn't know anything's been stolen. Listen, Judson, I can't just let this lie there. Hannah Jacobson was my client. If it gets around that a client of mine wound up dead and the goods pinched, it could be bad for business if I don't do something about it."

Sure, that spiel I just threw at him is the official line, but I know damn well Judson heard me trying not to gag on it, heard me struggle not to go soft over Mrs. J's death. I hear it in the quiet way he asks, "What do you want me to find out, Cantor?" But that's as sentimental as he'll get, which is how we both want it.

"There's a brother," I say, "a Marcus Stern. He was a professor of chemistry at some college or other here in town, maybe still is. But he's also a big deal in the plastics line. Stern's married, and there's a daughter. I don't know the wife's name or the daughter's name or how old the girl is, but I think the doorman at Mrs. Jacobson's building has eyes for her so she has to be at least a teenager. I want you to find out all you can about the Sterns, Judson. Who likes them, who doesn't. They're supposed to have money, but you never know, so take a good look inside their pockets. And get me an address on them, too. And listen, I know it's the middle of the night, but if you have to, wake people up."

When I hang up, I already have another nickel in my fingers, ready to drop it in the slot and call Rosie. She's probably still up. She's probably waiting for me to call. I should talk to her, tell her how terrific she is for thinking fast and smart and saving our skins. I should tell her all sorts of sweet things.

I put the nickel back in my pocket, walk out of the phone booth and into the night.

At the corner, I hail a cab.

❖

Vivienne Parkhurst Trent lives in the house she grew up in, an ornate number that's bigger than your average town house but smaller than Grand Central Station. It's on one of the swankiest blocks between Fifth and Madison, down the block from Central Park. The place is a three-story limestone confection in the Beaux-Arts style, meaning a little French, a little Italian, a bit of Baroque, a touch of Rococo, a dash of Classical Greek, and a whole lot of money, which more or less describes Vivienne, too. But she's no society dilettante. When it comes to art, especially of the European Renaissance, Vivienne knows her stuff. She's a curator at the city's most high-hat museum. It was Vivienne who brought Hannah Jacobson to me.

The door to Vivienne's pile of stones is a thick slab of black walnut carved top to bottom with forest scenes painted red. During the day it looks like the forest is on fire. At night, with just the glow of streetlamps raking the door in light and shadow, it looks like the trees are bleeding. The massive door is original to the house, commissioned by Vivienne's grandfather when he married the Parkhurst copper heiress during the Gilded Age. I once asked Vivienne why she kept such a spooky front door. "I like it," is all she said. She smiled when she said it, though. Like everything else about Vivienne, the smile was gorgeous, as sure of itself as all pampered things are.

The doorbell is silent from the street but I've been in the house before and know well the doorbell's rich cascade of chimes. Right now, I'm sure those cascading chimes are disturbing the sleep of the butler, a guy named George who also doubles as a cook. He's a very good cook.

He eventually opens the door. His face is one big frown of annoyance at the late intrusion, but the frown soon curves up in surprise at who's in the doorway, before his expression finally settles into controlled irritation that it's me. Despite all his facial permutations, George always looks like a butler. Even in his pajamas and brown robe, his graying brown hair pillow flattened on one side of his head and sleep tangled on the other, he maintains the formal bearing of those who live to serve.

"Good evening, George. My apologies for getting you out of bed, but it's important that I speak to Miss Trent."

"The hour is rather late," he says, in the dry tone of someone whose sleep was rudely interrupted but who's determined to carry out his duties with dignity, "Surely your business can wait until—"

"No, it can't wait. I wouldn't be on her doorstep at almost three in the morning if my business could wait."

"In that case," he says with a slightly irritable sigh, "you may wait in the living room. I'll inform Miss Trent you're here." Even George's well practiced butler lingo can't hide his distaste for the interruption I'm bringing to his carefully organized and civilized routine, not to mention his sleep.

George takes my cap and coat and hangs them on the coatrack, a scary looking row of elephant tusks, souvenirs of Vivienne's father's African safaris. Daddy Trent was quite an adventurer, hacking his way through jungles to stalk big game. The elephants got their revenge, though. On his last safari, when Vivian was fifteen and confined to boarding school, a big bull gored Daddy Trent to death. Vivienne's mother, whose mind was said to be fragile to begin with, was along for the ride and saw her husband ripped to pieces. She went nuts and stayed nuts. Vivienne visits her in the sanitarium.

I've always wondered if Vivienne inherited a trace of her mother's madness, but figured probably not; she's a respected member of a profession that requires disciplined brain power. Still, you never know.

George takes his leave of me and walks up the broad stairway to the second floor, where the private quarters and guest rooms are located. What the mansion set calls the public rooms—living room, dining room, library, and in this house a ballroom said to rival Mrs. Astor's—are down here on the first floor. George is billeted on the third floor, his bedroom in handy proximity to the house's linen closets and now-empty servants' quarters, used these days for overflow storage. Before the War, the house employed three additional servants. And according to Vivienne, before the *first* war back in '17, there was a staff of nearly a dozen. But with the exception of the requisite butler, live-in staff went out of fashion when chauffeurs and footmen went off to be soldier boys, and parlor maids earned higher pay in war-production factories. The fellas came back from their overseas adventures with bigger ambitions than servility. And when they came back from Europe and the Pacific this time around, first they bumped all the Rosie the Riveters out of their factory jobs, and then they sealed the deal by marrying them.

So it's just Vivienne and George rattling around here these days, giving the place an empty feel, which isn't helped by the echo of my shoes tapping along the checkered marble floor in the hall as I wander toward the living room. But Vivienne's money and George's ministrations, helped by weekly visits from hired house cleaners, do a great job of upkeep. On either side of me, the carved mahogany paneled walls are polished to a luster and lined with a coolly serene Vermeer interior here, a moody Caravaggio church drama there, a couple of Leonardo studies of hands, a small, jewel-like Van Eyck triptych of the Annunciation commissioned by a Flemish cloth merchant hoping to buy his way into heaven, and a honey-toned Madonna by Fra Filippo Lippi, the bad-boy friar of fifteenth-century Florence. The model for the Madonna was likely Lippi's mistress, a former nun. I acquired two of the works for Vivienne, even slipped the Lippi past the Vatican's watchdogs before finally making it out of the great arms of St. Peter's Square and into a cab for the short hop to the Tiber River and a waiting boat. It wasn't as hard as it sounds. I was dressed as a priest. A monsignor even gave me the eye.

Judson, of course, acquired the paperwork that stamps the acquisitions legit.

The living room is one of my favorite rooms in Vivienne's house, not that I've seen them all. For instance, I haven't seen Vivienne's bedroom. I'd like to, but to my disappointment she's kept our tête-à-têtes all business, even over elegant meals whipped up by George. But I've seen enough of the house to like some rooms better than others. Some are too stiff and stuffy for my taste, holdovers from Grandpa Trent's day, though the fussy decor was probably Grandma Parkhurst's doings. But Vivienne's been redecorating, and she's done up the living room in rich greens and browns and golds that complement the pale skies and dappled waterways of the seventeenth-century Dutch landscapes around the walls. When I turn on a couple of table lamps, the room is as welcoming as it is classy, congenial as a warm snifter of brandy.

I make myself comfortable on the sofa, a good-looking slate-green number with a row of black pillows fringed in gold. It's the first time all night I've had a chance to relax since I left Mrs. Jacobson's with ten grand in my pocket and arrived back at my apartment with Rosie.

Rosie…

I lean back into the soft embrace of the pillows, light a cigarette, and let the tobacco soothe me body and soul. I'm enjoying the smoke and my solitude—my first moments alone since I examined the Dürer on Drogan's tug more than six hours ago—when Vivienne swooshes in, her deep purple satin robe billowing around her like a storm cloud.

At thirty-two, Vivienne still isn't finished being beautiful, and with her perfect bones molded by a century or so of privilege and breeding, she probably never will be. She has big green eyes like those of a palace cat, and full rosy lips that missed their calling in the better brothel trade. Her shoulder-length chestnut hair is tousled from sleep, with wild strands curling down her cheek and highlighting the real zest in Vivienne's beauty, a bloodline inheritance that seeps through from her up-from-the-gutter great-grandfather, Malachi Trent, founder of the family dynasty. He was a brawler from the slums who had the brains to recognize the efficiency of steamships over sailing vessels, and the brute personality to steal his first ship and then kick competitors out of the way. Brutishness has since been bred out of the Trent line, but there's still something of the back alley in Vivienne, some vestige of the raw, vulgar life of the old New York slums. It's in the fullness of her body, the sinuous but slightly savage way she moves. It's a trait she's not even aware of, which makes it twice as delicious.

I get up from the sofa to greet her. Nearing me, she says, "If you're showing up in the middle of the night, it can't be good." That stings, even though it rides on a voice velvety as fine wine.

"Well, hello to you, too."

"So why are you here at this ungodly hour, and what kind of trouble did you have to get into to get that nasty bruise on your chin?" She says this as she sits down on the sofa, a move earthy and graceful at the same time, her body carving its curves around her, but touching down light as air on the sofa cushions. The woman makes me dizzy.

"Hannah Jacobson is dead."

Vivienne's "Oh—?" is part whispered, part choked. "Well…I mean, she was elderly and I guess she—"

"She was murdered." I'm still standing when I say it but sit down next to Vivienne when she reaches for my hand, clutches it, like grabbing a lifeline. She's holding tight enough to make the tips of her fingers go white, which makes her red-polished nails look even redder.

Slowly and with the difficulty that comes from dealing with rotten news, she asks, "Do you know who killed her?"

"No, and the cops don't know much either, except that someone cut her. Cut her face to pieces, too. And the Dürer I delivered to her tonight? Gone."

The mention of the Dürer grabs Vivienne's attention. "Cantor, do the police know about the picture?"

"No, but they know I had some connection to Mrs. J. They know I didn't kill her, but they'll knock themselves out trying to tie me in to it."

"Please, you've got to keep the police from learning about that watercolor."

"And keep your name out of it?" I say, more cruelly than I intended.

Dropping my hand and shrinking from me as if I suddenly smell bad, Vivienne leans back against the floral pillows but keeps her eyes on me, those big green eyes full of reprimand for my inexcusable nerve in talking back to my betters. Frankly, her high society act gives me a chuckle.

Slowly, though, that haughty look in her eyes softens, darkens with emotions turned inward. Almost sighing but not quite, she says, "Yes, of course you're right. I shouldn't be so cavalier about what happened to Hannah Jacobson. She really was a sweet old thing. But you must understand, Cantor, I can't allow my name to be mixed up with anything sordid."

"Oh, come on, Vivienne. The Parkhursts and Trents before you supplied New York with some of the city's juiciest society scandals. They found ways to ride out the notoriety, and so can you. Look, I'll do what I can to keep your name out of it, but let's face it—you come from a long line of scoundrels. There was even a murder, if I'm not mistaken."

"It was a *duel*," she says, defending the family honor with a sniff.

"Maybe in your neighborhood. Under the boardwalk we called it a shootout."

All she does is tsk and wave the comparison away, though weakly. Maybe sticking a fancy word like duel onto a plain old murder clogs the slum bloodline in Vivienne's veins. Anyway, the society snootiness is gone, or at least mellowed, replaced by the nervousness of a woman who feels vulnerable and isn't accustomed to the feeling.

I almost feel sorry for her. Vivienne Parkhurst Trent doesn't know how to survive weakness. She wasn't bred for it. It's interesting to watch her flounder in this unfamiliar territory, her attitude shifting from her usual haughty command of the room to that of a woman trying not to go weak in the knees. The pampered princess is gone, replaced by a worried Everywoman forced to face a threatening world. "It's not just personal scandal that worries me, Cantor," she says. "Well, not too much, anyway. It's the damage the scandal will do to my professional reputation. If I'm connected in any way to the stolen Dürer, I'd be ruined as a scholar. The museum would bury me."

I laugh. I can't help it. "After all the canvases and crockery I've brought them on your say-so? You can't wander around the place without tripping over something I've risked my life to get for them. Listen, if this Jacobson business blows hard enough to lift your skirts, guess who'll get caught hiding under there? Those guys at the museum will have a helluva time staying hidden behind your legs. And, anyway, even if they do make you the scapegoat, you won't starve, Vivienne." I spread my hands around the elegant room.

The look she gives me is the kind I usually see after I've given some puffed-up brawler a slam to the gut or a wallop to the jaw and they can't believe I did it. "Damn you, Cantor! Maybe *you* don't care that I'd lose everything I've worked so hard for, but I do. I've given my whole life to earning respect for my work. I've even passed up marriage—three times, I'll have you know—so I'd have no other claims on my time." The marriage news nearly floors me, but I don't let on. She's angry enough at me as it is, points a scolding finger at me and says, "You've been around the art game long enough to know how tough it is for a woman to get a curatorship, even with my doctorate and a research and publishing history that stands up to anything those bearded troglodytes at the museum ever wrote. Money didn't buy my curatorship at the museum, Cantor. I *earned* it."

"I know that, Vivienne."

"Do you? I wonder. Now give me a cigarette."

There aren't many pleasures in life as sweet as being told off—and deserving to be told off—by a beautiful woman in a shimmering satin robe that's clinging in the right places and sliding revealingly in others. The temptation to make my move and maybe finally get to see Vivienne's bedroom, or run the interesting risk of getting slapped in the face, is becoming as impossible to ignore as light strokes to the groin. But I'm here about the ugly business of murder, and that's a lousy pretext for romance.

So I just take my lighter and my pack of smokes from my pocket and offer Vivienne a cigarette. "All right, we're even now," I say. "Didn't mean to be so rough on you. I'm just tired. It's been a helluva night." She cups my hand between hers when I light her cigarette. Her touch is soft as silk and slips away too soon, those red-polished fingernails glinting in the lamplight. I wonder if Vivienne has the slightest idea how difficult she's making it for me to maintain my good manners and keep my hands to myself.

I figure I'd better do the smart thing and bring the conversation back to business. "Think, Vivienne. Did anyone else know that you were working with Mrs. Jacobson before she signed on with me? She has family here in New York. Did they know?"

"I've never met her family. And if she mentioned my name to them, she didn't say. Oh God, I hope not." Leaning toward me, cigarette smoke catching lamplight as it curls along her cheek, she says, "You know, I liked Mrs. Jacobson, Cantor. I really wanted to help her. I tried my best to get her family's art back. You believe me, don't you?"

"Any reason I shouldn't?"

"Of course not."

"Okay then, we can still help Mrs. Jacobson. We can honor her memory and we can help each other, too. I can help keep the cops away from you and you can help me track down the Dürer."

"Well, yes, of course, whatever I can do. Just what do you have in mind?"

"Listen, you're more than likely acquainted with all the interested parties in town. And frankly, I don't know if Mrs. J was killed for the picture or if the killer saw it in the living room and stole it as an afterthought or if it was the killer who stole it at all. But if we want to keep the cops out of our hair, we've got to figure out this business before they do. So try to remember, Vivienne. Did Hannah Jacobson ever mention anyone who seemed too inquisitive? Did she seem frightened?"

"Frightened? No, she seemed like the sort of woman who was on an even keel."

"What about the Dürer? Anyone besides Mrs. J ever show excessive interest in it? Maybe someone who knew the Jacobsons before the War?"

She stubs out the half-smoked cigarette in an ashtray on a side table and shakes her head. "I really don't know much about her former life or who she knew in those days, Cantor. You know, before the War the Jacobson collection was written about in a number of scholarly journals. I even wrote an article about it myself."

"Yeah, I read it."

"You did?" She looks at me like she just found out I read something beyond the *Daily Racing Form*.

"Sure. Don't be so surprised. I do my homework," I say, diverting the insult. "It's just good business. Now, you were saying about Hannah Jacobson?"

A little less haughty now—but only a little, which is okay by me, since a bit of haughtiness looks good on her—she says, "Yes, well, that article is how Mrs. Jacobson knew about me, why she thought I could help her get her family's art back. The problem was that after the collection was confiscated by the Nazis and the pieces dispersed, God knows where, the thread of information was broken. Most of the scholars who'd followed the Jacobson holdings turned their attention to more accessible collections. So I don't..." Her own attention wanders off then makes a slow U-turn and arrives back with a light in her eyes. "You know, there *is* someone who just might know if there's been any under-the-table interest in the Dürer. Max Hagen."

"Of the Pauling-Barnett auction house? Now there's a guy I'd like to do business with, but he's never let me anywhere near him."

"I'm not surprised. Max can be very exclusive in his associations, and he doesn't like to take risks. And believe me, you really are risky business, Cantor. But even though he doesn't do business with you, he knows all about you. He even told me he'd love to get his hands on the Dürer, but not through you."

"Oh, really?" I say, sarcasm dripping from me, thick as molasses. It's meant to cover my annoyance at being snubbed by Hagen, but it's not quite doing the job. "Just how did Hagen know I was bringing in the Dürer? Only you, Hannah Jacobson, and three other people in all of New York knew how the job worked, and those three work for me. They don't even know Hagen and wouldn't betray me to him if they did." I lean a little closer to her, bringing the last of it home for the kill. "So why'd you do it, Vivienne? After all our deals together, I thought I could trust you."

She shrinks away from me with the hurt feelings of a kid caught with her hand in the cookie jar. "You *can* trust me, Cantor. I've never betrayed you, and I didn't now. Not really. I know Max. He's as discreet as stone when it comes to acquisitions, so I knew he wouldn't blab about it. And I did it for Hannah Jacobson, anyway. Max said he had a buyer who would've made her a terrific offer, enough money to set her up for life. I told you, I really liked her. I wanted to help her!"

I let all that work through me, sort itself out into pieces I can handle, in part because I have no choice—I need to keep working with Vivienne if I hope to track the Dürer and maybe Mrs. J's killer—and in part because I'm a sucker for her gorgeous green eyes and everything that's behind them and below them.

So I soften my attitude a bit and say, "I assume you can get me to Hagen?"

"Of course." I suppose I'm flattered that she seems relieved to be back in my good graces. Anyway, an interesting smile slides across those brothel-worthy lips when she says, "For a price."

"Yeah? What sort of price? Maybe a Michelangelo you want me to put in your hands?"

"No, not a Michelangelo."

"What then? What little gem are you asking me to risk my life for, Vivienne?"

"It's not your life I want you to risk. It's your equilibrium."

"My equi—? Don't tease, Vivienne. All I need you to do is introduce me to Hagen, then you can be safely out of the rest of it. We can go to his office when the auction house opens this morning, say our hellos, and then you can say your good-byes."

"No, not at the auction house. Max won't see you there. It's too public. But he's having a small gathering this evening at his place. Very select, very discreet. Do you have a dinner jacket?" She fingers the lapel of my suit and says, "Yes, of course you do," almost in a whisper, and strokes the silk fabric slowly, even tenderly, then suddenly stops, as if she's afraid she'll wake the pinstripes and they'll rise up and snare her.

Before I can get a grip on Vivienne's first-time-ever intimacy with me or catch my breath at her abrupt stop, she's up from the sofa and almost to the door, calling over her shoulder, "Do something about that ugly bruise on your chin, Cantor, and be here at eight tonight. Escort me to Max's party. That's my price."

I haven't slept in nearly twenty-four hours. I'm exhausted from swinging in the wind in the harbor, and from the cops, the murder, Vivienne, the night. By the time I get home and crawl into bed, my bones drag along like lead pipes and my mind feels like dead space. The only thing I'm aware of as I fall asleep is that my bedsheets still smell of Rosie and me.

CHAPTER FIVE

*G*et up!*" stabs in my ears. My eyes pop open as the rest of
me is yanked from my pillow by a gorilla pulling me up
by the neck of my undershirt.

The gorilla is a thug named Screwy Sweeney. His stupid
eyes and lumpy face are so close to mine his hat brim is squashed
against my forehead. His stinking breath clogs my nose and throat
with the stench of cheap cigars.

I fight like hell to push him off, but he's got the bigger hands
and the better angle. I can't budge him. Screwy's a stubborn galoot
who earned his moniker after too many bruising bouts as a bottom-
of-the-card fighter screwed his brains up, which makes him the
best kind of thug: big muscles, powerful hands, too stupid to think
for himself.

These days, the guy doing Screwy's thinking is a hissing snake
named Jimmy Shea, the Mob's enforcer around the waterfront.
Jimmy and his gang of cutthroats make sure the Big Boys get
their bags of cash, and unless you want a bullet in the head, your
throat slashed, or your brains bashed in, you don't hold back from
skinny Jimmy. He's thin as a crowbar and just as hard, with ice-
blue slit-like eyes, murderer's eyes that I hope won't be the last
eyes looking at me but might, because he's sitting in my bedroom,
opposite the foot of my bed. His fedora's on his lap and his coat's
open, exposing a badly tailored gray suit that can't hide the bulge

of his gun under his jacket. Sure, Jimmy's got enough dough for better threads, he's just cheap.

"Good morning, Cantor," he says. His wheezy, high-pitched voice is as sociable as wind whistling through a dark alley.

"So far"—I manage to rasp through Screwy's tightening grip on my undershirt, strangling my neck—"there's nothing good... about this morning. Get Screwy off me...and maybe there'll be a...slight improvement."

Jimmy lets me gag a little bit longer before he finally calls it off. "Let 'er go, Screwy."

My head snaps back against the headboard when the galoot lets go of me, adding another indignity to my already undignified wake up. Getting Screwy's hands off my neck and escaping the stink of his cigar breath does improve the morning, but not by much. There's still the problem of Jimmy Shea in my bedroom. "How'd you get in here, Jimmy? My building super isn't the sort of guy who opens apartments to just anybody. Or maybe you left him lying bloodied in the hall, or did Screwy just break my door down."

Jimmy doesn't crack a smile or even bother with a nasty sneer. His attitude just stays flat and cold and hard. "Nah, nothin' so showy," he says. "Just like you, Cantor, I know a useful thing or two. Little inconveniences like locks don't stop us, do they."

"No, I guess not. All right, so you picked the locks downstairs and on my front door. Couldn't you just ring my doorbell?"

"I rang. I got no answer."

"Maybe I wasn't home."

"Maybe you was still in bed. Maybe I was interruptin' somethin'. You got a hot reputation, according to some." He says this through a humorless grin so thin and sharp it could shred my bedsheets. I pull the sheets a little tighter around me while he keeps talking through that razor-like grin. "How'd you get that bruise on your chin, Cantor? Rough trade, maybe?"

I've learned to ignore the crap people throw at me about who I am and who I bed. I don't give a damn what they think. I don't give a damn what Jimmy thinks. It's his smarmy way about it, though, that makes me want to bash his teeth in. But even with bashed-in teeth he'd be able to talk, and the first words out of his mouth would be to tell Screwy to break my neck.

My bedside clock reads just a few minutes after eight, which gives me an excuse to change the subject. "I didn't know you were such an early riser, Jimmy. I thought big shots like you lie around with breakfast in bed."

"I'm a busy guy, Cantor. I can't let the day slip away from me. Can't let people slip away, either."

"Uh-huh. So what's so important in your busy day that you had Screwy yank me awake?"

"Well, it's like this," he says with an offhand shrug that hints at the possibility that the length of my life might be abruptly shortened. "You're bringin' trouble where we don't want trouble."

"Is that so? I don't recall ever bringing you anything but cash and lots of it. I make sure you guys get paid before my goods ever hit the docks. As far as I'm concerned, my account's up to date."

"Oh, the trouble ain't money, Cantor. The trouble's a murder and a nosy cop. A certain Lieutenant Huber."

I can't let Jimmy see the deep breath I'm trying not to take or the swallow I'm trying to hide. The last thing I need is for Jimmy Shea to figure I'm jittery. The Mob doesn't like jittery people, can't trust 'em, and they have only one way of dealing with people they don't trust.

But yeah, I'm jittery, because now I know just how far Huber's willing to go to get me. The police usually avoid stirring up the Mob. It runs the risk of exposing the crooked deck the Mob, the brass, the judges, the politicians, and the big-money boys have stacked against the average Joes and Janes. Too much exposure means people have to be silenced. Bodies start piling up, which gets noticed by the newspapers, who shine a spotlight into the police department, sending the dirty cops scurrying like rats. If Huber's willing to risk all that, could be he's hoping one of the bodies in the pile is me.

So I have to keep my conversation with Jimmy steady, no sudden swings, no show of nerves. A cigarette will help. I take one from the pack on my night table, pick up the lighter lying next to it, and light the smoke while Jimmy and Screwy watch my every move.

After a deep drag and an exhale as slow and lazy as I can make it, I try a play, keeping my voice and manner as matter-of-fact as my jitters will let me. "Since when are you concerned about a nosy cop, Jimmy? You and your outfit own plenty of cops. Pay Huber enough and he'll probably go away."

"Probably ain't good enough," he says, not buying my play. "We don't throw money at people we don't know, and we don't know this guy Huber. Matter of fact, this is the first I've ever heard of the guy. He's not the usual dockside cop, not from any of the waterfront precincts. He seems to know a lot about you, though. According to my boys, this Huber knows you visited some old lady last night and the lady wound up dead."

"He also knows I didn't kill her."

"He don't care. And I don't care either. And neither do my associates. But we *do* care about this cop askin' too many questions about our arrangement with you on the docks. You understand what I'm trying to tell you, Cantor?" He's pointing at me, index finger extended and the other fingers curled up, his hand aimed like a gun. He lets it linger in the air before he finally lowers it slowly, sure he's made his murderous point. "This guy Huber is lookin' to tie you up in a murder any way he can," he says, "but he's doing it by digging for the kind of information that could get the attention of too many higher-ups, them reformer types always looking to clean up the docks. That kind of attention is bad for business, Cantor, very bad for business. We don't want business interrupted by no murder investigation. So I'm asking you: What's the story with this old lady?"

"She's dead. That's all I know." I keep my lie and my face steady behind a cloud of cigarette smoke.

Jimmy sighs like he's annoyed with a naughty kid in the schoolyard. "Maybe I haven't made you fully understand your situation," he says, getting up, his skinny frame unfolding section by bony section until he's looming above my bed, "but it sounds like the dead old lady was your client and that whatever you brought into port last night was meant for her. Now she's dead, and I figure the goods are in the wind, am I right? You see what I'm gettin' at, Cantor? Your client, your goods. That makes this your problem. Take care of the problem. Get rid of Huber."

"Whoa there! You can't seriously be asking me to kill a cop? You're worried your outfit's attracting attention *now*? Killing a cop who's been sniffing around the docks would bring the whole damn police department down on your head *and* mine. Even the cops you own would turn on you. Use your head, Jimmy. Cop killing crosses the line. And anyway, I don't like killing."

"Give me a little credit, Cantor," he says with a show of humility even his priest wouldn't buy. "My associates and I ain't askin' you to kill the cop. Just get him the hell off our backs. Give him someone that's good for the old lady's murder."

"You want me to find the killer."

"Or someone who'll go down for it. It don't matter to us. Just do it fast so this Huber can go away happy and we can get on about our business. What's the matter, Cantor? You look pale."

"I don't like sticking a frame on anybody any better than I like killing."

Jimmy puts his hat on and buttons his overcoat, taking his time about it, overstaying his welcome with each button. "You know," he says, suddenly good natured through a poisonous sneer, "you should get married, Cantor."

"Sure. There oughta be a law."

"I'm talking on the level, as a friend, you understand. You could be a nice-lookin' dame if you got rid of that undershirt and the rest of your bull-dyke wardrobe and got yourself some nice dresses and frilly underthings. Know what I mean?"

"Get out of here, Jimmy."

I watch his phony good cheer dissolve into the skin-crawling evil that's the true Jimmy Shea. "Give this Lieutenant Huber someone who'll fry for the old lady's murder, Cantor," he says. He motions to Screwy to follow him to the door.

"And if I don't?"

"We'll give him you."

❖

A long hot shower loosens the knots Screwy tied in my neck. The steam cleans the stench of his cigars out of my nose. Nothing, though, is going to get Jimmy Shea's threat out of my system. If I don't deliver what he wants, he'll either scapegoat me to Huber and have me thrown in the clink, or maybe he'll toss me in Huber's lap, already dead.

Huber. If I don't figure out what he's up to, I could wind up just as locked up or just as dead.

It's barely nine in the morning and I'm already squeezed between the Mob and the Law. Surviving the day could get tricky, and I'd hate to be standing at the Pearly Gates before I finally get my chance to twirl around with Vivienne Parkhurst Trent tonight. Some fantasies should come true before you die.

Since there's nothing in my closet that fulfills Jimmy's fashion suggestion or his best wishes for my domestic bliss, I get dressed in a light green pullover and a favorite dark brown silk suit which, unlike Jimmy's cheap goods, is custom tailored to hide the bulge of my Smith & Wesson .38. I load the chambers and slide the gun into its rig, snug under my left arm. Then I put my overcoat and cap on and slip the envelope with the ten grand I got from Hannah Jacobson into my inside jacket pocket.

Before I leave my apartment I grab extra rounds and drop them into my pants pocket. It's going to be a dangerous day.

❖

For a great big city made of steel and stone, New York still has its weedy places, out of the way patches where the landscape hasn't changed much since the dinosaur days. Drive beyond the piers on the Brooklyn shoreline and you'll find swampy inlets snaking through real estate where, if it wasn't for the view of the Manhattan skyline across the river and roadside billboards with pretty girls hawking Rheingold Beer and toothy guys smiling through Barbasol shaving cream, you wouldn't be surprised to see some toothy green thing slither round the corner, claws out.

Red Drogan berths his tug in one of the inlets, a boggy spot of tall reeds, soupy grasses, and a mist gray as dust. For a less experienced tugman, this inlet would be hell to navigate, but it's the perfect place to keep a boat out of sight. In other words, it's the perfect home for Red Drogan.

I park back from the water's edge where the land is still firm, and call out "Drogan!" when I get out of my car, a snappy dove-gray '50 Buick Roadmaster convertible I picked up this past February. She's a free spirit with her top down on warm sunny days, tight and cozy on brisk days like today.

Drogan emerges head and shoulders from the tug's cabin as I step onto his small, barely visible dock. He waves me to come aboard. Before I'm even on deck I catch the welcoming aroma of coffee.

"You look like you could use a cup," he says, pouring me one when I walk into the cabin. "Late night?"

"And lousy morning. Jimmy Shea paid me a visit and used Screwy Sweeney as an alarm clock. Oh, and by the way, here's your cut of last night's job." I give Drogan two grand.

He takes the dough and stashes it in one of the overhead bins built into the cabin. Knowing Red, who doesn't spend a dime unless it's for his boat or to buy a bottle, and maybe a little coffee, he probably has a fortune lying around up there.

The tug's cabin is a tidy spot that Red keeps to the essentials: a bunk to sleep in, an old wooden chair and a counter to eat at, a sink, overhead bins to stow gear, and his ship-to-shore phone.

Everything's clean as a whistle, though he really should treat himself to a new hot plate and coffeepot. The hot plate looks like it's been doing hard time since the invention of the electric plug. And the coffeepot, one of those blue enamel-over-tin jobs, is so beaten up Drogan has to tip it sideways to keep the coffee from spilling out of the dented spout as he pours himself a fresh cup. After taking a gulp, he says, "Now, what's this about Jimmy Shea?"

I give Red the whole story, from delivering the Dürer to Hannah Jacobson and all the way through to Jimmy's morning threat in my bedroom. When I'm done, Red says, "Always figured you might die young." It sounds even worse through that gritty growl of his.

"Not so fast with my obituary, if you don't mind."

"Well you made it this far and you ain't so young anymore, so I guess you're still beatin' the odds. I suppose you want me to keep my ear out along the waterfront, yeah? I'll be towing float barges round the piers today, so I'll be hearin' a lotta stuff from a lotta guys."

"Good, see what you can pick up," I say. "That freighter I came in on last night, she still in port?"

"Till tomorrow."

"Start there. I crossed her captain's palm with a thick slab of green grease, but who knows? Maybe somebody on the crew sold me out. And see if you can get a line on who Lieutenant Huber's been flashing his badge to along the docks."

"I'll look into it." After another pull of coffee, Drogan's mood changes, darkens with worry. "Listen, Cantor," he says, "those goods you brought in last night, you clipped it off some Nazi, yeah?"

"In a manner of speaking. Why?"

"Maybe Jimmy Shea's not your only problem, if you catch my drift."

"War's over, Red," I say, getting up to go. "Been over for five years."

"Not for everybody."

❖

My office is my place of business, my treasure chest, my sanctuary. It's in plain sight but you'd never spot it: a small, nondescript brick job with a blacked-out front door at a midtown corner of Twelfth Avenue, under the West Side Highway. The Hudson River docks are across the street, which has come in handy on more than one occasion. The stretch of piers nearest me is part of Luxury Liner Row. Some of the world's fanciest ocean liners come into port over there, carrying some of the world's fanciest people. The fancy folk don't linger after they've come off the boat; they hurry to their taxis and limousines to beat it out of the noisy neighborhood and its tangle of grimy piece-goods factories, cheap eateries, and rough longshoremen's saloons.

So in the midst of the neighborhood's hoopla, no one pays attention to my little brick corner or has any idea that down in the basement, behind a false wall, is a walk-in vault with treasures that would knock your eye out.

Only Judson, Rosie, and my lawyer know about my little building, and my lawyer made sure my name never appears anywhere in the paperwork. Even my clients don't know about the place. All I give them is the phone number. It's unlisted and in a paper name, can't be traced back to an address.

I pull into Louie's garage, up the block from my office, and park my car in my monthly rental spot, paid for in cash, no checks to trace back. Garaging it keeps my car off the street and out of sight of nosy cops and even nosier dockside gangsters. After I get out of the car, I start for the Twelfth Avenue door but change my mind and go out the back and walk through the alleys. No sense kidding myself, I'm jumpy. Jimmy Shea's threat is crawling all over me like lice. And then there's Huber. Who knows how many eyes he's planted around the waterfront?

Judson's already at his desk when I walk in through the steel door from the alley. In addition to Judson's aforementioned talents, he's a first rate guy Friday. He keeps accounts up-to-date, balances the books, deals with paperwork—and all of it in a code only he and I can decipher. If any of it ever falls into the wrong hands, they'll just figure we're big fans of Scrabble.

"You got two calls," he says when he sees me. He gets up and hands me two message slips.

About the first one, I say, "Tell this guy I'll think about it." About the second one, "And tell *this* guy that until I hear one way or the other from that broken-down Count What's His Name, I can't move the piece. Now, what've you got for me on the Sterns?"

Judson leans against his desk and takes a cigarette from the pack of Camels rolled in the sleeve of his T-shirt. He lights the smoke, speaks through the exhale. "You're right, Marcus Stern made a killing in the plastics business. He's got a plant out in Queens, Stern Chemical Products. Does a million-dollar business."

"What about Stern himself? Is he still connected to a university?"

"Nope. Not since '43 when his business started raking in buckets of dough in war production. He resigned from teaching to devote all his time to business. According to my guys, the plant retooled after the war to make plastic casings for all those new household appliances. The market for that stuff is booming."

"What about the wife and daughter."

"Wife's name is Katherine, maiden name Anderson. She's from some little town in Ohio. Came to New York to become an actress, became a secretary instead. Guess whose?"

"Uh-huh, and married the boss. And the daughter? What's her story?"

"Francine. Eighteen years old, a student at Barnard College uptown, and from what I hear, a handful. The State lifted her driver's license. Daddy had to pull some strings, pay off her fines, and grease some palms to buy it back."

"Just what the world needs, another wild eighteen-year-old."

"Weren't you?" Judson ribs me.

I get a kick out of the question, even get a little nostalgic. "Plenty," I say through a smile full of tomboy memories, "but not on my pop's dime. Speaking of cash, here's your cut and Rosie's cut, too. I'll tell her to drop by for it." I give Judson three grand from the remaining eight Gs in my suit jacket, fifteen hundred each for him and Rosie.

He pockets his half, puts Rosie's cut in his desk drawer. "One last thing," he says and hands me a slip of paper. "Here's the Sterns' address."

I pocket the paper and walk into my private office.

My spot is cozy as a favorite chair, which it has: a large, pale green club chair with leather so supple it feels like I'm sitting in a woman's soft lap. The chair's next to my oxblood sofa and near my big walnut desk. Considering how much time I spend here, even sleep on the couch sometimes if I have to lie low, I figured I might as well outfit the place with first-rate furnishings. Hell, what good is risking your life to earn a living if you can't reward yourself with top-of-the-line prizes like wine, women, and good furniture? There's even a refrigerator and a hot plate, a phonograph and a radio, and a good supply of Chivas scotch.

Snug as it is, I'm not here to hang around today. I'm only here to make a call. I sit down at my desk, dial the number, stash the receiver between my shoulder and my chin, and light a cigarette. Rosie answers on the third ring.

"It's me," I say.

"Good morning, Cantor." Her greeting is sweet as peaches and cream, just like Rosie. "You almost missed me," she says. "I'm on my way out, doing an early shift. See you tonight?"

"Sorry, can't tonight. I guess you know Hannah Jacobson's dead."

"Yeah, I overheard the cops last night."

"Well, things are getting rough. There's stuff I have to do, people I need to get to before the cops catch up with me. And the Mob's not too pleased with me, either. The cops dragged the Jacobson business to their doorstep."

"Sounds bad, Cantor."

"It is bad. But you were terrific last night, my girl. You saved both our skins with your smart move down the fire escape. It was a crappy thing to have to do. I wish things were different. I won't forget it, Rosie."

"I hope that's not the only part of last night you won't forget," she says in a whisper so ripe I can almost taste the sweet, warm breath behind it.

"No, it's not the only part I won't forget. I could never forget it."

"Tomorrow night, then?"

"Sure, maybe. But I have to get to the bottom of the Jacobson business first."

"Just be careful, Cantor, okay?"

"Aren't I always?"

"No. And…I wish…look, at least *try* to be careful."

"Yes, ma'am. By the way, drop by the office during your trips around town today. You can pick up your cut of the job. I meant to give it to you last night, but, well, we got caught up in other things and it slipped my mind."

"Yeah, mine, too." There's that whisper again.

"You can pick up your dough from Judson. 'Bye, Rosie."

"'Bye, Cantor," comes through the phone like she's blowing a kiss before she hangs up.

That went better than I deserve.

There's a safe built in to the wall behind my desk. The safe's behind a painting I liked enough to buy legit. I do that from time to time, especially if it's the work of a living artist, which this one is. After all, the guy's entitled to make a living. The painting's by one of the new abstract bunch who've taken to painting what goes on in their heads instead of what goes on in the world. About a year or so ago, this guy Rothko started painting fuzzy-edged rectangles and squares of different colors. They look like spaces I could crawl into, get lost inside a slot of brown or a chasm of green or a tunnel of black. I don't know what I'd find in there. Maybe Sophie.

Maybe that's why I hung the painting in front of the wall safe, because inside the safe, next to the strongbox where I stash cash, is a framed photo of Sophie and me that I kept on my desk for months after she disappeared, until it became too tough to look at every day.

I pick up the photo after I stash the remaining five grand. The sight of Sophie still nearly buckles me over, the way her dark hair falls to her shoulders like the mane of a gypsy's pony. I'm the happy idiot next to her. We're cheek to cheek, grinning after our first night together. We'd made love over and over until dawn, the wildness of it releasing the gods who lived inside us and who'd never show themselves to anyone else. I'd gone to heaven that night. I wish I'd never come back.

Chapter Six

Marcus Stern's town house on Riverside Drive is the odd Greek Revival number in a row of four gewgawed Beaux-Arts palaces on the block, the morning sun tracing a line of gold along their corniced rooftops. The Stern house looks as if it's been squeezed between its bigger, flashier sisters whose limestone curlicues do their best to ignore the brick-and-marble upstart in their midst. But the brickwork on the Stern place is as well cared for as the curlicued girls on either side of her. Her white-framed windows, marble front stairs, and fluted white columns are as trim and crisp as the new money stacked in Marcus Stern's bank account. The only smudges threatening this otherwise confident façade are the black hearse parked at the curb and the single black limousine parked behind it.

I pull into a parking spot across the street but don't get out of my car. I just stare at the limousine and the hearse. It's the smallest funeral procession I've ever seen.

Okay, so Mrs. J didn't have a lot of family in America, just her brother, his wife and kid. But what about friends? There must be other people besides me who knew her. Hell, even Vivienne knew her. A woman as sociable and smart as Hannah Jacobson must've had a pal or two, someone to have coffee with, or maybe play a hand of canasta. Where the hell are they?

Mrs. J deserves better. She deserves a standing-room-only sendoff on her way to meet the souls of her husband and children and probably the souls of old friends, too, all devoured in the Nazi frenzy. Maybe their ghosts will show up at her funeral. I hope so. A great lady like Hannah Jacobson shouldn't exit this world unescorted.

The tantalizing sight of a young woman, blond and pert, coming out the door and down the front steps of the Stern place blunts my brooding. Her short, bouncy hair glints in the sun and bathes her pretty face in a silky light that young women wear like a glowing second skin. In her dark blue coat with its fashionably turned-up shawl collar and a handbag tucked under her arm, she's lithe and graceful as silk in a breeze.

She must be the Stern daughter, Francine.

She's followed out of the house by a woman I assume is Francine's mother, Mrs. Katherine Stern. Her pinched-waist princess-style black coat, little black hat with a small silly feather, and her slightly haughty, slightly unsure posture give her away as the sort of dame who'll never accept that her fiftieth birthday is moments ahead or maybe already moments behind. She's blond like her daughter but her hair is longer, a more formal shoulder-length style spilling from her little hat in a tightly controlled wave. She looks as if she'd punish any strand that rippled out of place.

Marcus Stern is the last out of the house. The brim of his fedora shadows his eyes but the lower half of his face is visibly jowly. His black overcoat hangs with the discipline of expensive tailoring forced to cover a bulky, slightly stooped frame. I'd peg Stern at about sixty-five.

After the Sterns get into the car and the funeral procession drives off, I invite the ghosts of Mrs. J's family and friends into my Buick, then fall in line behind the limousine.

❖

New York buries its dead on the outskirts of town. Most of our cemeteries are in the borough of Queens, whose small old villages are nowadays in a chokehold of boxy suburban tract housing and stores crammed with household schlock that offer up the American Dream on the cheap. Driving along Queens Boulevard is like driving through an America that's burst her corset, freeing herself from the double-whammy constraints of Depression-era privation and wartime frugality, and now revels in the privilege of growing acquisitive and fat. As I roll through streets clogged with woodie station wagons and sedans gaudy with chrome, I wonder what these neighborhoods will be like ten, twenty, thirty years from now, if there'll be a tree left standing or all mowed down in the name of progress. I wonder if there'll even be a parking space.

Our little funeral procession finally breaks free of the commercial clutter and drives into the cemetery. Headstones and greenery take over, a front lawn to the Manhattan skyline shimmering in the distance across the East River like an apparition of the heaven awaiting the city slickers buried here.

Nearing Mrs. J's grave site, I hang back and pull over but stay in my car. Explaining my presence to the family will go down a lot better after they've buried Mrs. Jacobson without the distraction of a stranger.

Anyway, that's the story I tell myself, but who am I kidding? I'm hanging back from the funeral because the rabbi conducting the service would look me over and probably give me the stink eye, a look I've gotten from the God boys since I put on my first suit as a teenager prowling for love under the Coney Island boardwalk. If I get that look from this guy, I'll react the way I always do: I'll want to spit in his face but won't do it. I've never been able to spit in a rabbi's face.

So I watch the funeral from my car. I see Marcus Stern lower his head and cover his eyes with his hand, his bulky body sagging like a sack of old potatoes. His wife touches his arm but her gesture is stiff and mechanical and doesn't seem to give her husband much comfort; anyway, he doesn't acknowledge her. And Francine isn't paying attention to either of her parents, lowering her head from time to time then raising it again and taking a deep breath as she looks at her aunt's coffin.

The rabbi's voice, thin and reedy in the cadences of the ancient language, slides around gravestones and drifts toward me like a wraith. Those words, those old sounds, come at me as something foreign and familiar at the same time. I recognize only bits and pieces but the archaic chant pulls memories out of me, memories of burying my mother, and then a couple of years later my pop, both of them dead of overwork and disappointments.

The graveside service and the rabbi's chant drone hypnotically on, the sun glimmering off the polished coffin, making the air around it shimmer, or maybe the shimmer is the dance of the ghosts keening over Hannah Jacobson. The glow lingers as the coffin is lowered into the ground.

The funeral service is ending. Marcus Stern, unsteady on his feet and helped by the rabbi, is the first to toss the customary shovelful of dirt into the grave. It must be tough for the guy to bury the older sister who only a few years ago came back into his life.

His wife and daughter then toss their shovelfuls. Mrs. Stern gets rid of the dirt like it's—well, just dirt. Francine spreads her shovelful as if she's sprinkling flower petals over the coffin.

It's over for Hannah Jacobson's family, but not for me. I can't say good-bye to Mrs. J yet. Neither of us will know any peace until I track down her murderer.

I get out of my car, give the family a minute or two to gather their wits after the service ends, but I don't dare lose them before I have a chance to toss them a few questions. Funeral or not, I'm still squeezed between the Law and the Mob, and I can't let a little thing like good manners get in the way of saving my own life.

I've barely taken two steps toward the family when Francine Stern heads in my direction. Her parents call after her but she doesn't seem to give a damn.

The lithe, fresh-faced college girl I saw coming out of her house earlier today has turned into a worldly-wise dish advancing on me with a stride that advertises no-nonsense, but whose luscious green eyes hint at a rather robust taste for nonsense of various kinds. I guess it's true, what Judson said about her; she's an eighteen-year-old handful.

She's looking at me like I'm a banana out of place on an apple tree, though she doesn't seem put off by the mismatched fruit. Nearing me, she doesn't offer any greetings or any other niceties or even a smile, just asks, "You knew my aunt?" with the interrogatory politeness of a stranger asking for the time of day. Before I even get a word out, she follows it up with, "You don't seem like the type to hang around with Aunt Hannah. How did you know her?" Lack of confidence is never going to be a problem for this kid. I like her.

"We shared a love of art," I say.

"Uh-huh. Got a cigarette?"

I give her one of my smokes. When I light it for her she keeps her eyes on me. A smirk seeps into those green eyes.

Through an exhale that sends smoke in my face, she says, "You know what I think? I think you're the piece of bad news the police warned us about."

"The police think puppies and rainbows are bad news."

"You're no puppy."

"Sure I am. Give me a treat and I'll wag my tail."

"What kind of treat are you looking for?"

"Information."

Her eyes stay on me but the smirk fades away. I get the feeling I've disappointed her.

Another pull on her cigarette gives her cover for a minute while she recharges her attitude, then she says, "What kind of information? The same stuff the police wanted to know?"

"That depends. What did they want to know?"

"They said you're Cantor Gold and they asked if we knew what business my aunt had with you."

Things could get tricky here. If I play it too pushy about the cops, she might back off, scared that I really am the bad news the cops say I am. So I keep my tone easy, my attitude matter-of-fact. "And what did you tell them?"

"The truth, I guess. That we never heard of you."

"What do you mean, you guess?"

"I mean, I don't know who the hell you are. I never heard your name before the police mentioned it. But I can't say what my parents know. Maybe Aunt Hannah mentioned you."

"What else did the cops want?"

"Oh, the usual," she says with a shrug. "Did my aunt have any enemies, that sort of thing."

"Did she?"

She starts to take another drag of the smoke but can't, stopped by a sob that's suddenly clogging her throat. She tosses the cigarette away, catches her breath, and when she's finally able to speak she's the innocent college kid again. "My aunt was wonderful. Brave and wonderful," she says, barely getting the words out. "How could anyone hate her?"

"Your aunt *was* wonderful," I say, "but her killer didn't think so. Listen, Miss Stern, I can help you and your family—"

"Please just go away." She takes a handkerchief from her bag and dabs her eyes with it. "Look, you're not the police. What gives you the right to barge into my aunt's funeral and ask questions? What is it you want, anyway?"

"If I told you justice for your aunt, would you believe me?"

"I don't know. Should I?" With a girlish sniffle and a last dab at her eyes, she gets her tears under control, though they could spill again any minute. She's looking straight at me, the remnants of tears giving a sheen to the smirk sneaking back into her eyes. What goes on with this kid?

A rough shout, "Francine!" comes at us from Marcus Stern, lumbering toward us like an irritated bear. He holds his fedora so tight he's bending the brim. "Francine, I told you to get into the car." Except for the remnants of his German accent, he sounds as worn-out as any other American father of a modern teenage daughter. Looking me over, he says, "Just what is your business here?"

"Daddy"—Francine jumps in and does my talking—"this is Cantor Gold."

Stern's fleshy face goes gray as old dough. "Yes, yes, you're the troublemaker Lieutenant Huber warned us about." He turns again to Francine. "Go back to the car. Do as you are told."

The kid's not happy about it, but she's already ignored those orders once today, and as long as Daddy controls the purse strings, ignoring those orders a second time could come with too high a price. She goes back to the car, but not before she gives me a last look with those smirking eyes.

I do my own talking now. "I'm not here to make trouble, Dr. Stern. I'm here to pay my respects. Your sister was a great lady."

"And how is it you knew her?"

"She never mentioned me?"

"No, she did not."

"I see. Well, what did the police tell you about me?"

"They said you are a troublemaker, a criminal. And they told me to contact them if you show up."

"And will you?"

"I—" He shuts up so suddenly it's as if his throat's been cut. He's looking past me and over my shoulder, the expression on his face like he's seen a ghost.

I turn around fast, but whatever scared the hell out of Marcus Stern is gone. When I turn back, Stern has a handkerchief to his face, wiping away sweat, the oozy kind that stinks of fear.

"Dr. Stern, what did you see? Who's after you?"

He puts his hat on, says, "I must go. Do not bother me or my family again or I *will* call the police," then walks back across the cemetery and toward the limousine. The stench of fear coming off him could wither the grass.

But his fear can't be allowed to let him off the hook. He's the guy who survived, he's the last of his Old World family. He owes that family a survivor's legacy of truth. He can't just toss that burden away like an out-of-date suit.

So I go after him. "Dr. Stern! Dr. *Stern!*" I grab his arm with so much force his whole body shakes and his hat falls off and tumbles to the ground. "I'm trying to help you," I say. "If you want to find out who killed your sister, you're better off trusting me than the police."

"But they said—"

"Never mind what they said. You of all people should know not to trust the authorities. Your sister didn't."

That gets him. I might as well have called the cops the *polizei* by the look he gives me, this big, lumbering man with the expression of a mouse caught hiding in a cupboard. He finally says, "You have a car here?"

"The light gray Buick over there. That's mine."

"I will meet you at your car. Please wait there for me."

I get into my Buick while Stern explains to his family that he'll be driving back to town with me. His wife looks over in my direction, though she's too far away for me to read her expression. Francine is already in the car. After more prodding from her husband, Mrs. Stern finally gets in, too, and the limousine drives away. Stern trudges back to me. He looks so exhausted he might pass for dead.

❖

"Okay, Dr. Stern," I say when we're out of the cemetery and driving through Queens. "What scared you back there?"

He doesn't answer me right away, just looks out the window, fascinated by the flashy scenery. "So many places growing," he says, "so much in America growing so fast. You know, when I first came to this country twenty years ago, this borough, this Queens, it didn't have very much, just quiet little towns and some farms. A pretty place. Now look—stores and people everywhere. It's not as pretty."

"But it's making you very rich," I say. "All that stuff made of plastic that those people are buying off the shelves of those stores. Plastic that you supply. The American Dream is lining your pockets nicely."

"You know my factory? How would you know my factory?"

"Your sister mentioned it, and that your plastics formula was making you wealthy."

"Yes, that is certainly so," he says with a slightly guilty sigh. I've seen that act before, especially among educated Old World types, a discomfort with the brute facts of making lots of cash. His sister didn't seem to share that silly attitude. Good for her.

Stern's daydreaming out the window again. Sighing, he says, "I miss the quiet of the pretty little farms and villages I used to drive through on my way to work. So nice, it was."

Never mind the quaint past; I need to get this conversation back to the problem scaring the hell outta Stern's present. "Look, Dr. Stern, we're not here to discuss the effects of American capitalism. How about getting to the point."

"Yes, all right," he says, finally turning his attention from the scenery out the window and back to me, "but first I have a question for you. How does a person like you come to know my sister Hannah?"

I've run into this crap a million times but it still tightens my jaw. Through a tight smile, I toy with him. "A person like me? What do you mean, a person like me? You mean my good tailoring? My nice car? Or maybe you mean my appreciation for expensive art."

"Oh, you understand art?"

"Your sister certainly thought so."

"Yes, well, she would know. Hannah loved art. So did her husband. He had quite a famous collection. The Nazis took it. Hannah wanted it back. Did she tell you that?"

It's not time for me to come clean with the guy, not until I know he's a good bet, and so far he's not winning me over. "Listen, we could chitchat about museum pieces all day but that's not why you're here. So get to the point. What the hell scared you back there at the cemetery? What did you see?"

He looks out at the passing streets again, more as a way to avoid looking at me than with any real fascination with the shiny new suburban landscape. After he clears his throat—another way of putting a bit of distance between himself, me, and his fear—he says, "A woman. A woman in black. I have seen her before. She has threatened me before."

"Yeah? When? How do you mean, threatened you?"

"She warned me not to talk. And look, here I am, talking." He's sweating again, opening the collar of his overcoat, taking out his handkerchief and wiping his face with it.

"Talk about what? Dr. Stern, I'm not a mind reader. If you want me to help you, you've got to tell me what's going on."

We're stuck in a bottleneck, which further upsets Stern. "Ach, this traffic is terrible! My wife will be waiting for me. The rabbi is coming over."

"He'll wait. Rabbis are good at waiting. So let's put the time to good use. Give me the story about this woman. Who is she and what is it she warned you not to talk about?"

"I don't know who she is. She was waiting for me on the street outside my house when I came back from the police station last night. And she didn't say her name."

"The cops took you to the station? Why?"

"To show me pictures. In a book. Maybe I could recognize someone who knew my sister. Why would they think Hannah would know such disreputable people? Gangsters."

"And did you recognize anyone?"

"Of course not. At least, not until I saw you at the cemetery and my daughter told me your name."

Wonderful. Known by my mug shot.

Stern's still talking. "But the police didn't tell me how they connected you to Hannah, just that I should watch out for you. They didn't tell me anything, really. I guess they never do. They just ask questions. That's how they frighten people." He's getting more fidgety by the minute. "Can't you get out of this traffic? And must *everyone* honk their horn? America can be a very noisy country."

"Never mind the noise. What did this woman say last night?"

"She asked me if I had something. She kept saying, *Do you have it? Did you take it?* and things like that. She was in such a wild state she didn't even say what it was she thought I had. I told her I had no idea what she was talking about, but she didn't seem to believe me. And that's when she threatened me. She said she'd kill me if I was holding out on her or if I told anyone about her talking to me. Oh God, this traffic is terrible. My wife will be very angry."

"Settle down. Look, the lane next to us is starting to move. Okay, so let's talk about what this woman looked like. Can you describe her? Was she in one of the pictures the cops showed you?"

"I never saw her face. She wore one of those hats with a veil, a wide black hat with a veil, and it was nighttime. She wore the same black hat and veil now, too, at the cemetery. Ach, traffic is stopping again. We're getting nowhere. Maybe we could go around or something? Make a U-turn?"

"Dr. Stern, if I make a U-turn into oncoming traffic, the cops will hop on our tail and move us off the road and ask a bunch of questions neither of us would want to deal with and wind up giving me a ticket which I don't need showing up on a police blotter. So just be patient." That last word is lost in a bang as loud as thunder. Shards of glass fly past me, nearly take out my eyes. The passenger-side window is shattered into a million pieces, and bits of Marcus Stern's skull and brains are splattered all over my face and coat.

CHAPTER SEVEN

Barking dogs. Snapping alligators. Dirty brown clouds fat with storms. I see their shapes in the soot and tobacco stains on the window behind Lieutenant Huber's desk. Picking out shapes on the glass is all that's keeping me from going loopy from the drone of Huber's tedious grilling, or howling like a banshee at the memory of Marcus Stern's exploding head.

Marcus Stern, Hannah Jacobson: brother and sister whose family has suffered more death and destruction than heaven should allow. And Huber, for all his droning, all his grilling, doesn't know the half of it.

All he knows is that Mrs. J and Marcus Stern were murdered in the here and now and that I show up in both killings. Huber's knocking himself out trying to attach their deaths to me, to somehow find some scrap that will give him the satisfaction of sending me to prison, which seems to be every New York cop's wet dream.

So I'm stuck here in Huber's office, my face still sticky and stinging, and my coat still reeking with the bloody remnants of Marcus Stern's skull and brains.

Huber's had me going around and around about the Stern shooting for the better part of the afternoon, ever since he had me brought back to Manhattan for questioning after the Queens cops wasted about three hours of my time. The Queens boys weren't happy about handing me over to their more well-connected rivals in Skyscraper-ville, but their hurt feelings were nothing compared to how I felt about it. I wasn't crazy about them taking my gun, either.

My annoyance collapsed into bone-crushing tedium by the time Huber pumped me about the Stern shooting for the umpteenth time through that buzzy growl of his, though I've given him nothing new with each retelling. He's taking his frustration out on his unlit cigar, chewing the end like a dog working a piece of gristle.

He can gag on that cigar, for all I care. He'll never hear it from me about the mysterious woman who scared the crap out of Stern at the cemetery. I don't share anything with cops.

And I'm sick and tired of Huber's company. It's time to get the hell out of here.

So I reach for the phone on Huber's desk.

His hand slams on the receiver. "And whaddya think you're doing?" he says.

"Taking my rights as a citizen, Lieutenant. I'm entitled to a phone call."

"You're entitled to what I say you're entitled to." He pulls the phone away from me, parks it close to him.

"Sure, I forgot," I say. "You're Daddy Law. Mustn't disobey Daddy."

He finds that funny; anyway, he's laughing, sort of, if you can call that toothy rasp of his a laugh. "Daddy Law! Not bad, Gold. But I hope you don't think it'll make me like you any better."

"You've got a right not to like me, Lieutenant, but I've got a right to use the phone."

He's not laughing anymore but he's still enjoying himself, still playing petty with me. Maybe he can't make me talk, but he can control my use of the phone.

He finally lights his cigar, takes his time about it, too, letting the match hover at the burning tip. Then he sucks two or three times on the damn thing, the flesh under the day-old stubble on his skinny face creasing like a dirty pillowcase. He finally tosses the match away, saying, "Okay, sure, go ahead, make your damn phone call. Calling your lawyer, I suppose?" He pushes the phone toward me like he's offering candy.

"I guess you're just too smart for me, Lieutenant."

"Don't get cute, Gold. You know, it could be a while 'til your lawyer gets here, and in the meantime you're still mine."

I do my best to ignore that stomach-turning thought, just take the phone and dial the number. The whir and click of the rotary almost mask the sloppy pop of Huber's lips puffing the wet end of his cigar.

It's not my lawyer I'm dialing, it's my office. I get Judson on the line, but before I get a chance to say anything past hello, Judson says, "Hey, where you been? Drogan called. He wants you to meet him at Smiley's bar. You know the place, across from Pier 18 near the fish market. He said he'll wait."

"Yeah, okay. Listen, I need you to spring my car from the police lot in Queens and get the busted window replaced and the interior cleaned up. And tell the repair guy he'll see an extra fifty to get the job done this afternoon."

"How the hell did the window get busted?"

"Tell you later. One more thing"—I look straight at Huber, who's still puffing the cigar behind a cloud of smoke that can't completely obscure his smug disgust with me—"call my lawyer. Send him to Lieutenant Huber's office. *Now.*"

When I hang up, Huber's grinning around that cigar. Then he talks around it, tobacco juice pooling between his teeth. "You know, Gold, for all your big money and flashy style, for all the fancy women in your life—yeah, sure, I know all about that, sickening, if you ask me—for all that, you're nothing but a no-good lowlife who keeps lousy company. Death squads seem to follow you around. You visit Hannah Jacobson and she gets cut to ribbons. Her brother Marcus Stern gets into your car, and, bang, he's blown to kingdom come. And how many times do I have to ask you what the hell he was doing in your car anyway? Why wasn't he with his family after the funeral?"

"You're wasting your time, Lieutenant. My lawyer's office isn't far. He'll be here pretty soon to spring me, since you have nothing to hold me except your deep dislike of me, my love life, and my tailoring. So why don't you forget about all that and do something useful, like arrange police protection for Stern's wife and daughter? Or are you using them as bait? I wouldn't put it past you."

You'd think I'd have learned by now not to toy with cops, but it's too much fun and I can never resist an opportunity to stick a pin in their puffed-up chests, like calling Huber Daddy Law. But I've gone too far this time. I know it because I recognize what's going on in Huber's eyes and on his face—darkening, reddening—as he puts his cigar down, stands up so slowly, and moves his stick of a body around his desk so calmly that the air around him doesn't even ripple. I know what's coming and there's nothing I can do about it, because if I raise a hand to a cop in a police station I'll wind up broken and bleeding on the floor of a holding cell, worked over by every cop in the building, even the traffic boys. So when Huber's fist slams into the left side of my jaw I'm stung by the pain but not by surprise.

He grabs the armrests on either side of me, pins me to the chair. His flushed face and cigar-stained teeth are a grotesque study in red and yellow. Stick a picture frame around his bony head and he'd pass for an Expressionist portrait of meanness. "You got your nerve, Gold," he says through a predatory growl. "Everything about you is an insult to what's good and decent in this country, you hear me? You think you know my job? Well I'm way ahead of you. I posted a patrol at the Stern house while you were on your way here from Queens. *I* was free to do that, Gold, while *you* were stuck in a paddy wagon. You get my drift?"

The temptation to rip his lips to shreds and get that smug ugly smile off his face is so strong I figure it might be worth the beating I'd take in the slammer, but I'm distracted—and Huber's mouth is saved from disfigurement—by the musky tang of expensive men's cologne drifting into the room. Irwin Maximovic, my lawyer, is coming through the door, all three hundred elegantly fat pounds of him.

If you want a lesson in just how confident, quiet, and polite pure power can be, all you have to do is listen to the refined patter of Winnie Maximovic. "Good afternoon, Lieutenant Huber. Always a pleasure to see you. I know a policeman's lot is a busy one, so I wouldn't dream of wasting your time. May I inquire on what charge you are holding my client?" The smile on Winnie's fleshy face, like a fold in a satchel, would charm the stars out of the sky, and then he'd step on them.

Huber picks up his cigar again and chomps it between his teeth. "You can skip the theatrics, counselor. Just get lost and take your client with you. She's stinkin' up the joint, and so are you, if you want my opinion. The sooner the two of you get out of here, the sooner my office can air out."

Winnie, still smiling, says, "Well then, let's go, Cantor," but he immediately changes his mind and says, "Sit down again, Cantor." He's seen the bruise on my jaw, my split lip, the smears of Marcus Stern on my face. "Lieutenant? To what do we owe the injuries to my client's face?"

"Haven't you heard? She was behind the wheel when the passenger in her car was shot to death. Head blown to bits. Glass and flesh and pieces of the guy's skull flew everywhere. She must've caught some. Isn't that right, Gold?" It's not a question. It's a coded instruction not to make trouble for him. Ordinarily he wouldn't care; cops slap people around every day and get away with it. But he knows that Winnie Maximovic has more lines into City Hall than the phone company. Huber may not care who digs around in his personal life, a fact he lorded over me last night, but no cop really wants their name dangled like fruit in front of the higher-ups, even if their name is clean. It annoys those higher-ups, makes extra paperwork for them, puts blisters on their fingers, and if that happens, Huber would take it out on me. Maybe not now, maybe not soon, but down the line, when the heat's off him and no one's looking.

Winnie, dry as toast, says, "Is the lieutenant's account true, Cantor?"

"True enough," I say. "C'mon, let's get out of here." Getting rid of Huber feels as good as having a good shit.

Before Winnie and I leave the building, I stop in a restroom to wash up. There's nothing but cold water, and its chill stings the cuts on my face. Framed by the mirror, I look like a recruiting poster for one of those death squads Huber says follow me around. Last night's gash to my chin has new company: the patch on my jaw where Huber walloped me is red as raw meat and already turning black-and-blue; there's blood on my split lip and crusting remnants of Marcus Stern on my cap and overcoat. I wash the blood off, get rid of as much brain pulp and bone splinters as I can, but violence and death still cling to me like sweat.

❖

Winnie's black Lincoln, with its slathering of chrome and bright whitewall tires, is fat, heavy, and expensive, just like Winnie. It moves through midtown traffic with the ponderous grace of a whale in a tuxedo.

The trip downtown gives me time to fill Winnie in on everything that's happened since I left Mrs. Jacobson's apartment last night. The story's up-to-date by the time we're downtown and pull up to the East River waterfront.

"Listen, Winnie, any chance you can get my gun back from the Queens cops?"

"Is it registered to you?"

"No. It's clean."

"Then leave it. They can't frame you if the gun is ever used in a crime, accidental or otherwise. You're already in a tough spot. A passenger being assassinated in your car does not bode well for your health and safety, Cantor."

"Spare me the lecture. You sound like Rosie."

"Whom, I must say, you do not appreciate sufficiently."

"You can spare me the guilt angle, too."

"All right, but what can I do to get you to be less reckless in your work? Cantor, my friend, I can more than likely remove you from the Law's grip when you need me to, but keeping you safe from murderers or the likes of Jimmy Shea is outside my sphere of influence. In those matters, I'm afraid you're on your own."

"I know, Winnie. Just stay available for a while, yeah? Huber's not going to let up on me. I might need you to get me free of him again."

"Do you want me to contact my friends at City Hall? See about having Huber called off altogether?"

"No, let's give him his rope, see where he dangles it. I might see something useful there."

"You play dangerous games with the police, Cantor."

"And you don't? I've seen what's in your bedroom closet. Someday those gowns will get you arrested." I get out of the car to the sound of Winnie's guffaws echoing along the docks.

❖

Smiley's bar has been at this same spot on the waterfront for so long that river fog permanently floats through the room. Walk through the briny mist and the floorboards groan and sour fumes rise from an ancient broth of spilled whiskey, tobacco spit, and vomit. Several generations of Smileys have kept the place a bare-bones saloon where dockworkers and fishmongers do their light lunch drinking at noon and their serious drinking at night. Mornings and afternoons, the rickety tables and scratched-up bar stools are occupied by the out-of-luck guys who've fallen out of favor with Jimmy Shea's dockside Mob bosses, who pass them over for work. Someday maybe these guys will get smart, or at least get angry, and go to war to break the Mob's grip. Until then, they just smoke and drink and mumble.

I spot Red through the river fog and cigarette smoke circling a table in the back where he's sharing a bottle with a woman. As

I get closer, the woman's story gets clearer: she's a working girl, a still-attractive redhead with a good figure, which helps keep attention off the faded state of her floral print dress. And she's still trying to pass for a hot kid of twenty, but the sway of her hair against her face and along her shoulders can't completely hide her pinched cheeks and the thickening skin of her neck, which peg her just over the dark side of forty. That faded dress and those hollow cheeks tell me she's on her way down in the trade, but with her big blue eyes and round, plump breasts that push nicely against that floral dress, her goods are still sweet enough for johns to work on her in carpeted bedrooms. It won't be long, though, before she's sliding her backside along the dockside streets. Maybe she already is. Her story's an old one but it's a heartbreaker every time.

When I get to the table, Red asks, "You wanna drink? I'll get an extra glass."

"Don't bother," I say and just pick up the bottle of the no-name whiskey that he and the woman are drinking. I take a slug, hoping its rotgut fire can burn away the crappier elements of my day. It does, a little, blurs the tedious malice of Lieutenant Huber, but can't touch the memories of Mrs. J's bloody outline on her carpet or Marcus Stern's head exploding all over me.

I take a seat, say, "Where are your manners, Red? Aren't you going to introduce me to your lady friend?"

"Cantor, this here is Miss Iris Page."

"Hello, Miss Page. I'm—"

"I know who you are." Her voice is breathy and raw, fine-tuned by whiskey and cigarettes and sex. So when she says, "You're Cantor Gold," it sounds like a three a.m. proposition. The way she's looking at me, though, is anything but a proposition, more like a mother hen. "Uh, are you gonna be able to get through this conversation? You look like you need more than a drink. You look like you need an ambulance."

"I'm fine."

She takes that with a shrug and says, "Then let's get down to business. I have information. Information worth paying for."

"Is that so?" I take my pack of smokes from my pocket, shake out one for myself, and offer one to Iris, who takes it. That's when I notice her chipped nail polish, a five-and-dime shade of bright pink. I light the smoke for her, which brings a look of surprise into her eyes, and I get the feeling it's been a while since anyone's treated her like a lady. Well, maybe Drogan's been giving her the princess treatment. Whores tend to bring out his chivalrous side.

"Listen," Iris says after a deep drag on the cigarette, the exhaled smoke veiling her face, "word gets around, and the word around the docks today is that Red here's been asking questions on the quiet about a certain cop. Now, I trust Red. Everybody on the waterfront trusts Red, so I figure I can't go wrong telling what I know. But a girl's gotta eat, so after Red and I meet up, I told him I heard your name mentioned in a certain conversation. But sharing that conversation and who did the talkin' is going to cost: first from him, just for my coming forward—like a service charge, you understand—and then from the interested party, meaning you. So here we are. We've been waiting here for you for over an hour."

I take another slug of whiskey, then ask Drogan, "How much did she take you for, Red?"

"Coupla sawbucks. But like she says, a girl's gotta eat."

"You're quite the businesswoman, Miss Page," I say. "All right, what'll this cost me?"

"Fifty. Up front."

"That's a lot of green for this neighborhood."

"Yeah, well, the information's first rate. The life-or-death type. *Your* life or death, and I'm not kiddin'."

The negotiation just swung in her favor. Iris Page has been negotiating tough deals all her life, and she knows when she's holding the aces. "Twenty-five up front," I say, "the rest if I like the information."

"How do I know you won't cheat me for the other half?"

I pull my wallet from my pocket, take out twenty-five and hand it to her. "I don't cheat women."

She takes the bills as if I've just offered her flowers.

She gets over the sentimental lapse pretty quick and stuffs the cash into her handbag, a black beaded number that isn't threadbare yet but will be, inside of a year. She snaps the bag shut with the solemnity of someone about to give a death sentence, or maybe hear one. "You can't ever say you heard this from me," she says. "I'm dead if it gets around. My skin may not be real sweet anymore, but it's the only skin I've got and I still like walking around in it."

"I know how to keep my mouth shut."

She nods, takes a drink, swallows it slowly, like maybe the whiskey will stop time, but when it doesn't after all, she says, "That cop Red's been asking about is in cahoots with Jimmy Shea."

The only reason I don't fall off my chair is because suddenly I'm clutching the edge of the table, holding it so hard my fingernails dig into the crummy wood. "That's a helluva statement, Miss Page. Can you back up a thing like that?"

"Oh, I can back it up," she says. "I was there when they were talking. Well, sort of there."

"What do you mean, sort of there? Either you were there or you weren't."

"It means," she says with dramatic exaggeration, "that I was in Jimmy's apartment. In the bathroom, washing up. I, um, well, Jimmy had hired me for the night." She's actually embarrassed when she says this, cringing like a schoolgirl who just found out she's been spied on naked in the girls' locker room. Embarrassment is out of tune for a working girl, but I guess spending the night with Jimmy Shea could humiliate even the most desperate soul. Iris Page just broke my heart again.

She takes another swallow of the rotgut to restore her. "Anyway, while I'm in there, in the bathroom—"

I break in, "Hold it. When was this? What time was this?"

"Real early this morning, before seven o'clock, maybe a quarter 'til. So while I was in the bathroom, I heard the front doorbell ring. Jimmy was good and annoyed. First of all, the guy was able to come upstairs from the street door, like he broke in or something"—I doubt he'd have to work hard to break in. Jimmy's

as cheap about his living quarters as he is about his tailoring—
"and really, what a helluva nerve, showing up at that hour, the
crack of dawn. I heard Jimmy grumbling all the way to the door.
The bathroom is next to the bedroom, right off the living room,
and you have to go through the living room to get to the front door,
so you can hear what goes on pretty good in there. Well, Jimmy
opens the door and the guy comes in, and boy, did I get an earful."

She's got me and Red wrapped around her little finger and
she's enjoying every bit of our rapt attention, especially Red's,
angling, I guess, for his business, until she remembers that I'm the
paying customer at this table. Taking a last drag on her cigarette,
she drops it to the floor, stubs it out with the toe of her shabby
pink shoe, and shifts her attention to me. "And that's when your
name came up," she says. "The guy, the one who came in without
so much as a good morning, says to Jimmy, *I want Cantor Gold.
You're gonna give her to me.* The guy has one of those sawtooth
voices, the grating kind that could cut you in half. Gave me the
creeps, I can tell you. Anyway, then Jimmy says, *Who the hell
are you?* And the guy says, *Lieutenant Huber, New York Police
Department. And if you don't want the cops breathing down your
neck, Shea, you'll play ball with me.*"

I should've ripped Huber's face apart when I had the chance
back at the precinct. I should've killed him. I'd have fried for it,
but one less cop, one less sneaky officer of the dirty-playing Law
would be around to stalk people.

I have to quit that daydream and get back to Iris's story. She
says, "And then neither of them says anything for a minute until
Jimmy says, *How about some coffee, Lieutenant? Come into the
kitchen.* And that was it. As soon as I hear them go into the kitchen
I get myself back to the bedroom. I really wanted to just scram but
figured if I run out behind Jimmy's back he'll know something's
up, that maybe I got big ears, so I just get back into bed and make
like I went back to sleep, like I didn't hear a thing."

Smart girl. "And you're sure they didn't know you heard them?"

"I'm alive aren't I? Now give me that other twenty-five."

❖

Red was happy to make sure Iris got home safely, and Iris was happy to have him take her there. By now, she's probably got her hands in Red's pockets—that is, if he's still wearing his pants.

I catch an uptown subway at Fulton Street for the ride to the garage where they're patching up my car. No cabbie is going to pick up a fare sporting a gashed chin, a bloodied lip, and a black-and-blue jaw, except maybe Rosie, but letting Rosie see me in this shape isn't the best idea right now. She'd mother hen me about my latest injuries. And besides, getting ferried around town by one woman before going out for the evening with another isn't exactly chivalrous.

It's still the early end of the rush hour, barely past four o'clock, so the train's not too crowded. A few passengers give me the look-over when I step into the car, then turn back to their own business, this being the New York City subway, where odd passengers, even beat-up and bloodied ones, are common as soot. So I settle down in a seat whose woven cane isn't too torn up and scratchy, between a sweaty guy dozing into the afternoon *Journal-American* and a middle-aged woman whose attitude is as pinched as her face.

I nurse my aching jaw as best I can against the subway's lurch and rattle, settle in for the trip uptown. I used to ride the subway a lot more than I do these days, ride it in from Coney Island as a kid with pennies and nickels in my pockets. Then I'd ride around town like a little big shot with dollars in those same pockets after I'd fenced the stuff that fell out of people's bags at Coney's beach. I liked to read the ribbon of ads running the length of the car above the windows and imagine myself buying some of the stuff, like the fancy whiskeys and the colorful packs of cigarettes, just to impress the pretty women in some of the ads, who in my fevered pubescent imagination would find me suave and irresistible.

The women in the subway ads are still pretty, and so are the sweeties in the trains' underground beauty pageant: the monthly winner of the Miss Subways title. The current winner is right above me, a sweet-faced blonde who's a salesgirl at a stationary store, the sign says, and who likes movies that remind her of her childhood back in Iowa. Not really my type.

Iris Page might've been my type at one time or another, before she hired herself out, got careless about holding on to what must've been a sweet soul. All she's got now is the gut instinct to survive. She knows which tools to use and how to use them. Truth is a tool, and so is a lie. She used a lie on Jimmy Shea this morning by hiding what she overheard. That lie saved her life. She used the truth to get fifty bucks outta me.

But Jimmy knows how to use those same tools, knows how to use them even better than Iris. Jimmy knows how to twist the truth and polish the lie so that one looks like the other.

So who's he lying to? Me, or Huber?

It hurts my jaw and split lip when I smile, but I can't help it; I'm smiling. I'm smiling because the bombshell Iris Page just dropped might not explode in my lap after all but in Huber's lap, and that would make me grin from ear to ear.

❖

The guy did a good job on my car, cleaned her up and polished her good as new. There's no trace of blood or brains or broken glass, nothing to catch the eye of the garage attendant in my apartment building when I drive in. And if my car looks its usual spiffy self to Sam, who notices even the smallest thing about a tenant's car that'll earn him a few bucks for a wax job, it'll look good enough to ferry the very classy Vivienne Parkhurst Trent.

But even a hot shower and dressing in the smooth threads of my black trousers and white dinner jacket can't polish up the violence that's been carved into my face. The old scars just keep getting more company.

CHAPTER EIGHT

Vivienne's butler George is less annoyed at seeing me at eight o'clock this evening than he was at three o'clock this morning. Instead of rumpled pajamas, he's his impeccable self in his butler's finest, tailcoat and all, when he opens that spooky carved door of the mansion and lets me in. "You may wait in the living room," he says. "Miss Trent will be down directly."

So it's once more along the checkered marble floor and past the Renaissance treasures that line the hall. A minute later, I'm back in the living room and on the sofa.

I light a smoke. That first deep, satisfying inhale does a good job of calming the body, but it can't chase away the horrors clawing around in my mind. Thoughts of Hannah Jacobson, cut up. Marcus Stern, blown to bits. That piece of shit Huber smacking me around. This isn't a state of mind I want to show Vivienne. I've got to play her smooth so she's easy in my company when we're at Max Hagen's tonight. If Vivienne doesn't play along, Hagen could dummy up about any possible leads to the stolen Dürer, and without that lead, I'm stuck between the long, hulking shadows of the Mob and the Law.

So I get up and pour myself a Chivas at the small bar behind the sofa, hoping the good whiskey will work its magic and improve my mood. A swallow or two helps a little, helps me put on an easy face—my suave act, as Drogan calls it—when Vivienne swooshes into the room in a swirl of black silk, ruby jewels, and a red lipstick that begs to be smeared in the dark. She's very classy. She's very sexy. And she's no fool. "What's wrong, Cantor? I haven't seen you look this miserable since…I mean—"

"You mean since Sophie disappeared."

"Yes, well—yes. I'm sorry. I didn't mean to reopen such a painful subject."

"Skip it."

"Of course. But you do look like you've been chewed up."

Bringing up Sophie doesn't help my disposition, but then Vivienne lifts her fingers to my battered face, strokes my wounds, and looks at me through those big green eyes of hers as if I'm an orphaned pup. "You've had a tough day," she says. Her touch doesn't take the hurt away; it even makes each cut and bruise hurt more. But it's a sublime pain.

And then it's gone. Her fingers are gone from my face. The tenderness in her eyes simmers into something darker, a deep green that lures like an open cave. Softly, in almost a whisper, she says, "Aren't you going to offer me a drink?"

"What's your pleasure?"

"Bourbon, with a splash of soda. But make it a short one. We really should be going."

I hand her the drink. Her red nail polish glints in the lamplight as she wraps her fingers around the glass. And then, in a manner that's at the heart of Vivienne's charm, that blend of ladylike class and the ancestral gutter streak at her core, she downs the drink in one pull. Putting the empty glass on the bar, she says, "Shall we go?"

I take her arm, chivalrous to *my* core, and escort her out of the living room.

George is waiting for us at the front door. He has Vivienne's black silk clutch bag and her evening coat, a deep purple number he's holding at the ready.

"Please give my coat to Cantor, George," she says. "She'll help me on with it."

Obedient at the bidding of his mistress, he hands me the coat.

I slip the coat along Vivienne's arms and settle it on her shoulders. The whisper of the silk lining against her skin is as seductive as breath in my ear. I'm having a helluva time reminding myself that tonight is a business date.

Vivienne takes her clutch bag. George opens the door. As we walk through, Vivienne doesn't wait for me to take her arm; she slips her arm through mine.

I don't know if it's because a streetlight has caught the white of my dinner jacket, but in any event, I'm glowing.

❖

Max Hagen doesn't have a butler. He has a maid. She takes Vivienne's coat when we arrive.

Hagen's apartment is everything you'd expect an art connoisseur's Park Avenue apartment to be: big, impeccably furnished in well-chosen historic periods if heavy on the fussiness of French Baroque, the lighting carefully arranged to show off all the good art on walls the color of old blood. The walls throw a weird red tinge around the edges of the Baroque picture frames.

Most of the paintings have the muted luster of the Renaissance masters, Hagen's specialty at the Pauling-Barnett auction house. Scattered among the Dutch and Italian landscapes, there's an elegant Mannerist Madonna by Parmigianino, with the artist's typical taste for a Madonna who's more fashion mannequin than Holy Mother; a couple of Frans Hals's cheery, red-faced drunks to give the living room a party mood; a Rembrandt biblical scene to keep Hals's revelers from getting out of line; and a Holbein portrait of an English nobleman in full sepia regalia, a filigreed gold and ruby sash stretched across his fur-trimmed cloak. I wonder if the guy is one of Hagen's ancestors or if Hagen just wishes he is. Maybe Hagen gathers high-quality antique ancestors the way he gathers pricey antique frames and furniture.

Hagen's guests are as well appointed as the Holbein nobleman, the men in perfectly tailored tuxedos or dinner jackets, the women in colorful silks and satins, jewels swaying on their well-tended flesh. All in all, between the priceless art, the treasury of jewels, and the bank accounts of the guests, there's enough money in this room to buy a reasonably sized museum or a small country, say, Luxembourg.

A cultured male voice, deep and smooth as warm syrup, rolls toward us through the refined chatter of guests and the tinkling of cocktail glasses. "My dear Vivienne, I'm delighted you could make it." The voice belongs to the approaching figure of a tall, elegantly attired and groomed man whose white dinner jacket shimmers in the light of each lamp he passes, and whose carefully trimmed mustache sits on his lip with the perfection of two delicate brushstrokes. His blue eyes are impish and steely at the same time, giving him the air of a fun-loving aristocrat with a murderous streak. It's our host, Max Hagen.

He and Vivienne exchange suavely Continental greetings—a light kiss on each cheek—and then Hagen extends his hand to me, buddy fashion. "And you must be Cantor Gold," he says. His apparent comfort with me is surprising. Well, maybe not so surprising: there's a svelte young man nearby, dark haired and pretty in his close-fitting black tuxedo, who's looking at Hagen with an expression I've seen in the eyes of some of the more impatient women I've dated.

Well, well.

Hagen, the perfect host, says as he moves between us and takes Vivienne's arm and mine, "I'm sure you both need a drink. Come, let's move to the bar," and leads us across the living room. The svelte young man watches us but keeps his distance.

After the hired bartender fixes us up with a bourbon and soda for Vivienne, a martini for Hagen, and a neat scotch for me, Hagen says, "Forgive me for mentioning it, Gold, but you look as if you've been in some sort of accident. Are you quite all right?"

"I'm fine, thanks."

Vivienne, with a nod toward the pretty young man with the impatient eyes, says through a sly smile, "You know, Max, you're really ignoring Vern, and he doesn't look at all happy about it."

"He'll just have to get over it. He shouldn't even be here, and he knows it. This is a working evening for me. My guests are clients of Pauling-Barnett. Really, sometimes that boy has no discretion. I'm sure Gold understands."

Dry as sandpaper on stone, I say, "Sure, I understand."

Hagen ignores that, just says, "As a matter of fact, we should move to somewhere more private. You're attracting the wrong kind of attention, Gold. Let's go into my study, shall we? Come along, and please bring your drinks."

Vivienne's earlier description of Hagen as a cautious man barely describes the panic he's doing a reasonably good job of swallowing. A few arched eyebrows and I'm shunted off to a side room. I don't like it, and ordinarily I'd hold my ground, but this is Hagen's home, his castle, his risk, so his rules. And I need his cooperation.

I follow Hagen and Vivienne across the living room. The stares of several guests swipe me like sword blades as we walk by. Some stare at my battered face. Some stare at my dinner clothes. One of the stares is from a particularly delicious blonde in a strapless low-cut pink silk number revealing a creamy cleavage I wouldn't mind crawling around in. The outlaw in me can't resist giving her a wink. She shrinks from it. Pity.

I notice, though, on my way into the study, that Vern of the impatient eyes lifts his drink to me in a smiling toast.

Hagen's book-lined study is the baronial sort where a sixteenth-century Medici prince would feel right at home. Drifting around the books and framed antique maps is the meaty aroma of fine old leather bindings. Hagen motions me and Vivienne into two club chairs and leans his long body against his desk, an ornate mass of dark wood with medieval-type carvings of gargoyles running down the corners. "So," he says, before swallowing the rest of his drink and setting the glass beside him on the desk, "you are the infamous Cantor Gold. I've avoided doing business with you, as I'm sure you realize, but it seems I finally require your services, unseemly as they are."

"Why don't you climb down off that high horse, Hagen. My unseemly services have supplied Pauling-Barnett with more than a few pricey knickknacks. Not everyone in that house is so, uh, dainty about doing business with me."

"True. But your reputation for taking undue risks doesn't mix well with my reputation for delicacy. So you'll excuse me if I generally prefer to deal with a less danger-prone supplier."

"Suit yourself," I say, "but I'm not here tonight to win your business. According to Vivienne, you might have some information I'm looking for. Has she filled you in?"

"She's told me that a Dürer watercolor's been stolen, if that's what you mean."

"That's only part of what I mean. The other part's about murder."

He doesn't even blink. "Yes, Vivienne mentioned that, too. Your client—Mrs. Hannah Jacobson, was it? Unfortunate. So sad."

"And her brother, too. Had his head blown to bits this afternoon." I just described a horror scene, but Hagen doesn't look horrified. Instead, he gives me haughty look, as if he'll dismiss me from the room if I say anything else distasteful. I can't tell if his aristocratic armor is a cover for his fear of all the death that's trailing the Dürer or he's really just a cold and snobby fish.

Vivienne's face has gone so white her ruby necklace looks like open wounds. "Cantor, really, must you put it—I mean, that poor family."

"Yeah," I say and take a swallow of my drink. Maybe if I drink enough it'll finally drown my revulsion at yesterday's rotten night and today's equally rotten day.

Hagen moves around his desk to his chair. He seats himself and lets the desk between us shield him from whatever vulgar danger I've had the gall to bring into his home. He says, with a dismissive wave, "Well, I don't know what sort of information you expect from me, Gold. I certainly don't involve myself with murder."

"It's the Dürer I want to ask you about. Vivienne tells me you already had a buyer."

"Yes, that's so. He was prepared to pay handsomely for it."

"And you'd take a cut, yes?"

"Of course. Just what is it you're getting at, Gold?"

"Just covering my bases," I say. "Did Vivienne also mention that the Dürer had deep sentimental value for Mrs. Jacobson and that she probably wouldn't sell it? Of course, if you sold it to your buyer directly, without Hannah Jacobson in the picture, you wouldn't have to settle for just a cut of the money."

Vivienne pipes up, "Cantor! Really!" at the same time Hagen springs forward in his chair. But being the tasteful man he's obviously schooled himself to be, he leans back again, regains his elegant calm, and says, "Just covering your bases, yes, of course. Well, let me cover this base for you, Gold. I don't acquire artwork by violence, and I don't need to increase my bank account by stealing art, either. My bank account is healthy enough through legitimate earnings, thank you."

"Good for you," I say, unimpressed with Hagen's self-righteous brand of honor. "All right, now that that's out of the way, do you have any ideas about who else might covet the Dürer? You're connected to some of the richest, most aggressive collectors of Renaissance goods in town, Hagen."

"And so are you."

"Sure," I say, "so let's talk about the clients we share. And right now, no one in my stable is a candidate for a heist of this particular artwork. So it's your clients, the ones we don't share, that I'm interested in. Anyone come to mind who might want the Dürer so much they'd kill for it? And don't give me a cock-and-bull story that your crowd is too dignified and risk shy to get their hands dirty. You and I both know how cutthroat the art game can be. There's a thousand years of murder behind it."

Vivienne, the color struggling to get back in her cheeks, says, "Cantor, please. Let's just discuss the missing Dürer and leave out all this talk of death. It's upsetting."

Hagen chimes in, "Quite right. Let's pursue a more productive line, shall we? Frankly, Gold, I really can't think of anyone among my clients—even, as you call them, the more aggressive ones—who'd stoop to murder. So I have even less of an idea about where the Dürer is than you do. Which is why I need your services." He leans forward now, his blue eyes cold as an Arctic sea. "I want that watercolor," he says, the syrup in his voice congealing into waxy condescension, complete with a sniffy raise of his head, the better to look down his nose. "I want to engage you to find it on my behalf. My client is still willing to pay a fortune for it. Finding it could prove profitable for us both, Gold." He leans back again, awkwardly though, aware that his snooty manner is annoying me more than impressing me. The next time he opens his mouth, he corrects his attitude, reverts to being the genial host again, his tone silky as a debutante's dress. "What I mean to say is, since you're already looking for it, why not make the search profitable?"

I polish off the last of my scotch while I take a good look at Hagen, at the smile that now shows too many teeth and spreads his mustache like a tortured moth. "*How* profitable?" I say.

"I could cut you in for, say, ten percent."

With my own genial smile, I say, "Fifty percent."

"That's rather steep," he says.

"Fifty percent," I say. "Or find it yourself. I've already risked my life lifting that Dürer from an embittered old pal of Hitler's, slipping it out of Europe and bringing it into New York. And now you're asking me to risk my life again, put myself in the crosshairs of whoever's murdering anyone connected to that watercolor. So if you want me to hunt for it, you can just think of my fifty-percent cut as combat pay."

Hagen slips into his perfect-host persona again, hoping, I guess, to draw me into a more reasonable negotiation. He's so cordial now, so oily smooth, I'm surprised his dinner jacket doesn't slide off his shoulders. "Can we say thirty percent, then?" he says. "A fair compromise?"

"Maybe you didn't hear me, Hagen. The risk to my life is not up for horse trading. Fifty percent. That's what it'll take for me to turn it over when I find it. *If* I find it."

Vivienne's hand moves along my arm in a way that's friendly and scolding at the same time. "Don't be greedy, Cantor. Max is making you a fair offer."

"Sorry, Vivienne, but we're in a greedy business. Hagen certainly is, but so are you. Your museum's collections and prestige are built on scholarship and greed. So don't get all moral on me. It's unattractive in you, and you're too beautiful to let that get in the way."

I've barely finished talking when the chatter of Hagen's cocktail party rolls into the room as Vern of the impatient eyes and svelte tuxedo walks into the study. The chatter disappears when he closes the door behind him.

With a drink in one hand and a cigarette in the other, Vern moves across the room with the grace of a tango dancer and the attitude of an opera diva. He arrives at Hagen's desk and, supple as a swan, leans his hip against it as comfortably and possessively as if it's his own.

Vern says, "Really, Max, you shouldn't be ignoring your guests, or me, for that matter. Hello, Vivienne. Nice to see you again, but you're keeping Max away from his guests too long. And won't you introduce me to *this* interesting person?" He's looking at me. His eyes aren't impatient now. They're narrowed but slightly glowing, looking me over as if trying to memorize me.

I don't wait for an introduction. "My name's Cantor Gold. And you are—?"

"Vern Sichelle." He spells it out. "Yes, that's right, it's pronounced *seashell*. An old Huguenot name according to my mother, but Mother was better at style than truth." He puts his cigarette out in an ashtray on the desk and then extends his hand to me. His fingers are long and thin, fluid as a ballerina's, so his strong grip and steady handshake come as a surprise.

Hagen is clearly in no mood for this intrusion of his usually well-hidden private life, despite the ease with which he knows I'll take it. "If you don't mind, Vern," he says, pushing Vern's name between his teeth, "this is a business meeting."

"Oh," Vern says more to me than Hagen, "are you discussing the little picture Max wants so badly?"

Hagen cuts off that line of chatter. "Vern, since you insisted on joining the party tonight, you can make yourself useful and entertain my guests for a few minutes. Please be your most charming self and go away."

Coolly, as if he's just heard a joke that fell flat, Vern, his hand on his hip, turns to me and Vivienne and says, "You mustn't take Max's dark mood seriously. I certainly don't," then he moves around the desk to Hagen, placing a hand on his shoulder.

Hagen says, "Not now," and brushes Vern's hand away.

If Vern is insulted by Hagen's brush-off, he doesn't show it, at least, not on his face. But his head is down just a little, his shoulders not as straight. "You'll feel better when we go to the country house this weekend, Max. We always enjoy ourselves there." His voice is as light spirited as a prom queen's.

Hagen glances at me and Vivienne and says, with more bite than pleasure, "Vern can be quite the country sportsman. Almost as good at country sports as you, Vivienne."

Vern brightens at the compliment, and at an idea. "You know, Vivienne, you should join us up there in the country sometime. This weekend's hunt is booked, but maybe later in the season?"

"Thank you, Vern. I'd be delighted. I could use a break from town."

"Then it's a date. Well, I see my lord and master has had about enough of me, so I suppose I'd better go out there and earn my keep. It's been nice meeting you, Cantor Gold," he says on his way to the door. "I hope to see you again. We can discuss tailoring."

With Vern gone, Hagen leans forward again, his composure restored. "So, Gold, we were discussing thirty percent."

"No, you were discussing thirty percent. And I told you it's fifty percent or there's no discussion at all." A final swallow of my drink and a loud thunk of my glass on Hagen's desk end my conversation. I extend a hand to Vivienne as I get up from the chair. "Vivienne, care to join me for a drink elsewhere, or will you be staying on at Hagen's little soiree?"

"I, well, I think I ought to stay."

"Suit yourself." I say it as breezily as I can, covering my disappointment. I was hoping for more of Vivienne tonight. A lot more.

Nothing to do now but get out of here. On my way out of Hagen's study, over the cocktail-party noise coming from the living room, I say over my shoulder, "Thanks for the good scotch, Hagen. Anytime you want to get serious and do business, let me know."

The classy crowd in the living room is a little more sloshed now, their chatter more high pitched. Miss Cleavage in Pink is on the arm of some jowly bald guy who has the look of a third or fourth husband. I'd feel sorry for him except he gets to crawl around in places I can only dream about.

"Gold!" My name comes at me from across the room. It's Vern. He's on his way over. "Gold, I'm glad I caught you before you—oh, Vivienne's not joining you?"

"What's on your mind, Vern?"

He takes my arm as we walk across the living room. I get a kick seeing all those society eyebrows go up as we pass. "Well," Vern says, "I just hope you didn't get the wrong impression about Max."

"Was there a right impression I was supposed to get?"

When we're alone in the vestibule by the front door, Vern finally lets go of my arm. The sashaying diva of the study is gone, replaced by a young man whose heart has apparently been taking a beating. "I know Max can be, well, chilly," he says, his head down, his hands in his jacket pockets like a schoolboy. "But you mustn't be too unforgiving of him. He can be a very lovely man."

CHAPTER NINE

There's a chill in the air on Park Avenue. It stings the still-raw bruise on my chin, courtesy of last night's crash landing on Drogan's tug. But it's a good pain, the sting that wakes you up from your delusions, because I must've been deluded to think the aristocratic Vivienne Parkhurst Trent would really leave Hagen's party with me for a night on the town and maybe even tumble with me later. All that teasing at her place, her fingertips on my face, her eyes on me, was just that: teasing. Some women do that, get a thrill from tickling forbidden fruit. Vivienne's not the first woman who's used me to massage that thrill, but she's the first one to get under my skin. I can still feel her crawling around under there.

And I must've been deluded to think that the high and mighty Max Hagen—he of the scrupulously untainted fingers, greedy tastes, and a love life he abuses—yeah, I must've been deluded to think Hagen would give over information, that is, if he had any information at all. A guy like him, so prickly about the slightest risk to his fastidiously cultivated image, he'd have no idea about what gets passed around on the street, no less in the gutter. And the gutter is where I'll have to look for information, maybe even find who killed Hannah Jacobson and Marcus Stern. Murderers are natives of the gutter. It doesn't matter if they sleep in a shack or a penthouse.

So I have to find out what's going on in the gutter, talk to its citizens, or those who do business with them. There's nothing for me here among the golden apartment buildings of Park Avenue.

I get in my car and drive away.

❖

It's nearly nine thirty by the time I get to the Lower East Side. The change of neighborhood, with its neon-lit delicatessens sending out sharp smells of mustard and pickles, the overhead rumble of the Third Avenue El playing background for Billie Holiday singing the blues on my car radio, helps me get rid of my delusions, only to be replaced by a rehash of dirty facts still sticking to me like toilet paper under my shoe: Hannah Jacobson, dead; the Dürer she trusted me to find, gone. Her brother, Marcus Stern, buries his sister only to get his head blown off right here in my car, a blood-and-brains spectacle that might keep me awake nights for the rest of my life. Jimmy Shea and the waterfront Mob are happy to feed me to the cops for Mrs. J's murder, and Lieutenant Huber is happy to eat me alive. And according to Iris Page, Shea and Huber are in cahoots, getting ready to salt and pepper me before they toss me into the pan to fry.

I pull into a parking spot in front of a brownstone on Second Avenue. The house once had sweet memories for me, memories that might've soothed my troubles tonight. I used to think there was genuine welcome and even motherly concern for me from the old woman who's lived here and plied her larcenous trade here since New York was lit by gaslight. Way back when I was a tomboy kid from Coney Island bringing her my pilfered goods to fence, she'd serve me warm honey cake while she picked through my treasures, instructing me on the finer points of thievery. I knew I was a damn lucky kid to do business with her because Esther "Mom" Sheinbaum was then—and still is—the most well-connected fence in New York, maybe even the whole country. But those sweet memories of honey cake and cozy afternoons soured about a year and a half ago when her daughter was killed. In her grief, Mrs. Sheinbaum's true feelings for me seeped out, and those feelings weren't loving. As far as she was concerned, I'm nothing more than a mug, and worse, unnatural, even unclean, no matter how well tailored. *And* she was willing to let Rosie be held hostage, even die, as vengeance for her lost daughter. *And* she was willing to throw me and another woman to the wolves to boot. I managed to get Rosie out of the situation alive, but the other woman, Celeste Copley, whose lies were as seductive as the rest of her, wasn't so lucky.

So coming here to this house to ask a favor of the old woman feels crummy, but it's my best chance to get a line on the missing Dürer, because nine times out of ten there isn't an item that moves through New York that Mom Sheinbaum doesn't know about. And if it's that tenth time, if it's something that didn't actually pass through her chubby fingers, she'll know which sewer grate to look under and whose rear end is warming that grate.

There's light coming through the lace window curtains on the first floor, so the old lady's obviously still awake. As I walk up the front stoop, I wonder if she'll even let me in. I haven't been here or talked to her since that ugly night in March of '49.

I ring the doorbell, then cool my heels longer than I'd like until the lock turns and the door opens. An aroma of warm honey surrounds the plump silver-haired old dame in the doorway, who I used to be glad to see.

"Well, will you look who's here. Cantor Gold." Her greeting comes at me in the old familiar Lower East Side immigrant singsong, a melody that slides up and down and curls around like a roller coaster. "The last time you were in my house, you held a gun on me. A gun!"

"Yeah, well, you broke my heart. Can I come in?"

She stands there like Cerberus guarding the gates of Hades, then turns to walk back into the house. "Sure, come in," she says over her shoulder. "Why not? Wipe your feet."

The frilly pink housecoat Mom's wearing flutters like feathers on a fat chicken as we cross the hall on our way to the dining room, where a half-full glass of tea, a floral teapot, and a pot of honey are on the table. A lace cloth covers the table, as always, letting only hints of the polished mahogany beneath peek through. Everything in the old-fashioned room, all the fussy mahogany furniture, even the rosy flowers on the teapot, shimmer in the room's amber-shaded lamplight. The place is still cozy, on the surface; underneath, the mood is cold as a Russian night.

Mom sits down in her usual chair at the head of the table, pours tea into the glass, and stirs in a spoonful of honey, leaving the spoon in the glass to absorb the heat, a habit leftover from the Old Country. As I pull out a chair and sit down, she says, "Don't sit if you want some tea. Get yourself a glass from the sideboard."

"No thanks. I don't want any tea."

She looks me over while sipping her own tea, her small green eyes crinkling above the rim of the glass. When she puts the glass down, a chilly smile accompanies the crinkling eyes. "Still with the men's clothes, I see. And fancy-shmancy ones tonight. A bow tie, even. You got a big evening, Cantor?"

"Maybe I got all dressed up for you, Mom."

"Hah. Don't make me laugh. Almost—what?—maybe two years you don't come to see me or do business with me, and suddenly you're all dressed up like Clark Gable come to say hello? *Mommaleh*, don't try and fool an old lady. So tell me, Cantor, why is it you're here? You got some nice goods to show me after all? Or you want me to find you a good buyer?"

"I want information. And I want something to drink, something a lot stronger than tea. You keeping it in the same place?"

"Yeh, over there, the cabinet in the sideboard. What kind of information you want from me?"

"A watercolor was stolen last night," I say on my way to the whiskey cabinet, "stolen from a client. That's bad for business. And whoever stole my client's watercolor also stole her life. Cut her up." Saying it, thinking about my visit last night with Mrs. J, I pour myself a badly needed double. After pulling down half of it in one swallow, I say, "She was a sweet old lady, a real—"

"Wait," Mom says, sitting up, "you mean that woman over on West End Avenue that's in the newspaper? An old lady knifed or something?"

"Yeah, that's her."

"The news article says she has a brother here in New York. Yeah, that's it. She was one of yours? Huh. From what the newspaper says, she didn't seem like the type of person to get mixed up in business with you."

"Did the papers also say she survived Hitler? That her husband and children burned in the ovens of Auschwitz?"

The color fades from Mom's face, fast, as if all of her blood simply dried up and blew through her skin like dust. Everything about her suddenly seems weak, even the way she puts down her glass of tea, even the way she speaks. "Cantor, you're looking for this woman's killer?"

"Her name was Hannah Jacobson, and I'm looking for a Dürer watercolor I brought into town and delivered to her last night. It used to belong to her husband, before the Nazis stole his art collection. Could be if I find her killer, I'll find the art."

"And what will you do when you find this killer? Cantor, be careful. A person who would do that, who would do such a thing as that to a woman who survived that Hitler"—the Yiddish word for murderer shoots out of her mouth like she's spitting stones—"this is not a person who is a human being."

The only other time I saw Esther Sheinbaum look this shaken was the night her daughter died. And now tonight, this woman who generally has the fortitude of a mountain that can't be breached or a safe that can't be cracked, tonight she sits here in her own dining room as if monsters are under her chair, ready to devour her.

But a few deep breaths, deep enough to flush the poison of ancestral fear from her marrow, restores her. She sits up straight, her bulk imposing as a fortress, her eyes narrowing, once again the Empress of the Underworld. "So," she says, "you think I might know something about this watercolor picture by whatsisname?"

"Dürer."

With a tinge of renewed alarm, she says, "A German? You're tangling with Nazis? You think because Hitler is gone that all those mamzers are finished? Five years the war's over, but that monster Mengele is still running around loose. Maybe he's even here in New York."

"Don't worry about it," I say. "Dürer's been dead over four hundred years. He wasn't a Nazi. Look, have you heard anything about a Renaissance watercolor moving through the pipes?"

With a shrug and a wave so dismissive it feels like I'm being pushed out the door, she says, "I can't help you, Cantor. You know I don't deal in paintings and the like. That's your line. I deal strictly in hard goods like jewelry and antique tchotchkes. So if you're looking for information from me about a fancy painting, you might as well go home now. Shoo."

I finish my drink but pour another. I'm not ready to go yet, not ready to let her off.

She watches me drink as if I'm an amusing disappointment, then says, "Better you should have some tea, Cantor. Too much whiskey will kill you."

"Your concern warms me all over, Mom. Listen, with all your contacts and all the people who owe you favors, you can probably pick up even the quietest whispers about anything that's floating around, even a Dürer watercolor. I'm asking you to listen to the whispers and tell me what you hear."

"And who have you talked to so far?"

"Mrs. Jacobson's brother, and Max Hagen, from Pauling-Barnett."

"Max Hagen? That *faygeleh*?"

"You know him? He made a big deal about not dirtying his hands with our kind."

"He doesn't. But he's cozy with people who do, people who've sat right here at this table."

"Anybody you can muscle for information?"

She takes another sip of tea, looking at me over the rim of the glass, then takes her time about putting the glass down before she finally answers me, keeping me in my place. "You hold a gun on me," she says, "you don't talk to me nearly two years, and now you come around asking for favors? Maybe you could tell me why should I do this for you, Cantor?" She practically sneers it.

"Because—oh, hell, never mind." Annoyed at myself for even thinking the old stone mountain would give a damn, especially if there's nothing in it for her, I polish off the scotch, put the glass down on the sideboard with more force than the furniture's used to, and start out of the dining room.

Before I'm out though, I get an idea. I turn back to Mom, say, "Don't do it for me. Do it for Hannah Jacobson, and for her brother, who's dead now, too, by the way. Murdered. Do it to spite the monsters."

She's still sitting there like stone, but there's just enough of something, some emotion creeping into the corners of her mouth, that forces her to mumble, "I'll see what I can do."

❖

It'll be a while until Mom gets back to me with any information she manages to scavenge, and until then there's really nothing more I can do tonight. It's been a lousy day, I should just pack it in, but I'm restless and it's too early to cash out the night.

So I'm headed for the Green Door Club, a favorite spot where the women are willing and the music is sweet, hidden away in an alley off the tawdry hip of Fourteenth Street.

I find a parking spot nearby, then walk into the shadowy alley, the only light coming secondhand through windows in the surrounding buildings, oblongs of light that linger or fade. A dim glow rises from the bottom of a stairway leading down to the basement of a building on the right of the alley. Lounging along the railing at the top of the stairs are sharp dressers in tailored suits and rakishly tilted hats, enjoying a smoke, conversation, and the embrace of women whose evening wraps and cocktail dresses could rival even the taste of one Miss Vivienne Parkhurst Trent.

Corners of light find a red hem, a gold bodice, the upper edge of an aqua elbow-length glove. I hear, "Evening, Cantor," here and there. Someone asks if the banged-up state of my face is the result of an act of chivalry or a jealous dame. The question gets a few laughs.

At the bottom of the stairs is a pale green door with a polished brass handle. Weak light from a single bulb glows above the door. There's no sign. If you need a sign, you don't belong here.

I walk in.

Every nightspot has its own feel. The Green Door Club feels like an intimate party where your day job won't come up for discussion. There are always familiar faces, a sprinkling of new ones to keep the night interesting, and everyone is comfortably enough juiced to let life's dramas play out. The Green Door Club has seen dramas of hand-wringing emotional zeal.

The red leather booths are full, so are most of the little white-clothed tables with couples in assorted varieties of evening wear: some in tuxedos or dinner jackets, some in suits, their dates and lovers in cocktail dresses and high heels. The unattached but hopeful assess their chances from positions at the long coppered bar, some seated on the bar stools, some standing, all of them posturing like dandified bucks or babes from Broadway. Blue music from a three-piece combo—the piano and saxophone dressed in pale green taffeta, the drum in a tuxedo—drifts through the smoke and the chatter and the laughs. Faces are caught by the light of small pink-shaded lamps on the tables. Jewelry flashes. Lipstick glistens. Couples dance. Bottles and glassware sparkle on the wall behind the bar. Forbidden love has a place to call home.

Peg Monroe is behind the bar. Peg is tall, strong, and well padded, with skin the color of caramel, her short hair always neat with pomade. She has dark brown eyes that notice everything and a finely shaped mouth on a face too sweet for her swagger. It's a face better suited to somebody's virginal aunt, the one with the tough streak. Peg's dark eyes will drill holes in you while a velvet trace of a Georgia drawl fondles you. Sometimes Peg wears a tie.

Sometimes she wears a dress. Sometimes she wears a tie and a dress. You never know with Peg. Tonight she's wearing a green-and-gray plaid tie open at the collar of a white shirt, sleeves rolled up to the elbows. A big gold watch on her left wrist glitters as her large hands move with quickness and grace mixing drinks, handing them to a cocktail waitress, then pouring a highball for a pretty blonde in a strapless silver dress at the far end of the bar.

"Evening, Slick," Peg greets me as I slide onto a stool at the bar. Peg's called me Slick since the night I sweet-talked an irate ex out of scratching my eyes out right in the middle of the dance floor. Peg described my contrition act as slick, and her name for me stuck. That was four years ago. "Shot of Chivas?" she says, already reaching for the bottle.

"Yeah," I say. "Make it a double."

She looks me over while she pours the drink. "Nice dinner duds," she says. "Fancy evening?"

"Maybe too fancy."

"And what's with your chin? Every time I see you, Slick, there's another gash on that handsome face of yours."

"I came in for a rough landing last night, that's all."

"Interesting. You gonna share the story?"

"Nope. I'm gonna drown it." I down the double scotch in one pull. "Pour me another, Peg."

She holds the bottle above my glass but doesn't pour. "Maybe you should take it a little slower this time," she says.

"What's this? I'm not drunk."

"No, but you're gonna be real fast, too fast, if you down doubles like that. Now take it slow, you hear?"

I give her my most courtly smile. "Well, yes, ma'am," I say. "Slow and easy."

Peg pours the double but keeps her eyes on me while I take a drink, careful not to suck it up in one pull.

I take a look at that pretty blonde in the strapless silver number at the end of the bar. She has delicate shoulders, soft eyes, a cute mouth, and a dainty way of holding her highball glass. Her dress is the slinky sort, at least what I see of the upper half of it above the bar.

Peg, catching me eyeing the blonde, says, "So, you ready to make your move?"

Maybe that's just what I need, a little warmth from a stranger, maybe a roll in the hay with no strings and no expectations to smooth out the jagged edges of my crummy day. I slide off my bar stool and walk toward the woman in the silver dress at the end of the bar.

The closer I get to her the more I'm aware that her soft blue eyes have dark depths of sadness. Someone's hurt this pretty little sweetheart, recently, I'd guess, and now she's here to drown the pain. I should tell her there's no drowning it, there's only washing it clean enough not to poison the rest of you. It's taken a lot of scotch over the last two years to wash my pain over Sophie, and it's still not fully clean. Maybe it will never be.

I wandered over here to ask the woman if I could buy her a drink, but I'm surprised to find myself saying instead, "Would you like to dance?"

The sad eyes look me over like maybe I'm a leaky boat that's washed up on her shore.

Maybe if I introduce myself, take the *Who the hell are you?* element out of it, I'll come off as courteous suitor and not that leaky boat. "My name's Cantor Gold."

She says, "I know who you are," through a voice that's soft and distant, like someone whose body is here but whose mood isn't. "Those scars on your face give you away. Your scars are famous. And your chin looks like you've recently added to the collection."

"Then we have something in common," I say.

She looks at me like I've just said something in a foreign language, one she's not familiar with.

"I mean, I think we both could use some soothing," I say and extend my hand. "So, would you like to dance?"

She pauses to think about it, looks at my hand, then my face, then back to my hand again, and decides I'm not such a leaky boat after all, or at least one not in danger of sinking both of us quite yet. She takes my hand and slides off the bar stool.

Yeah, that strapless silver dress is slinky from top to bottom.

"What's your name?" I say.

"Tess McBain."

"Pretty name, Tess." I lead her to the small dance floor near the band. It's crowded with couples moving body to body to a slow and melancholy tune that has plenty of sex sliding through the crooning saxophone. I take Tess in my arms, and we dance, cheek to cheek, heartbreak to heartbreak.

She's a wonderful dancer, smooth, her body responsive. My hand presses gently against the softness of her back, guiding her in the dance. Her hips fold themselves into mine. Her body is sexy and warm, its heat coming through the thin fabric of her dress, seeping into me, oozing into my most tender places. I can tell by the way she's moving against me that she's aware of the effect she's having on me and that she's pleased with it, which arouses me even more. I press more of me against her, absorb the swell of her breasts, slide my hand down her back to the delicious roundness of her ass. The longer we dance, the more slowly we sway, the music wraps around us and closes us off in our own erotic world.

But it's no good.

My body is willing, but my soul needs a safer place to harbor after the horrors of last night and today.

I stop dancing and pull away. "I'm sorry," I say.

With a nod of disappointment but not surprise, she says, "Yeah, me, too. I thought we might distract each other from our troubles for a while. I guess not."

"I wish we could. I really do. Look, I don't know who hurt you or why, but I have the feeling they're a fool."

That gets the first smile from her since I saw her at the bar. "Why, thank you, Cantor Gold. You know, they say you're dangerous, but I don't think so. But I could be wrong."

❖

Home beckons.

By the time I park in the basement garage and ride the elevator up to my apartment, I figure maybe Rosie can salvage things a little, at least soothe my bruises—the ones on my skin, the ones the Jacobson and Stern murders clawed me with, and the one Vivienne delivered to my ego by staying at Hagen's. Maybe Rosie is that safe harbor I need tonight.

Taking off my dinner jacket and untying the bow tie that feels like it's choking me now, I don't even bother turning on a light in the living room on my way to the bedroom. I don't turn on a light here either, just flop down on my bed. A shaft of city light through the window guides my hand as I dial Rosie's number on the bedside phone. Sweet Rosie. When I called her from my office this morning, she was on her way out the door for an early shift, so maybe she's home now. And it's only a little after eleven thirty. She's probably still awake.

The minute she picks up the phone and says hello, I feel better.

"It's me, Rosie," I say. "You busy?"

"What do you have in mind, Cantor?" If she said it any more seductively, I'd crawl through the phone and slither through the wire all the way to her place.

"Well, we could—wait, hold on, someone's at the door."

Out of habit, my heart races, because like last night, like any night during the last two years when there's a buzz at my door, I hope and pray and imagine it's Sophie: Sophie escaped from God knows who and what, Sophie coming back to me.

But also like last night, it could be Lieutenant Huber and his lackey, Tommy the Cop, come to twist my arm some more. Or like this morning, it could be Jimmy Shea and *his* lackey, Screwy Sweeney, come to twist all of me some more.

But when I switch on a lamp in the living room and open the door, it's none of those people. It's someone I'd least expect, *never* expect. It's Vivienne.

She says, "May I come in?"

Dumbstruck, I step aside to clear the way, and in one of the great graceful moments of womanhood, she slides her clutch bag into her coat pocket and removes her purple evening coat as naturally as a snake slithering out of its skin as she walks through the door.

I take her coat, drape it over the back of a club chair while she looks around my living room. I can't tell if she expected it to be more tasteful or less.

She finally turns to me, her dark hair swirling, her ruby necklace and black silk dress catching lamplight. My living room never looked so good.

"Wait here," I say.

I go back to the bedroom, pick up the phone. "Listen, Rosie, I'll have to call you back." How long, I wonder when I hang up without explanation, until Rosie sees me for the heel I can too often be?

Back in the living room, Vivienne's still standing there like a little kid who's lost her way, maybe wondering if she should backtrack out of here.

"How about a drink?" I say. "Bourbon with a splash of soda, right? Make yourself comfortable, have a seat."

She remains standing and seems to have a hard time trying to talk to me, even bites her lip, making a tiny scratch in her red lipstick. "Cantor, I…I came to apologize. Max was very rude to you, and well, he shouldn't have been."

"Then it's Hagen who should apologize." I hand her the bourbon and soda, then pour a scotch for myself.

Whenever I'm around Vivienne, in her office at the museum or when I've been in her house, two things are always clear to me: she's really savvy about her Renaissance art and I really want to get her into bed. But earlier tonight, a third thing became clear: she's one of those out-of-reach dames who teases. So if I want to keep my wits, I'd better take this party in a different direction. "All right, Vivienne," I say, "you've fallen on your sword for Hagen. Real noble of you. Too noble for *him*, if you want my opinion. For that matter, Vern is probably too noble for Hagen, too. That boy's heart is pretty beaten up."

"Vern can hold his own. At least, I've always thought so," she adds with a shrug before disappearing into her drink. After an awkward sip followed too quickly by another, she says, "Well, it's getting late. Perhaps I'd better go."

"Yeah, perhaps you'd better."

"I'll just get my coat."

"Let me help you." I take the coat from the chair, hold it out for Vivienne to slip into.

Except she doesn't. Facing me, she says, "Cantor, are you really going to find the Dürer for Max?"

"I'm going to find the Dürer, whether it's for Hagen or not. Why? You want it, too?"

"Well, the museum certainly would. And securing it for them would strengthen my position there."

"Yeah, but I'll get more money from Hagen."

She doesn't like my answer, her pretty green eyes flashing her annoyance. "Is that all you care about? Money?"

"All? No. Mostly? Yeah. I remember what it's like to go hungry, and I didn't like it."

She waves that away with the nonchalance of someone who has no idea what I'm talking about and never could and just keeps going with her own concerns. "If Max gets the Dürer, it will go to a private collector God knows where, and no one else will see it. But at the museum, everyone can see it!"

"You're pretty passionate about that."

"Yes, I am. You know how I feel about museums."

"Sure, I know. And I also know you're even more beautiful when you're passionate about something. Which means you're damned beautiful right now, which means you'd better go." I press the point by holding out her coat again.

"All right. If that's what you want." She slips an arm into the coat.

"Uh-huh. That's what I want." Her hair smells of lilacs.

After a deep, aristocratic breath of what I expect is condescending resignation, she turns around to me, one arm still in her coat, the rest of the coat draping down her back to the floor. But it's not the aristocratic Parkhurst lineage looking at me; it's the back-alley line of Trents. "No," she says, "that's not what you want. This is what you want."

My fantasy of smearing Vivienne's lipstick in the shadows is suddenly real. She's kissing me, my mouth sliding along hers. I knew, in my imaginings of Vivienne, that her lips would be warm, that her body, against me now, would be supple in its movements. I knew all those things, but what I didn't know was just how badly I wanted her, like an insistent, rutting animal.

And so I pick her up and carry her to my bed.

❖

I'm in an ecstasy of Vivienne, of her lavish breasts in my hands, her hard nipples in my mouth, her legs around my waist, turning and rolling with her, hearing her moan, feeling her shiver. She's still hungry, and so am I when she pushes me down and grabs my head between her legs, pressing her sweet juiciness into my mouth. She's hot and swollen. She's screaming.

There's just the night and the flesh, Vivienne's and mine, sliding along each other, enveloping each other, blocking out anything outside of us, blocking out thought. I don't remember reaching into the drawer of the beside table. I don't remember strapping on. There's only *now*, a relentless *now*, and Vivienne's groaning rasp in my ear, "Yes, Cantor, fuck me."

❖

Noise is invading my dozing, something loud, over and over again, until I'm not dozing and I know the sound. It's the phone.

I have to roll away from Vivienne to grab it. Her arm, limp with sleep and catching light from the window, is still across my leg when I pick up the receiver and mumble, "Hello."

"Cantor? It's me. Red."

"Yeah, sure…okay Red, what's up? And what the hell time is it?"

"Almost one a.m. You sound groggy. Sorry to wake you, but I know you'll wanna hear this. Listen, I'm still here with Iris at her place—you remember Iris Page, from this afternoon at Smiley's joint?"

"Yeah, I remember." I wonder, grinning, how much of his dough Red's turned over to her by now, assuming she charges an hourly rate.

"Yeah, well, she's in the kitchen, makin' coffee," he says, "so I figured I'd give you a call. Anyway, we was talkin' a few minutes ago, I asked her about, you know, her life and all on the docks, and she tells me about all the funny business she's seen down there, and one night stuck in her mind 'cause it scared her plenty."

"Sure, Jimmy Shea's Mob guys can do some pretty scary stuff," I say. "What's Iris got on them? Anything I can use?"

"Cantor, it ain't about Shea. It's about Sophie."

Chapter Ten

The last of my sleep and any remnant glow from my tumble with Vivienne are gone, ripped away by the sound of Sophie's name.

"What about Sophie," I say, almost barking it but squelching it down so I don't wake Vivienne.

"It's something Iris saw one night, a coupla years ago," Red says, "by the downtown docks on the East Side. Yeah, March of '48 she says. She's sure of it because it was the last night to see that Tyrone Power pirate movie in her neighborhood before the theater changed features and she was annoyed she'd missed it 'cause she likes that pretty Tyrone Power. Anyways, she'd just finished a little business with a longshoreman in Cuyler's Alley when she sees these two guys drive up in a truck and park by a freighter docked at Pier 8. So she hangs around, figuring she'll pick up another coupla tricks, make a few more bucks."

"Drogan, what the hell does this have to do with Sophie?"

"I'm gettin' there, Cantor. Just listen. So at first Iris thinks the truck is one of those fruit-'n-vegetable rigs that pick up produce for early morning deliveries. But this truck wasn't for no fruits and vegetables. It's carrying live cargo, *human* cargo. Women, maybe a dozen of 'em, pulled outta the back of the truck by them two guys. You know what I'm saying, Cantor?"

I do, and it's scaring me.

"You still there, Cantor?"

My throat tight, I manage, "Just keep talking, Red."

"Okay. Look, Iris knew right away what was going on and it shook her. She knew about the flesh-slavers working the city, grabbing women off the streets and shipping 'em off on freighters and trawlers to nobody knows where. She knew all about the captains paid off to hide women with the legit cargo and deliver 'em when they reach port. So Iris ain't no fool—she slides into shadow against a wall so them guys won't see her and take her, too, but she could see everything goin' on. She says the girls were screaming and crying, but they was chained together like a prison gang and couldn't get away, and the guys are slapping them around, telling them to be quiet and—"

"Drogan, what's this got to do with Sophie?"

"I'm gettin' to that, Cantor. So Iris remembers one of the women being different than the others. Instead of crying, she fights back, kicking and spitting at them guys until one of 'em puts a knife to her throat and threatens to kill her right there on the dock and toss her body in the river. But she don't shut up. She keeps on fighting and yelling and the guy gets madder and madder, and Iris is sure it's curtains for that dame until the other guy pulls off the guy with the knife and says something about the dame being worth a lotta money. Then the two guys pull all the women to the pier and onto the freighter. And I tell you, Cantor, the way Iris described that girl, the one who fought back—"

With every word out of Red's mouth, every nerve and muscle in me twists into knots, my brain trying to build a wall against what I know deep down is going to be the unbearable finale to his story.

"—the way Iris described her with dark hair, wearin' the sorta polka-dot dress I remember she fancied and the way she hollered at them guys in what Iris is sure was Spanish, that girl sounds a helluva lot like Sophie."

I can barely breathe. I'm even afraid to breathe, afraid of letting time move forward and bring this nightmare with it.

Somehow I muscle enough air up from the pit of my stomach to say, "The freighter, Red. What was the name of that freighter?"

"I dunno, Cantor. I asked Iris, figuring I could get a line on her, but after them guys got the women on board, Iris wasn't about to hang around and risk getting spotted when they came back to their truck. She got the hell outta there. She never saw the name of the boat. The next time she was down that end of town, the freighter had already sailed."

I can't speak, not a word, not even to say good night to Red when I hang up, not even a word to Vivienne, who's awake now, sitting behind me and turning me to her, her face pale in the city light coming in through the window. I don't know what she heard, I don't know if she heard me say Sophie's name, but she heard enough to realize that the pain of my life just invaded the night we shared and destroyed it.

Shipping the women off to nobody knows where, Red said. Well, somebody knows where, and that somebody is Jimmy Shea. He knows every port of call of every ship in New York Harbor and scrapes a percentage of profit from every ounce of their cargo. Even human cargo.

I don't care if it's after one thirty in the morning, when all upstanding citizens are asleep. Jimmy Shea isn't asleep. The gutter crowd's not asleep. Time to go deeper into the gutter, to Jimmy's place.

Vivienne doesn't question me or try to stop me when I get out of bed and get dressed. She doesn't say anything, and I don't either. I don't even look at her. A few minutes later, after a quick washing up, after putting on a clean white shirt and zipping up a pair of pants, I grab one of my spare .38s and a shoulder rig along with a handful of extra slugs from my bedroom safe, take an overcoat and cap from the closet, and walk out the door.

I park my Buick near Jimmy's place on Stone Street, a cobblestoned alley of small sagging buildings near the downtown docks. Jimmy's place isn't any fancier than the other architectural cadavers on the street, just an old brick job he owns with an apartment above a hardware store. But Jimmy's not a fancy guy. His neighborhood's as cut-rate as his clothing. I guess the only thing he spends his money on is whores, and if Iris Page is an example, he even does that on the cheap.

"He's not home," a guy says behind me when I'm at Jimmy's door. I turn and see a regular sort of guy, a working-stiff type in a lumber jacket and beat-up fedora. "You must be lookin' for Shea," he says through whiskey breath, "'cause I don't know you so you ain't lookin' for me. And the only other person who lives in this building is Shea."

"And who are you?"

"Shea's tenant. This here's my hardware store. I live in the back."

"Uh-huh. So if you're just getting home, how do you know Jimmy's not here?"

"'Cause I just saw him. In fact, he even bought me a drink," he says as I bolt away. "Hey, don't you even wanna know where he is?"

I know where he is.

❖

Coenties Slip is four blocks from Stone Street and around the corner from Cuyler's Alley, where Iris entertained her longshoreman. The slip ends at South Street along the East River's downtown docks. Right at the corner, in one of the wooden buildings still hanging around from New York's sailing-ship days, is a saloon as old and crusty as Smiley's but with an even tougher clientele. Up until about five years ago the place used to be called Joe's, but if there was ever a Joe he's long gone and now the joint doesn't have a name. It doesn't need a name, because the only people who go in there under the present ownership are friends or associates of Jimmy Shea. He's the owner. The back room of the saloon is his general headquarters.

When I walk in, the bartender gives me the once-over while the half-dozen tough customers smoking and drinking at the bar put their whiskey glasses down and slide their hands inside their coats to the bulge of their guns. One of those tough customers is Screwy Sweeney, who stops looking at the boxing pictures in the sports pages of the paper, reminiscing, maybe, about the days when he was beaten silly by smarter fighters. He puts the paper down, pushes his hat back as he gives me a dopey snicker, and says, "Hey, boys, look who's here. It's the pree-vert Cantor Gold. Ain't you in the wrong place, Gold? This ain't no pree-vert bar."

The twisted faces of the murderers' row at the bar is a pretty good hint of their twisted brains, which tempts me to say, *I'm not so sure about that,* but there's more of them than there are of me, so all I say instead is, "I'm here to see Jimmy."

"He ain't seein' nobody," Screwy says. "He's busy." Screwy's buffoonish self-importance is laughable, but I'm not in a laughing mood, and except for the snickering Screwy, who'd laugh at a flat tire, neither is anyone else, the air in the room thick with smoke and malice. The boys at the bar stare at me like I'm their guns' next meal. Screwy ambles toward me through the smoke, gives me a sweaty sneer, and looks down at me from the roughly four inches he's got on my height. "Get outta here," he says.

But Screwy and the boys make the mistake of looking at all of me instead of certain parts of me, like the part of me that's imperceptibly bending just enough at the knees, the move hidden by my overcoat, and when my head is just below Screwy's chin I lurch up fast, ram my head into his throat, pull my .38 at the same time, and spin around and aim it at the thugs, who aren't happy about suddenly being useless.

Screwy, gagging and tumbling backward, falls against a bar stool, knocking it over with a loud crash.

The noise brings Jimmy through the door from the back room and into the bar, shouting, "What the hell—?" in that high wind-through-an alley voice that makes my teeth grit. He's still wearing the same cheap gray suit and rumpled white shirt he wore this morning when he ordered Screwy to rouse me from bed. Only difference now, his tie and collar are open, exposing his ropey neck. And he could use a shave, and probably a shower, though no amount of soap could wash away the savagery that festers in his every pore.

Jimmy's slit eyes rake me over, finally settle on the gun in my hand. Looking at me but talking to Screwy, he says, "For chrissake, Screwy, get up off the floor and take Gold's gun."

"Nobody's taking my gun," I say. "I'll shoot Screwy's fat hand off if he tries it. And boys," I say to the thugs at the bar, "go back to your drinking. In fact, barkeep, pour the boys another round, on me."

Nobody moves. Screwy stays sprawled on the floor. The bartender stands stock-still. My gun's still aimed at Jimmy's thugs, who keep staring at me.

Jimmy's the only one smiling, giving me a knifelike grin that could add more cuts to my face. "Glad you could drop by, Gold," he says. "I wanna talk to you. C'mon back to my office." Before he goes, he nods to the bartender, says, "Go ahead, Sammy, pour the boys a drink. Only don't take Gold's money. What sorta host would I be if I let a dame pay for a round?"

I follow him to the back room, my gun still out, still aimed at the boys at the bar. Before going through the door, I say, "Screwy, you heard your boss. Get the hell off the floor." Then I spit a small but highly satisfying laugh and walk into the back room, closing the door behind me.

Jimmy's office is nearly bare except for a long wooden table with a strongbox on it, a couple of dirty ashtrays, a few chairs, a shelf with a few whiskey bottles and a half-dozen glasses. In the glare of the single overhead bulb hanging from a cord, the room feels less like a place of business and more like a slow night at the morgue, the air waiting for the next death.

Jimmy reaches for two glasses from the shelf, pushes the strongbox away, and puts the glasses on the table. The day's take must be in the box, money clawed from the shippers and longshoremen, the loan sharks and hookers, and all the bandits like me along the waterfront. "Scotch. That's your drink, right?" Jimmy says in his whiny wheeze. He pours two glasses, pushes one toward me and lifts the other. "Bottoms up," he says.

"I don't want your whiskey, Jimmy."

"No? Suit yourself. But put that gun away. Killin' me ain't gonna solve either of our problems."

"Not right away," I say.

That gets his attention, stops him from sitting down in mid-sit, his skinny frame slinking back up like a snake ready to strike. "You're not gonna kill me, Cantor. You got more brains than that. It would bring too much trouble on your head from my associates. And I don't mean the lugs out there at the bar, but my associates higher up, the guys who run this city with steel guts and iron fists. You know the guys I mean."

"Yeah, I know. And if I don't get the information I want from you, maybe I can get it from them. And even if I do get the information from you, if I don't like what I hear I might kill you anyway."

His laugh, sharp as razor blades, cuts through me and feels like it's slicing its way up my spine. "I never figured you for such a lousy bargainer, Gold! You'll kill me if I talk about whatever it is you want me to talk about, you'll kill me if I don't talk about it. Some deal. And anyways, just this morning you told me you don't like killing. If you ask me, you ain't got a hand to play. So why don't you just sit down and have a drink, tell me what's on your mind." His good humor all dried up, he adds, "And then I'll tell you what's on mine."

I don't sit down. I don't have a drink. And I don't put my gun away. I just say, "Are you in the flesh business, Jimmy?"

"Ain't you? Ain't everybody? Lotta money in flesh." He sits down at the table as casually as if I'd asked him if he's good to his mother.

My hatred of him now runs through me like fire, burning around my trigger finger, curling it to shoot. But I can't let my hate get the better of me, at least not yet, not until I get what I came for. So I'd better stiffen up, choke back my hatred of Jimmy, my desperation to find Sophie. I'd better be hard as stone.

Cold and steady, I say, "Then you'll know about a boat, a freighter that hauled women off Pier 8 about two and a half years ago, March of '48. One of the women fought back, made a scene until one of the slavers threatened to slice her. Word about that night might've gotten around. Somebody might remember the story, even the name of the slaving outfit or the freighter."

"And you think I know such a story?"

"Cut the crap, Jimmy, you know every boat that comes in and out of this port, and Pier 8's right down the street. You can see it from the front window of the bar, so maybe you even saw that boat on that night. I want the name of that freighter, Jimmy, and I want to know where she sailed."

He's looking at me like he's about to laugh again. It's all I can do not to blast the smirk off his bony face, char it to a blackened skull.

He says, "You want me to tell you about some flesh boat that sailed two years ago? You must think I'm Mr. Memory."

"I told you to cut the crap, Jimmy. You've got eyes and ears on the docks. There's very little that goes on along this waterfront that you don't know about. And what you don't see yourself, you've got written down somewhere. Every nickel's worth of cargo, every kickback, every boat that comes in and goes out. You have those books in here, Jimmy? Maybe in that strongbox you pushed out of my sight? The secret books with all the Mob's deals? Look up the shipping news for a night in March of 1948 and tell me the name of the freighter that sailed from Pier 8 and where it went."

Even with a gun aimed at him, Jimmy's calm as an airless night. It's me who's feeling edgy, so close to finding out what happened to Sophie, so close...

"Why?" Jimmy says.

That's it. The scary question. The one I didn't want him to ask. I don't dare show my hand, and worse, my heart. Love cuts no ice with Jimmy. Jimmy *is* ice.

But he's not stupid. And he's not blind. "Well, how about that," he says, smirking again, his eyes crinkling around a vicious twinkle. "I'm guessin' you knew someone on that boat, right? Maybe a girlie of yours? Sweet Jesus"—he's actually chuckling now, a nasty sound that could make people run for their lives—"it must be eating you alive, Gold, knowing your girlie's getting pawed over and fucked day and night by guys who all got something you ain't got. Not a real one, anyways!"

I'm as close to murder as I've ever been, trigger close, close to madness, tangled up in the ugly scenes Jimmy's thrown at me, scenes of Sophie that—yeah—eat me alive.

I want to put several bullets into Jimmy's filthy mouth, blast his tongue to a pulp and his teeth to splinters, but I know that same mouth can give me the information I need. And Jimmy knows it, too. His smirk dissolves into something lazier, a smile more easygoing and confident, and even colder.

In the glare of the overhead bulb, his face and neck bleached white, his arms and hands dissolving in the shadows across his lap, he looks like the Grim Reaper. He sounds like it, too, his wheezy whine drifting through the gloomy room like a noxious gas. "Now you listen to me, Gold. Here's what's on *my* mind. You know how I operate. You know I don't give somethin' for nothin', not even with a gun in my face. You want information from me? You gotta give something back. Only now, you ain't got much to give. You ain't given me anybody for the Jacobson killing like I asked you this morning. And now there's that messy business with the old lady's brother. Yeah, I know all about that. That's what's on *my* mind, Gold, that guy's head blasted right there in your car. That's not the sort of result we had in mind, you understand? More bodies brings more attention from the newspapers, brings more cops nosing around."

It's my turn to smirk, throw the lie back in Jimmy's face about his worry over unwanted attention from the cops. But I pull the smirk back as soon as it creeps into the corner of my mouth because if I let on that I know about Jimmy's early morning meeting with

Lieutenant Huber, then Iris Page is as good as dead. It wouldn't take long for Jimmy to figure that Iris must've overheard Huber's visit and turned the story into a little cash.

Jimmy's left arm moves, just a little, his rumpled suit jacket catching light, but when I figure it, when I realize he's pressed a button hidden under the table, it's too late: I hear the buzz in the barroom, hear the door burst open, and feel a meaty arm around my neck, squeezing the air out while Jimmy pulls the gun from my hand. The glare of the light bulb gets dimmer. Jimmy's shout, "Don't kill her, Screwy!" sounds like it's coming from far away.

Then the pain around my neck lets up a little, the darkness that almost swallowed me opens up again. I can breathe a little easier and I can fight back, so I jab behind me at Screwy, my elbow digging into his fat belly over and over again, but he doesn't let go, even when there's a sharp slam across the left side of my face from something cold and hard. When my head snaps back I see what it was: Jimmy's slammed me with the butt of my own gun.

Jimmy's sneer could sour milk. His hiss is the stuff of nightmares. "Do I have your attention, Gold? Look at me. I said look at me!"

The left side of my face stinging, my choked throat pulling in all the air it can, I look at him, at that sneer, that icy brutality in his eyes, and then I spit in his face. It counts as one of life's more satisfying moments, even when the inevitable punch to my gut comes from Jimmy's fist.

With Screwy still on my neck, I can't even double over. I just have to take the pain while Jimmy hisses at me, "I could kill you right now, Gold," before he even wipes my spittle from his face with his pocket handkerchief and restores his stony calm.

He says, "I'd love to kill you right now, take your body apart and scatter it in the harbor from here to...well"—he's sneering again, a lewd curl stretched along his teeth—"to wherever that freighter sailed. But I'm not finished with you, and you haven't finished what you're supposed to do."

"Why don't you just hand me over to Huber, Jimmy? You want to."

"I might, if you don't come through. But I'd rather give the cops the real killer. It's neater and cleaner that way. No inconvenient questions later. If we give them you, well, that might work in the short run—but hell, maybe that's good enough." His sneer curdles into a smile, sharp, brittle, and deadly.

He's still smiling when he opens my coat, slips my gun into its rig. "You're gonna need this out there, Gold, if you're goin' up against a killer. Now be a good—what do I call you? Girl? Bull?" Laughing, he says, "Get her outta here, Screwy."

With his arm around my neck, I can't see Screwy's face, but I can tell he's enjoying dragging me out of Jimmy's office and across the bar while I shout, "You're gonna tell me, Jimmy! You're gonna tell me about that boat!"

Screwy would kill me, too, just to shut me up, if his boss would let him. But since Jimmy's decided to keep me alive, at least for now, Screwy will just have to be satisfied with some minor vengeance for the humiliation of me getting the jump on him in front of the thugs at the bar. He takes that vengeance when we're at the front door. First he tosses me out to the street with enough force to send me tumbling to the gutter, my face scraping the cobblestones. Then he comes outside and kicks me, first in the ribs, then to the gut, then to my face. He doesn't stop until I roll away from the next blow, pull my .38 and aim it up at him, shouting, "Listen, you galoot, Jimmy wants me alive! You, though, I'm not so sure about. You'd better get outta here, Screwy."

❖

Driving home was one long and brutal ache, and I'm not sure which hurts more, my beaten-up body or my beaten-up soul.

Vivienne is gone from my apartment. I'm alone in my bed, alone except for my visions of Sophie. They follow me into sleep.

There's a woman screaming but I can't see her, can't get to her. It's Sophie, screaming from somewhere inside a black cloud that's drifting all around me, circling my body, rising up to surround my head, blinding me with black nothingness. There's only Sophie's scream, shrill and seeping through the black, a wail that tumbles into something thinner, weaker, older, Hannah Jacobson crying... crying...crying for her lost husband, her murdered children, Hannah Jacobson wailing. I can't see her, just hear her, hear her horrible wail that keens through the blackness surrounding me like a whirlwind. The whirlwind roars, suffocating Hannah Jacobson's cry, the deep roar getting louder, changing, becoming a howl, a terrifying howl flung at me from inside the black cyclone, the howl of a man dying, Marcus Stern dying, exploding, exploding the whirlwind—

I bolt up from my bed. The nightmare scares me awake.

CHAPTER ELEVEN

Morning comes too early—a little after six by my bedside clock—after my lousy night's sleep, if you can call it sleep. My bedsheets look like there was a war on. And I guess that's what it was: a grinding, toss-and-turn war between my battered body and my nightmares.

A long, hot shower soothes some of the ache left behind by Screwy's pummeling, and strong coffee clears my head. But as I get dressed, finish tying my tie, slip my .38 into my shoulder rig, and put on my black suit jacket, what's looking back at me in my bedroom mirror is a horror show. My face—already bruised from my crash on Drogan's tug, nicked by flying glass and Marcus Stern's exploding skull, and marred by Huber's fist—is now rough with red scrapes from getting tossed onto the cobblestones outside Jimmy's saloon, and blotchy where Screwy mashed my face with his foot.

But the same urgency that woke me at an unholy hour this morning is pressing at my back now. There's no time to wallow in my pain. I have to get to the root of last night's nightmares. I have to find a murderer and the stolen Dürer. And I have to find Sophie.

I start by phoning Judson.

He mumbles, "What time is it?"

"Nearly seven. I've got an important job for you, Judson."

"At this hour?"

"At every hour from now on. There's a boat you have to find."

Still groggy, he mutters, "Boat?"

"A freighter. It sailed from Pier 8 on a March night in '48. I need to know the name of the freighter and where it was going. Captain's name, too."

"March?" He's more awake now. "In 1948? You want me to trace a freighter that sailed two and a half years ago? Why? What was it carrying? Something of ours?"

"It was carrying Sophie, Judson. It was a slaver, and it was carrying Sophie."

❖

There's something terribly wrong in the soul of the world when you have to go to the same cemetery two days in a row to bury two members of the same family. The same rabbi who buried Hannah Jacobson is chanting the same prayers for her brother. Marcus Stern's coffin glints in the same glow of morning sunlight. His wife wears the same dark coat and feathered hat, his daughter Francine is in the same blue coat she wore to her aunt Hannah's funeral, the sunlight again dancing on the waves of her short blond hair. But there are more people at Marcus Stern's burial than there were at Hannah Jacobson's. Some look like front-office and executive-suite types, probably from Stern's plastics factory. A few others look like workers from the factory floor come to pay their respects to the boss. But the extra attendees aren't only mourners. There's a handful of uniformed cops.

So Huber's as good as his word; he's assigned a protective detail to what's left of that family. If he wasn't a cop, I'd kiss him.

I stand back from the crowd, not as far away as I did from Mrs. J's funeral, but far enough not to be noticed. Except I am noticed. Francine sees me after dropping her shovel of dirt into her father's grave. She's too far away for me to read the look on her face, but I get the general gist that it's not warmly welcoming.

When the service ends, and everyone heads back to the line of cars, Francine defies her mother and comes marching toward me.

That's when the cops notice me, too. One of them gets right to his protective duties and tries to stop Francine from approaching me, but she waves him off, evidently telling him she recognizes me.

Angry at the world for destroying her family, yesterday's pert and flirty college girl shows me another side of her: a young woman with a hard shell and a fierce heart. "You. What are you doing here? Haven't you caused enough trouble for my family?"

"Miss Stern, I'm here to—"

She doesn't give me a chance to finish, just starts hitting me, pounding me with her fists, calling me an animal, a criminal. I move to grab her wrists to stop her, then change my mind, just let her spend her anger on me. Her flailing blows are mostly absorbed by my overcoat, but they're so careless in their fury, they wouldn't do much damage, anyway. Francine Stern is no Screwy Sweeney.

Her fisticuffs wind down when her anger is overwhelmed by what I'm sure is her immense grief. The curses she threw at me contract into choked sobs that sound so painful I'm afraid they'll rip her throat. The strength to withstand her grief crumbles right down to her bones, and she falls against me, crying. "Why did you do this to us? What do you want from us?"

"I want to help you, Miss Stern, I really do. But there are things you need to understand. If I'm going to help you, there are things we need to talk about, things you and your mother need to know. And you may even have information that I can use, information which could help free us, all of us, from all this death."

She pulls away and looks at me through eyes so filled with tears I'm sure I'm just a blur. But maybe that's better. Maybe she can't see the violence that's been pummeled into my face, some of it the residue of her father's killing.

Whimpering, she says, "The police were right. You're nothing but trouble. All your so-called help has brought this family nothing but misery and murder."

I take hold of her shoulders as gently as I can but firmly enough to make her face me and listen. "Miss Stern, believe me, I can help. There are things I know that might lead us to whoever killed your father and your aunt. You and your mother need to hear them. Maybe what I have to say can connect you to things you might remember, people you might remember, maybe even the killer. I know this is a rotten time, but the three of us have to talk."

Wiping her eyes with the back of her blue-gloved hand, her sniffling eventually peters out, her pretty face settling again into the sweet pathos of youth. "I still don't get what's your interest in this," she says. Her distrust of me taints the conversation. "Yesterday you told me you liked my aunt Hannah. Well, so what? A lot of people liked her, but they're not running around stirring up whoever killed her and...and..." She's sniffling again, choking on her own words until she finally spits out, "And my father, too."

I take out my handkerchief and wipe her tears, ready for Francine to grab the handkerchief and defiantly do it herself. But she doesn't. She just lets me wipe her tears away. Gently, feeling protective toward this young woman who's been walloped by too much pain and grief in so short a time, I say, "I'll explain all that when we talk. C'mon, let's go get your mother." I take her arm to escort her, but she pulls it away.

"No, not here," she says. "If you want to talk to us, come to the house. There'll be a crowd of visitors, but we can escape into another room." She gives me the address on Riverside.

I don't tell her I already know where she lives.

❖

Two uniformed cops are at either side of the stairs outside the Stern town house. They're eyeballing everyone who walks in.

One of the cops blocks me from the stairs with his billy club. He doesn't know who I am any more than he knows the other visitors to the house, but it doesn't matter; he doesn't like what's going on on my battered face. Cuts and bruises like mine always raise the hackles in a cop's suspicious brain. "What's your business here?" he says.

"I just came from the cemetery. Here to pay my respects."

"You know the family?"

I'm about to give him a story I hope will get me past his billy club when Francine appears at the front door. "It's all right," she says to the cop. He reluctantly lowers his stick.

I tip my cap on my way past him and up the front stairs. "Officer."

As I walk into the vestibule, Francine says, "My mother's waiting for us in the library."

Against my better judgment, but part of my nature, I catch that she's adorable in her black flared skirt and a white blouse buttoned to the neck under a black button-down sweater left open, a sweet outfit I bet she'll discard in favor of something more daring inside of a year. And when she does, heads will turn.

Francine leads me through the stately living room where the rabbi and guests chatter in muted voices. I start to take my cap off out of respect but decide to leave it on, even pull it low. I'm not in the mood for stares at my battered face.

We eventually arrive at the library's highly polished double mahogany doors. As Francine opens the doors, she leans into me and whispers, "I hope you don't terrify my mother. You look like someone's used you for combat training."

Mrs. Stern, bleak in a black suit, her blond hair as obediently in place as when I first saw her yesterday, is seated in one of the room's big brown leather chairs, looking out a window. She's wearing a dark red shade of lipstick, her lips glistening with it, as if she's recently refreshed it. If she's been crying, there's no sign of it—no red eyes, no smudged makeup, no streaked mascara. Maybe tears will come later, after the guests leave, when the house is unnaturally silent and she and her daughter are unnaturally alone. But the more I look at Katherine Stern, I doubt it. She's hollowed out, either by grief or because there was nothing inside to begin with. I hope it's the former and her emotions eventually come back after she's come to grips with the reality of her husband's death. I'd hate to think that the young Francine, alive with the spunk of youth, is stuck with a mother who's dead inside, feeling nothing.

Francine says, gently, "Mom, this is Cantor Gold."

I was wrong. The woman isn't dead inside. She feels plenty, all of it focused on me, deciding I'm just plain rotten under my scars and bruises, worthy of nothing but her hate.

I'm used to feeling people's hate, but I've never had so much of it thrown at me at one time from one pair of eyes. The blue in Katherine Stern's eyes is cold as a frozen lake. And there's hate in her voice, too, each parched word scratching out so slowly I wonder if she'll make it to the end: "You've...ruined...my... family."

"Mrs. Stern." I say her name with all the respect I can muster, but I remember her chilly indifference at Hannah Jacobson's funeral, and my respect frays like a ragged sleeve. And besides, it's tough to stay polite to people who hate you and wouldn't mind if you simply dropped dead, which Katherine Stern clearly wishes I'd do right now. But I give it my best shot; she's a widow, after all, and I need this widow to open up to me. "Mrs. Stern, I'm here to help you figure out who took the lives of your sister-in-law and your husband."

"Isn't that the job of the police? Why would I want a"—she stops and looks me over as if she's smelled something rancid—"a sick person like you butting into our business?"

"Think what you like about me, Mrs. Stern. But if you want to know who killed your husband, I'm a better bet than the police. The cops only know half the story, and they'll use that half to close the case without caring a fig for justice."

I'm not getting anywhere with Mrs. Stern, whose face remains as hard as stone, until Francine says, "At least listen to Cantor, Mom, okay?"

That seems to soften the hard line of Mrs. Stern's mouth a little bit, and I figure I'd better keep talking before she thinks about it and cuts me off. "I'm pretty sure the same person killed your husband and Hannah Jacobson," I say, "and I have a good guess about the reason why. Do you know anything about a watercolor by Albrecht Dürer?"

"Who?" I didn't think Katherine Stern's hate could get any worse, but it has, made bitter by her annoyance at not knowing who or what the hell I'm talking about.

"Albrecht Dürer," I say. "He was an artist in Germany in the late fifteenth and early sixteenth centuries."

Francine says, "Isn't he the guy who did those scary etchings of some knight and a devil or something?"

"Yeah, or something, among other pictures," I say, "not all of them scary."

Mrs. Stern gets up from her chair in a way that advertises that grace and elegance aren't natural to her but she's mastered enough over the years to pull them off, if stiffly. She goes to a small bar cart set up near a wall of books where she pours herself a tall stiff bourbon—no ice, no water, no soda—without asking me if I'd like one. "Is this Dürer picture valuable?"

"Very," I say. "So valuable your husband and his sister were likely murdered for it."

A hefty swallow of bourbon helps her soak up what I just said. The ease with which she swilled the straight liquor tells me she's a good friend of the bottle. "Well, where is this picture now?" she says. "The police didn't say anything about it when they spoke to us yesterday." It's not lost on me that the widow Stern hasn't said one word about her husband or sister-in-law, or asked about their relation to the Dürer watercolor or why it led to their deaths. I don't think I've ever met such a cold woman. I didn't think there even was one.

"I don't know where the picture is," I say.

She still doesn't offer me a drink, just swallows more of hers, her lipstick smearing the glass.

Nodding toward the bar, I finally say, "Do you mind?"

"Help yourself," she says too quickly, as if caught with her socially aspiring panties down. Recovering with the help of another swallow, she says, "So you're looking for this Dürer picture?"

"I am," I say and pour myself a Chivas.

"And what happens when you find it?"

"That depends."

"Depends on what?"

"On what I decide to do with it."

Francine says, "But what does this have to do with Aunt Hannah and Daddy?" finally putting some humanity into this conversation.

"Well, Miss Stern—"

"Please, stop with this Miss Stern business," she says. "It makes me feel like a file clerk. Just call me Francine." Nice to see the kid's sass coming back. I liked her spunk yesterday and I like it even better today.

"Francine," I say with a chivalrous nod, "your aunt Hannah hired me to retrieve the Dürer watercolor from Europe and bring it back to her here in New York. It was part of her husband's collection of German art, a collection that was stolen by the Nazis."

"Yes, she told me about my uncle Theo's art collection." The girl's youthful warmth is a welcome addition to the air in the room after the chill of her mother. "Aunt Hannah was sentimental about it, but she never said anything about trying to get it back."

"That's because she couldn't, at least not after she hired me."

The looks on the faces of Francine and her mother start out the same way: confused, slowly shifting to unsure. But as each of them arrives at the truth, their faces are as different as a sunny day and a rainy night. Francine gives me a mischievous smile; her mother looks like she just heard about a party she wasn't invited to.

Francine, with some delight, says, "You're a smuggler, right? Aunt Hannah hired a smuggler? Good for her!"

Her mother just swallows more of her drink. The lipstick smear on her glass gets thicker.

I don't bother to acknowledge Francine's good guess, just say, "When I told you yesterday, Francine, that I wanted justice for your aunt, I wasn't kidding. Hannah Jacobson was one of the greatest ladies I've ever met. Despite all the horror that life threw at her, she was loaded with grace and warmth. I had the pleasure of seeing her face when I gave her the Dürer. The picture worked its miracles. Great art always does. And the miracle it gave your aunt was the restoration of life, not a life of flesh but a cherished life remembered."

Francine's eyes fill with tears, but they don't spill. I guess she's spilled too many tears in the last two days. She's smart to hold some back, keep her spirit from completely drying out. "And somebody killed her to steal the picture? How cruel."

"I can't be sure yet why they killed her," I say, "but the Dürer watercolor's definitely tied up in it." I turn my attention to the widow, who's pouring herself a second tall drink. "Mrs. Stern, after Hannah Jacobson's death, I understand your husband was questioned by the police and brought to the station to look at mug shots."

"Yes," is all she says.

"When he came home, did he mention anything about a woman in a black veiled hat stopping him outside?"

"It was quite late when he came home. I was already asleep."

Francine says, "Me, too."

I say, "And he said nothing about it the next day? Before all of you left for Mrs. Jacobson's funeral?"

Both women shake their heads. Mrs. Stern says, "Who is this woman? What did she want? You think she killed my husband?"

"I'm not sure who she is. It's possible she killed Mrs. Jacobson, and your husband, too, but I know she sure scared him plenty. He told me about it after the funeral. He said a veiled woman was waiting for him outside the house when he got home from the police station, and that she kept asking him if he had it, only she was hysterical and wouldn't say what *it* was. Your husband told her he had no idea what she was talking about, though I'm pretty sure she was talking about the Dürer. But the Dürer was already gone when the police arrived at Mrs. Jacobson's apartment, so neither the police nor your husband knew a thing about it."

The bourbon helps Katherine Stern understand the tale of high art and crime I'm spinning. After a deep swallow, she says,

"Do the police know about it now?" There's a slurry trace in her speech now, the bourbon finally thickening her tongue.

"No, and it's better that they don't, understand?" I say it with my full criminal force. It might scare mother and daughter just enough to keep them from mouthing off to the police. The less Huber knows, the better.

After I let my little threat sink in, I say, "This veiled woman didn't believe your husband and threatened to kill him if he was lying to her. He saw her again yesterday, at his sister's funeral. I'm sure she was there to scare him, remind him she can get to him anywhere, anytime, if she decides he'd lied to her."

Francine, exhausted by the double whammy of death, sits down in another of the big chairs. "Poor Daddy. Why didn't he tell us? Why did he keep it to himself?"

"He probably didn't want to frighten you," I say. "Look, Francine, Mrs. Stern: Marcus Stern was probably marked for death the minute that Dürer went missing."

Francine, puzzled, says, "Well, if that woman didn't steal it from Aunt Hannah, then who did?"

"That's the million-dollar question."

"I don't understand. If the woman didn't get away with the picture, why did she kill my aunt?"

"I'm not a hundred percent sure she did kill her," I say, "or your father either, though it's likely. Whoever killed Mrs. Jacobson must've really hated her. Cutting up her face was a way to obliterate her identity, erase her. Maybe the same for your father, by…um, shooting him the way they did." I decide it's better not to mention the man's exploded head. Francine and her mother—well, Francine, at any rate—have had enough of that horror.

Katherine Stern puts herself back into the conversation. "You say my sister-in-law hired you to retrieve this Dürer artwork that was stolen from her in Europe?"

"Yeah, that's right."

"Then if you find it, I assume it would go to her family."

I don't answer until I light a cigarette, let the tobacco calm me and restrain me from thrashing this cold and mercenary widow whose heart isn't a bit warmed by the golden bourbon. After a long pull on the smoke, I drag things out further with a deep swallow of scotch. And then I answer her. "Like I said, it depends."

She gives me a stare so frigid her face might freeze and crack. "You have no right," she says.

"Maybe not. But I don't live by what's right and what isn't. So now that we understand each other, I'll be going. I hoped you'd have some information I could use, but I guess we can't have everything we want, right?" After a last swallow of scotch, I say, "I'll see myself out," and walk out of the library as Francine puts her hands to her eyes, sad and exhausted, I guess. The widow Stern pours herself another drink.

Fewer guests are in the living room. With fewer people to dodge, I make my way quickly through the house. But there's a sudden tug on my arm when I'm in the vestibule, just about to open the front door.

It's Francine. She says, "Will you do something for me?"

"If I can. What is it?"

"Stay alive." She gives me a quick kiss on my cheek, her lips making a direct hit on an old jagged scar, and I wish I was a lot younger.

CHAPTER TWELVE

Judson's on the phone when I walk into the office. His penny-loafered feet are propped up on the desk, his dungarees neatly cuffed, a pack of Luckies rolled into the sleeve of his white T-shirt. His end of the phone conversation consists of, "Uh-huh...I see...Well, can you—oh," and similar bits of chatter. He motions me over while he talks, waving three slips of paper in his hand. The sight of those slips, Judson's scrawl across each of them, sets my heart pounding.

But when I grab the slips of paper, none of them have information about the freighter that took Sophie away. My heart slows down, one pounding beat at a time, like a fist getting in its last punches.

One of the slips has a message from Max Hagen, says he got my phone number from Vivienne, wants me to call him at his office at Pauling-Barnett. Another message is from Vivienne. She wants me to call her at her office at the museum. But it's the third message that grabs me by the lapels. It's from Mom Sheinbaum. She wants me to come over around noon. That's less than an hour from now.

Judson gives a final instruction on the phone, "If you hear anything, anything at all, call me, you understand?" then hangs up, takes a smoke from the pack folded in his sleeve, and looks me over as he lights it. "What the hell happened to you? You look like you spent the night in a meat grinder."

"A meat grinder named Screwy Sweeney."

"Jimmy Shea's muscle?"

"Yeah. He doesn't like me. And neither does Jimmy. Who knew?"

Judson chuckles through exhaled smoke. "You'll just have to change your social calendar."

"I may never live down the disgrace. Listen, you have anything yet on that freighter?"

Judson leans back in his chair like all the air's seeped out of his skinny frame. "So far, nothing," he says. "It's like that ship just evaporated in the mist."

"We can't give up, Judson."

"Who said anything about giving up? But finding a ship two years later is tough, especially a ship that sailed on the quiet. But I'll keep digging. I promise, I'll keep digging."

I give him a nod on my way into my private office. I don't have to say anything else. I know he'll dig all the way to China if that's what it takes.

I light a smoke and spread the message slips across my desk. Two of them ask me to return a phone call, and one of the two is a call I can't make. At least not now. I can't call Vivienne now. My lust for Vivienne and my love for Sophie collided last night, and Vivienne came out the loser, pushed to the side of the road.

So I call Hagen.

"Good morning, Gold," he says, smooth and cheerful. "Do you always get such a late start to your day?"

"I had to attend a funeral this morning. Now, what's on your mind, Hagen?"

"Oh yes, of course. I'd quite forgotten. The unfortunate Mr. Stern." His contrition is slight and useless as a weak breeze. "Did you learn anything from Stern's widow about the whereabouts of the Dürer?"

"She never heard of it. Get to the point, Hagen."

"Certainly. Well then, we're getting ready to leave for my country house upstate for the weekend—"

"By *we* I assume you mean you and Vern?" I can't resist pulling the weakest link in Hagen's too carefully constructed chain.

"As I told you last night," he says, irritated, "Vern enjoys country sports, as do I, and the wild game on my acreage is plentiful this season. Now look, Gold, before I leave, it's important for you to understand that I'm quite serious about pursuing that Dürer."

"Have you reconsidered my terms of a fifty-percent take?"

My question's met with silence, except for the sound of Hagen's breathing, leaving me to imagine the hairs of his mustache twitching under his nostrils like nervous Nellies. He finally says, "I'm willing to entertain the idea of discussing it further."

"Yeah, well, discussing it further isn't exactly boffo entertainment. When you're ready to come through with the full fifty, maybe you'll have a hit show. Good-bye, Hagen. You and Vern have fun with your country hunt," I say and hang up. With any luck, Vern will mistake him for a bear and shoot him.

Getting up from my desk, I stub out my smoke, crumple all three message slips and toss 'em in the trash.

❖

Mom opens her front door wearing a housedress with pink and green diagonal stripes that threaten to give me eyestrain. She greets me with a rabbity smile that makes me distrust her more than I already do. The smile changes to mild surprise, then to not-so-mild disgust once she has a good look at the damage to my face. "Come in, Cantor," she says, a sneery undertone in her Lower East Side singsong expressing her distaste for my decayed state.

The aroma of honey cake wafts through the house, seeps into me like a memory I can't get rid of.

As we get closer to the dining room, Mom's uneasy smile explains itself by the sound of a spoon stirring in a glass and the sight of the jowly middle-aged man in a dark suit who's doing the stirring as we walk in. Sitting at the lace-covered dining table, stirring the lemon in his tea, the remaining half of a golden loaf of honey cake in front of him, is the most powerful man in New York, and it's not the mayor; the mayor isn't dangerous. The man stirring his tea is very dangerous. He's Sig Loreale.

Sig is everybody's boss, even the mayor's, even Jimmy Shea's, and when you get right down to it, even Mom's and mine. He doesn't run our rackets, has no involvement in my business at all, except as an occasional client in the market for a painting or antique. But from the kickbacks I give to Jimmy's dock mobs, to the money Mom uses to buy judges and City Hall pols, and all the other money—legit or dirty—that changes hands in New York, a percentage of every dollar finds its way into Sig's pockets. If you hold back even a nickel, you're dead. Sig's assassins will find you in your candy store in the Bronx, your rag-trade factory in Midtown, or your bagel joint in Brooklyn. They'll shoot you or knife you, dismember you and scatter you.

Sig's presence in Mom's dining room doesn't bode well for my current troubles. It also doesn't bode well for my memories: Mom's daughter Opal, whose killing last year was the cause of the breakup of our happy history, was also Sig's fiancée. He was crazy about Opal. Mom, though, was not so crazy about her American-born bundle of joy marrying a mobster, even if he's the most powerful mobster in the country. She wanted better for her pampered daughter, preferably a square-jawed icon of the American Dream. But Mom and Sig agreed on one thing, revenge, and I was the jerk who gave them the opportunity to exact it. Without realizing it, I handed over on a silver platter the woman who was responsible for Opal's death. She's dead now, too, gunned down right in front of me. Sig saw to that.

He stops stirring his tea when he sees me, his heavy-lidded, gray-eyed stare coming at me with the force of a train about to run me down. "Have a seat, Cantor," he says in that slow, precise way that's been giving me the creeps since I was a little kid making mischief in Coney Island and he was a young operator muscling in on the neighborhood's amusement park action. Sig's old-time, carefully learned English gives every word equal power, all of them threatening. "Have some tea," he says. "And honey cake. It is very good cake. It might make you feel better. You look terrible, all banged up."

"Hello, Sig," I say and sit down at the table, though I don't bother with tea or cake. "I assume Mom called you."

"You assume wrong."

Before I have a chance to ask what he's doing here, Mom snipes at me, "And take your coat and cap off in my dining room, Cantor. What, you think my house is a stable?" Raising one flabby arm and pointing around the room, she adds, "You see any horses in here?" When I was a kid, she used to call me her little American savage. I guess her opinion of me hasn't changed.

Mom's scolding strikes Sig funny, and his head tilts back, mouth open, in that weird, silent laugh of his that makes my skin crawl. Escaping that laugh is a good excuse for me to get up from the table to take my coat and cap off and lay them over the back of a chair.

His laugh finished, Sig motions me to sit back down. He says, "Mrs. Sheinbaum did not call me. She did not need to call me. A great many people have kept me informed of your activities. You are causing trouble, Cantor. That is why Jimmy Shea let that goon of his give you a going over outside his bar in the middle of the night."

I've known Sig for a long time, watched him carefully construct his web through the city, enlarging it year by year until it reached every corner of every borough, and it still amazes me that whenever any string of that web quivers, even a little, he knows who's disturbed it. This time it's me. I'm the one dancing along a thread, causing vibrations through his web, disturbing Sig's contentment at its center.

He gives me a smile that makes me wince. Satisfied that I get the picture, he says, "It was brought to my attention that Mrs. Sheinbaum was asking around on your behalf, calling in favors, even. Now, you know Mrs. Sheinbaum has my full admiration and respect, and if she's trading inquiries for favors, then I know that whatever is going on is serious business. You understand me, Cantor?" It isn't a question he wants answered. It isn't really a question at all. It's a warning. "That is why I arranged this meeting, to see if we can get to the bottom of your trouble, and make it go away for everyone concerned."

Against my better judgment, but maybe it'll lighten the mood, I say, "Are you offering to help me, Sig?"

He lifts his glass and takes a sip of his tea, looking at me over the rim. The bags under his cold eyes are magnified by the glass, making his stare grotesque, intensifying his evil.

So it's a relief when he puts the glass down and his eyes resume their merely hard-as-stone stare. "Let us just say I am offering to keep you alive."

I'm tempted to say, *I didn't know you cared,* but figure it's better to keep my humor to myself. I've already tried the mood-lightening gambit once, and it's not a good idea to press Sig's sense of humor too far. I've never been sure if he even has one.

He says, "There has been too much bloodshed in this situation already. That poor old woman, Mrs. Jacobson, cut up like that. A terrible thing. I understand she survived Hitler."

Just hearing the monster's name makes Mom shift in her chair and mutter, "Mamzer," cursing him as a bastard in Yiddish.

The sudden tenderness on Sig's face surprises me down to my socks. I've never known him to have a tender moment in his life, though maybe his dear, departed Opal did. I've never been at the receiving end, though. Probably never will be. "Forgive me, Esther," he says, patting Mom's hand. "I did not mean to upset you."

Mom gives him a nod, but that's all. She doesn't like Sig. She never did. But she's smart enough to let him think otherwise.

Sig's tenderness is short-lived, and the hard stare is back when he turns his attention again to me. His quick change from predator to humanitarian to predator again is terrifying. "And then her brother, Marcus Stern," he says, giving his tea another slow stir. Only Sig Loreale can make the scrape of a spoon against a glass sound sinister. "Mr. Stern was a scholar, a scientist, I understand, before he was a successful businessman. Very sad, the way he died. And his death was rather dramatic, from what I hear." He stops stirring his tea. The sudden silence is even scarier than the scrape of the spoon. I swear the air in the room actually cracks when he says, "Far too dramatic, Cantor. I am having to twist a lot of arms to keep it out of the newspapers and not attract the wrong attention. And another death, your death, would complicate matters further."

"Yeah, it would be a tragedy," I say, more or less muttering it.

Sig ignores my little joke. He just takes a cigar and clippers from his inside pocket, but before he clips the end of the cigar, he leans toward Mom and says, "May I, Esther?"

"Sure, go ahead. Wait, I'll get you an ashtray, you shouldn't make a mess on my table."

"No, please, sit," he says. "Cantor will get it for me."

I'm never sure if Sig treats me like a kid because he's known me since I was one, or it's just another way of expressing his power. But I get the ashtray.

After I sit down again, Sig clips his cigar, lights it, and puffs it a few times to get it going. The red tip burns like a warning from the devil, the glow crawling up the heavy flesh of his face, ringing his eyes. He eventually takes the cigar from his mouth, and when he speaks, his words ride on puffs of smoke, just like Satan's. "Your death would bring more attention from the police."

"Cheering all the way," I say.

He gives me a quick version of his grisly silent laugh, then says, "Yes, they might be very happy about that. But they are police, after all, Cantor. They would have to make a dumb show of pursuing justice, looking for your killer, or they risk losing face, and losing face is something policemen will not tolerate. They would be forced to start one of their troublesome crackdowns on crime."

Mom, more curious than alarmed, says, "And since when is that a problem? You have every precinct captain in the city on your payroll, no?"

"I can only restrain the police just so far, Esther, as long as it suits their interests. But this current situation does not suit their interests." He puffs his cigar and shakes his head with the concentration of an Einstein tackling a knotty problem. At the end of this line of thought, he turns to me. "And did you know, Cantor, that you are a hot gossip item? Oh yes, you are. You and your fancy suits and women on your arm. The Law might hate you for it, but you are a reporter's meal ticket."

"Lucky me," I say. "You think my funeral would draw a crowd as big as Al Capone's?"

"Go ahead, go think it's funny," Sig says. "But you will not be laughing when some eager policeman hauls you in and you wind up dead in a jail cell. Or Jimmy Shea puts a gun to your head and pulls the trigger. Your death or even just your arrest would be far too juicy for the news people to resist. They'd pry into everything in your life, Cantor. The girlie stuff," he says with a dismissive wave, "I don't care about, but there are places in your life where I don't want them to go. And I'm sure you don't either."

"All right, Sig, you've made your point."

"I hope so," he says, "because let me tell you, controlling those press people is no easy business these days. It used to be just the newspaper scribblers, then they added the radio yakkers, but now they're even showing up with bulletins on the television. A person can't relax with a cuppa coffee anymore without gruesome pictures showing up in their living room. Disgusting."

He puffs on his cigar again, fast and with deep inhales this time, the cigar's red tip a beacon of his anger, his exhaled smoke carrying that anger into his words. "What is worse," he says, "the politicians are even more untrustworthy than the police. If they smell an election issue—and crime is their favorite election issue—they will unleash the full force of a City Hall investigation, maybe even a state investigation." He leans across the table, his eyes boring into me, forcing me to feel the weight of his displeasure at his predicament. "I will not fight a battle on so many fronts, Cantor. It costs too much money, and the outcome is not guaranteed. You know I do not care for outcomes which are not guaranteed."

I'm about to ask him just what he expects me to do about it when Mom says, "Calm yourself, Sig. You'll give yourself a heart attack. Maybe even a stroke. I don't need such aggravation in my dining room. Calling the ambulance for you would attract as much attention from those Cossack police as this business Cantor's got us into."

If I'd challenged Sig that way, I'd be marked for dead. But Sig's an Old World kind of guy, and Mom is an Old World grand dame, and underworld royalty to boot. But most of all, she's the mother of Sig's beloved dead fiancée.

Now I know: Mom Sheinbaum is Sig's tender spot. That might come in handy someday.

But Mom's little interruption broke Sig's rant and lets me into the conversation on firmer footing. "Look, Sig," I say, "the last thing I need is you breathing down my neck, so let's get down to exactly what you have in mind about getting rid of my trouble."

"What do I have in mind, Cantor? Money is what I have in mind."

"I'm not sure I understand. You want me to give you money?"

"Don't talk nonsense, Cantor," he says, his head going back into that silent laugh again. That's three times in this conversation. I'm not sure I can take another without screaming in horror. When he's done with the laugh, he says, "I can already buy and sell you. What would I do with your piddling few thousand dollars? No, what I want is for you to help me *make* money."

"And how am I supposed to do that?"

"Well, I know that you are looking for a famous picture by a Mr. Dürer, yes?"

Like I said, there's nothing in this town Sig Loreale doesn't know.

Giving me the full force of his will, he says, "When you find it, I want you to give it to me. I have plans for it. Profitable plans."

"Give it to you? If I want to make a charitable donation, Sig, I can always write a check to the War Widows and Orphans Relief. And besides, I can get good money elsewhere."

"I am not speaking of charity, Cantor. I am speaking of business. Consider it my fee for cleaning up the mess you've made—"

"Hold it. I'm not the one who's made the mess. There's a killer on the loose, and a thief. It's their mess I'm caught in."

That gets his attention. For the first time in this conversation, he looks at me like I might have a brain in my head. "You are telling me that you think the killer and the thief are two different people?" he says.

"Yeah, that's what I'm telling you. I think Mrs. Jacobson was killed because the Dürer was already gone. And I think her brother was killed because he didn't have it either, and the killer thought maybe Stern was falling in with me to find it."

Sig takes a deep pull on his cigar, lets the smoke out slowly, giving him time to sort out what I said.

Mom, meantime, pours herself a glass of tea and cuts herself a slice of honey cake. The tap of the knife rouses Sig from his thoughts, irritating him. But when he realizes it's Mom who's disturbed his thinking, his attitude softens. The guy's really mush in her hands. Sooner or later, Mom's gonna play him again, just like she did last year in the hunt for her daughter's killer. Just like she played me.

Sig doesn't bring his tender attitude with him when he turns his attention back to me. With me, he's all hard business. "What about this fellow from Pauling-Barnett Mrs. Sheinbaum's been looking into, this Max Hagen. You think he may have killed for the picture?"

"He's certainly cold enough," I say. "And he's supposedly good with a gun, at least, according to him. He's on his way upstate to shoot a bunch of little animals this weekend."

"No, not animals. Birds. It is grouse-hunting season."

Well, well. Sig Loreale, gentleman sportsman. This jowly man with heavy shoulders and thick flesh must be quite a sight in tweeds. I wonder if he feels the same thrill hunting birds as he does hunting people.

"Fine, have it your way," I say, "birds. But I doubt Hagen killed Hannah Jacobson or Marcus Stern."

"Why do you say that?"

"Because it's possible the killer is a woman."

By the surprise on Sig's face, you'd think I told him the killer was a kangaroo. Funny, a lot of people can't imagine the fair sex as murderers. But I can run you a list a mile long of women who kill, from ancient queens who stabbed or poisoned their way to the throne, right up to a crafty dame who goes by the name of Miss Martha Beck, currently on death row for the brutal murders of a bunch of lonely women she and her boyfriend swindled. She did it for love, she said, and oh yeah, the women's life insurance money.

Mom, though, doesn't look surprised at all. And soon, neither does Sig. Instead, his hard eyes register a memory, the memory of his beloved Opal's death by the woman who was supposed to be her best friend.

Sig's figuring another angle, too, turning his cigar in his fingers while he thinks. He says, "Well then, what about this fancy curator you've been seen with? Is she a killer?"

There it is, the question I've been tiptoeing around almost since this whole thing started, the question whose answer could eat me alive. Vivienne may be at the side of the road, but she's not out of sight, the lust we shared certainly not out of mind. But the time's come to face some truths about Vivienne, like the truth that she wants the Dürer, and the truth that there's a crazy streak in her family, a madness she may have inherited from her mother, who's currently marinating in a sanitarium. The murder of Hannah Jacobson was certainly an act of raging madness. If Vivienne inherited her mother's wild mind and the violence of the rough-and-tumble slum Trents, that combination could be lethal. And according to Hagen's boy Vern, Vivienne is as good at those country sports as they are, a crack shot in her own right. And the last truth, about those warm feelings Vivienne said she had for Mrs. Jacobson: she should've been at her funeral, but wasn't.

Or was she? Not as a mourner, but as the mysterious woman in a black veiled hat who scared Marcus Stern out of his wits and later killed him.

Mom's voice cuts through my miserable musings. "Well, Cantor? Sig asked you a question. What about this woman, this—what's her name? Park? Park something?"

"Parkhurst Trent," I say. "Vivienne Parkhurst Trent. A killer?" I don't dare let on what I've been thinking about Vivienne. Sig might decide she's good for the murders, guilty or not, just to get the heat off. He might hand her over to the cops, as a gift that will end their disruption of the rackets. Or maybe he'll kill her himself just to get rid of the problem, save the cops the trouble of an arrest and trial. I've already done that dance of death with him, last year. I won't do it again. So I just answer Sig's question with, "I doubt it."

"What about the thief?" he says. "Any ideas?"

"Not yet. I'd hoped Mom could come up with something. She has ways of hearing about any goods that move through town."

Sig asks, "Esther?"

Mom gives him a shrug that wiggles those pink and green stripes of her housedress, a sight which could give the whole neighborhood a headache. "Nah. Except for this Hagen person's interest," she says, "I haven't heard a word, not a whisper, except everyone telling me that this Hagen is a *faygeleh* with fancy tastes."

"So we are nowhere," Sig says, articulating each word as if they smell bad.

Resuming his habitual courtesy toward Mom, he says, "My dear Esther, Cantor is correct about your knowledge of goods moving through town. Please continue your efforts to track this Dürer picture. In the meantime, I will see what I can do to restrain the police. Cantor, I understand you have had difficulty with a Lieutenant Huber?"

The meeting has finally turned my way, and I smile, a big, brash smile that hurts the bruises on my face, but it's a satisfying pain. "Yeah, I've had difficulty with Huber. You can see some of that difficulty right here in the split in my lip and the black-and-blue beaut on my chin."

Mom mutters, "What did I tell you. Cossacks."

I say, "But he's more than just a Cossack. He may be dirty, too."

Sig waves that away. "They are all dirty," he says. "Maybe he's just greedier, wants more money."

Like a kid with a secret that could win me candy from the grownups, I say, "Nope, that's not it. It's not money he's after. It's me he wants. And to get me, it seems he's thrown in with Jimmy Shea. So now he's Shea's man, Sig. Or worse, Shea may be Huber's."

Most people, when they hear they've been betrayed, register some degree of shock, or at least disappointment. Their eyes might open wide, maybe their eyebrows go up, or maybe those eyebrows go in the other direction and dive into a frown. Not Sig Loreale. He just sits in his chair, breathing slowly, steadily, and very, very quietly.

The tension in the dining room is stretched tight as a rubber band, until Sig finally says, "How do you know this?"

"I won't break a confidence, Sig," I say, "but the source was there when the deal was made. The tip is good. You know me long enough to know that I can tell if a story is good or bad, and this story is a good one."

He considers this for a minute, then gives me a nod in acknowledgment of my judgment. "I will look into this," he says, stirring his tea again, each scrape of the glass announcing bad news for either Shea or Huber or both.

This is my moment, my chance to get something back for the shocker I just tossed in Sig's lap. So I say, "While you're looking into that, there's another matter concerning Jimmy Shea I'd like you to look into, Sig."

Slowly, he stops stirring the tea and looks at me. "About a freighter that sailed two years ago," he says.

Here it is again, that reach of Sig's, as deep as it is wide. It's not enough that he knows what everybody in the city is doing, he knows what everybody is saying, even the whispers. And it's a sure bet that hearing about my interest in the freighter didn't come from Jimmy Shea or anyone in his outfit. Why pass along a tidbit they could hold over my head for their own gain? And it didn't come from Drogan. The way Loreale picks all the pockets along the waterfront, Red's no friend of Sig's. And it certainly didn't come from Iris Page. She couldn't get to Sig no matter how many guys she serviced on her way to the inner sanctum. No, it came from a source even deeper, maybe someone Judson nicked while digging his way to China. So I've got another assignment for Judson: find the leak and plug it. I won't ask how.

I say, "That's right, Sig. I want to know about a freighter that sailed from Pier 8 in March of '48 with a bunch of hijacked women aboard. I want to know where it went and who received the flesh on the other side. Jimmy might've been in on it. And even if he wasn't, he knows more than he's saying."

I catch Mom out of the corner of my eye. She's chewing a piece of honey cake, cutting another piece with her fork. Anyone walking into the dining room would think she's just an old lady enjoying her cake and paying no attention to the conversation at her table. But they'd be wrong. Mom's not missing a trick. She's hearing it all, storing it away.

I control a smile that wants to creep into the corner of my mouth. Sig would ask me why I'm smiling, and I don't want to be the one to tell him that his soft spot for Mom Sheinbaum could some day be his undoing.

His attention still fixed on me, Sig says, "This is about that woman you've been looking for, yes? If I remember correctly, her name is Sophie."

I hate hearing her name through his killer's mouth. But his saying it was his way of acknowledging that he owes me a favor, a favor not from tonight's revelation about Shea and Huber, but an almost two-year-old favor, when I delivered Opal's killer to him, whether I meant to or not. I hate trading on such a sleazy debt, but if it means finding Sophie, I'll do what it takes, even swim in slime. So I say, "That's right, her name's Sophie. And I have reason to believe she was on that boat."

Sig stubs out his cigar and drinks the last of his tea, enjoying that final swallow as if it was the high spot in his afternoon. "All right," he says, "I will look into that freighter business for you, Cantor, after you find that Dürer picture and hand it over to me."

He knows, I'm sure, by the look on my face, that I want to say, *But one thing has nothing to do with the other!* I know because of how he's looking at me, smiling, while he gives me his stone-hard stare. That stare pushes back at me with the force of a fist.

He says, "So if there is no other business, then you should be on your way, Cantor. You have much to do." Turning to Mom, he says, "And so do you, my dear Esther," though his tone is slightly less courtly than it was earlier. Maybe he's wise to Mom. Maybe there's no maybe about it.

CHAPTER THIRTEEN

Everyone has their favorite luncheonette. Mine's a sliver of a joint down the street from my apartment. The food's good, the marble counter's clean, the black-and-green checkerboard linoleum floor's not peeling or sticky, and the boss is smart enough not to bother fixing the neon sign out front, which now reads PE E'S instead of PETE'S. The busted sign gives the place a seedy look, which keeps the tourists away. This makes the regulars happy, locals who don't have the time to wait for a seat at the counter while Mom and Pop Hayseed make up their minds between the blue-plate special and the split-pea soup. It also makes the counter help happy, because the locals are good tippers and Mom and Pop Hayseed aren't.

But the best thing about Pete's is the coffee—rich and strong, with plenty of zing to keep a body going and a brain tip-top. Having finished my chicken on rye, I'm enjoying a cup, letting the tinny clatter of silverware and the quiet chatter of the other customers surround me like a cozy blanket while the caffeine sharpens my thoughts.

The trouble is I have lots of thoughts but none of them lead anywhere. I'm no closer to untangling this mess than I was when Huber came to my door and told me that Hannah Jacobson was dead. That was two nights ago, and now it's Friday afternoon and all I've got to show for it is another murder, the squeeze from

Huber, Shea, and Sig Loreale, and a busted-up face. And oh yeah, suspicions about Vivienne, suspicions that eat my heart out. What I don't have is the stolen Dürer or the name of the freighter that stole Sophie from me.

"What's the matter, Cantor?" The cigarette voice of Doris, my waitress, pierces my gloom. "You look like someone killed your dog. Only I know you ain't got a dog." Doris has been behind the counter at Pete's since it was Mike's, and before Mike's, Izzy's. Above her pink uniform, her perm-waved salt-and-pepper gray hair frames her thin face, a friendly face with a toothy smile and faded red lipstick that's seeped into the age lines around her mouth. Her brown eyes, narrowed like she's studying you, are alert to her customers' needs and moods, which is why she's holding a pot of coffee in front of my cup. "How 'bout I hotten it up for you."

I give her a nod.

Doris raises the pot and pours the black gold from on high, letting the air cool the steaming coffee on its way down into the cup. She doesn't spill a drop. "So what's on your mind, Cantor? Heartbreak? Dough? Gotta be one or the other. Always is, 'cause there ain't nothing else in this life worth worrying about except love or money."

A dull, "Mmmm," is my general agreement.

She puts the coffeepot down, rests her elbows on the counter, her chin in her hands, and looks me in the eye, a hash-joint psychiatrist waiting for me to spill what ails me. "Give over, Gold," she says.

There's no arguing with Doris once she's made her mind up, and she's clearly made her mind up to dig my troubles out of me. So after a fortifying sip of coffee and a resigned breath, I give over. "If a whole bunch of people were after you to do something—do the same thing, really, but for different reasons—and you had nothing to go on except a story with too many pieces and none of the pieces fit with the others, what would you do?"

With a shrug that's the diploma of Doris's sidewalk education, she says, "Well, I guess I'd just find the beginning of the story."

Suddenly the coffee tastes even better, Doris's cigarette voice sounds smooth as Ella Fitzgerald singing at Birdland, and my stool at the counter is classier than a booth at the Ritz. "Doris, my sweet, they should give you the Nobel Prize."

"Yeah? What for?"

I give her a smile, an extra fiver along with my buck-twenty-five tab, and say, "For untying the Gordian knot."

On my way out the door, she calls after me, "Who's Gordon?"

❖

After a quick stop at my apartment and a short drive across town, I'm at the tradesmen's entrance at the back of Hannah Jacobson's building, where a couple of items I picked up at my place—my lock picker's hook and tension wrench—are doing their job. A few strokes of the hook later, the last pin clicks, the doorknob turns, and I'm in the basement of the building.

There's a radio on somewhere down here, broadcasting the afternoon races at Belmont. The announcer's excited, almost hysterical, as a long-shot takes the lead. I wish I had money on it, but I'll settle for my good luck that the announcer's screech and the cheering crowd are covering my footsteps while the building super is hunched over the radio, too caught up in the race to notice me walk by. In just a few long strides, I'm through the door to the stairway.

I get out at the second floor, buzz for the elevator and take it the rest of the way to the twelfth floor.

The lock picks come out again and get me into Mrs. Jacobson's apartment.

It's like Doris said: I have to find the beginning of the story, a story that started here.

I take my cap off in acknowledgment of the sadness that hangs in the place, a darkness that doesn't go away no matter how many lamps I turn on in the living room. But I can't let the sadness paralyze me, can't let the dark mood obscure any details I might've missed when I was here with Huber.

So I stuff my cap in my coat pocket and start looking around.

Nothing's changed since Huber and I stood in this room two nights ago. The super hasn't cleaned the place yet and won't, until the family—or what's left of it—finally collects Mrs. J's belongings. The walls are still spattered with arcs of Mrs. J's blood. The bloodstain's still on the carpet between the sofa, the coffee table, and the side table that was chipped during Mrs. J's death struggle. The bloodstain is even darker, now that it's soaked in and dried, a large bulb-like shape of blotchy red-brown where a life quietly drained away after a fury of savage madness.

I've seen blood before, the dripped blood of the wounded and the staining blood of the dead. I know what it looks like, know its colors, and there's something not right about the colors on Mrs. J's carpet. There shouldn't be pale watery-looking splotches, and there shouldn't be tiny pinpricks of white.

I get on my hands and knees, bringing a lamp down from the side table for a better look.

The watery splotches are where another liquid must've fallen to the floor and mixed with Mrs. J's blood, diluting it in spots. The liquid was nearly colorless, or at least not as dark as blood. There's no odor of alcohol, but a faint scent of green tea. The white pinpricks are really tiny splinters of a hard but brittle substance, the splinters breaking when I try to scrape them up from the carpet. I know what that substance is and what the splinters are, the remains of a broken porcelain cup, maybe a cup and saucer. The crime-scene boys must've taken away the larger shards by the time I came back here with Huber. I guess they didn't find any fingerprints on the shards other than Mrs. J's or they would've already made an arrest. But it doesn't matter that the cops knew before I did that Mrs. Jacobson was seated on the sofa, enjoying a cup of tea, when her killer came to call. It doesn't matter because the cops are only concerned with Mrs. J's murder, not a stolen artwork, which they don't know a damn thing about.

I get up from the floor, put the lamp back on the side table, and sit down on the sofa. There's a miserable lump in my throat, but I'm smiling.

The lump in my throat is from a tearless, choking grief for the grand lady who shared tender moments with me here, a woman of strength and calm dignity who loved life despite the horrors it threw at her. My smile is for her courage and her determination not to let any more monsters rob her of her legacy and memories. Because if Hannah Jacobson was enjoying a cup of tea just before the monster killed her in frustration and rage, then the Dürer was still in Mrs. J.'s possession. It hadn't been stolen.

It never was.

I'll never know if Mrs. Jacobson told the intruder that the Dürer wasn't here, or that she never heard of it, or some other tale to keep the monster from getting their hands on it. Whatever she said, they believed her, which is why the killer's next stop was Marcus Stern's place. What Mrs. J couldn't know was that the intruder was possibly a madwoman.

I squelch the lump in my throat as I get up from the sofa, take my coat off, and start searching, silently congratulating Mrs. J on her sharpness of mind. Until she could secure the Dürer watercolor, maybe in a safe-deposit box, and then have it insured, framed, professionally secured to the wall, and alarmed, she did the smart thing and hid it.

Starting with the vestibule closet, there's nothing in there but a few coats, galoshes, and an umbrella. No false walls, no hidden nooks.

Back in the living room, I start with the usual places: under the sofa and chairs, under the bookcase and behind the books, in drawers, and under the carpet. Then in the not so usual places: the underside of the small dining table and chairs, between the walls and the furniture, and behind the framed floral and landscape prints. I even open the frames, take the prints out to see if Mrs. J hid the Dürer between the picture and the backing. Nothing. I knock the walls but don't find any hidden spaces, no concealed safe, no secret cubby.

My next stop is the kitchen and dinette, where I look in cabinets, drawers, behind the refrigerator, behind the oven, the underside of the enamel-topped dinette table and the steel chairs with gray Naugahyde-covered seats. I even unscrew the seats.

The kitchen and dinette proving a bust, I check the bathroom, even though I'm sure Mrs. J was smart enough not to store something so delicate in such a damp environment, but you never know.

I'm right; it's not in the bathroom.

And it's not in the linen closet in the hall.

So the last stop is the bedroom. It's got to be in the bedroom.

It's a pretty room, with afternoon sunlight through windows that face the street. The light falls across the blue and gold Chinese rug, electrifying the colors, and runs across the blue chenille bedspread. The sunlight touches the photograph on the night table, a recent photo of Marcus Stern, his wife, and daughter, the remnants of Hannah Jacobson's family. There are no photos of Mrs. J's husband and children because there are no photos to be had. They were left behind in Germany, to burn.

I shake myself out of this melancholy reverie and start searching the room, first on hands and knees looking under the bed, the night tables, the blue satin slipper chair, the bureau, and lifting the Chinese rug. I stand up, look behind the mirror, then go through the bureau drawers, which makes me feel lousy. Rifling through Mrs. J's most personal garments, pushing them aside, looking for hidden compartments or secret latches, feels like a violation, a soiling of her dignity. I'm relieved when I'm finished.

The closet's the last place to look. There's nowhere else. It's got to be there.

But there's nothing in the closet but clothes, the simple but elegant dresses Mrs. J favored, shoes neatly arranged on a rack, and some luggage on the shelf. I take down the luggage, three valises in all, and open them. The delicate scent of a floral sachet drifts from the quilted peach satin lining and into the room, breaking my heart.

Except for the sachet in the pockets, there's nothing in the luggage—no false bottoms, no Dürer watercolor.

I collapse into the slipper chair, annoyed at how I could get it so wrong. The Dürer's gone, stolen after all, by a thief so sharp they've outsmarted me, even outsmarted Mom Sheinbaum.

Miffed at being so cocksure of myself, the smart-alecky outlaw who thinks I know a good game when I see one, I kick a valise, hard, sending it sliding across the carpet and crashing against the bureau. I immediately feel crummy about it, as if I've put my foot in Mrs. J's hospitality. I get up from the chair and check if I've damaged the valise, and that's when I see it: a corner of the quilted lining knocked loose.

I'd been looking for false compartments, false bottoms, but never guessed there might be a false lining, so carefully sewn and padded it passed for the genuine article. I carefully pull the rest of the threads away and stop breathing when the lining finally slips down, the folio sliding into the valise.

When I start breathing again, I also start smiling again, a smile for my restored trust in my instincts, but mostly a smile for Hannah Jacobson, whose intelligence I should never have doubted. She must've prepared this valise while I was still out of the country, confident that I'd succeed in bringing back her prize.

A last pang of doubt tells me to open the folio, check if the Dürer is really there.

It is, in all its graceful splendor, its scene of grasses waving as if taking a fresh breath.

It's nearly three thirty in the afternoon, and I have plenty yet to do, so this isn't the time to linger over a great piece of art. I close the folio and put the luggage back into the closet.

Back in the living room, I put on my coat and cap, and after a last look around, a last sad glance at Hannah Jacobson's blood on the floor and the walls—all that's left of her—I put the folio inside my coat and walk out of her apartment.

Chapter Fourteen

Judson's working the phone again when I come in. He shrugs and turns his palms up to let me know he's got nothing new on the freighter. I nod acknowledgment on my way into my private office.

I toss my coat and cap on the couch, pour myself a stiff scotch, and bring the scotch and the Dürer folio with me down to the basement.

With its glaring overhead bulb, dusty concrete floor, bare brick walls, and assorted boxes of spare bulbs and electrical cords lying around, it looks like any other basement. So if the cops ever get lucky and find out about this place, all they'll see is a clerical office upstairs and an ordinary basement downstairs. Except it's not an ordinary basement. When I press a brick near the bottom corner of the back wall, a section of the wall opens like a large door. Inside that door is another door, a vault door. I dial the combination, pull the vault door open, and step into my treasure chest.

Shelves on either side hold a king's ransom of art, antiquities, and jewels that once sat snugly in museums, churches, castles, or villas of the well-to-do. Assorted royalty, presidents, prime ministers, and lesser lights among the world's elite are still scratching their heads wondering how this stuff disappeared from their clutches, and they'd surely hang me if they knew. Some of these treasures are waiting for shipment, some are waiting to be paid for, and some I'm still negotiating among various buyers. Among the latter is a curator of Medieval art at Vivienne's museum who's interested in a small ivory Madonna I brought over from France about six months ago. It's barely eight inches high, dating to the fourteenth century. The carving is as smooth as silk, the curve of her body under the folds of her robe as sensual as it is motherly, which is a good indication of the difference in how Europeans and Americans think of motherhood.

I take another pull of the scotch, put the Dürer folio on a shelf, and wonder what to do with it. The obvious choice is to give it to the Stern family. If it's anyone's, it's theirs. I'm sure Francine would treasure it, but if her mother gets her hands on it, she'd sell it, and probably to just anybody and certainly too fast and too cheap.

My bank account would best be served by dealing with Hagen. With his connections, he'd get top dollar, and my 50 percent would keep me in silk suits and new Buicks for quite a few seasons.

Vivienne's museum would probably come up with the dough, too. The Dürer is quite a prize, a masterpiece by one of the most important artists of the Northern European Renaissance. I bet the museum's trustees would rather rob their own banks than let it go to a rival museum, or worse, to a private collector outside their own old-money social circle. And Vivienne's right about one thing: if it's at her museum, everybody, every average Joe and Jane—not just Katherine and Francine Stern, not just Hagen's cash-rich collectors—could see and experience Dürer's brilliance.

But it's my personal interest that has the strongest pull, and my personal interest urges me to hand the Dürer over to Sig. It will buy his power to find the freighter that sailed away with Sophie.

And if I don't turn it over to Sig, he might kill me.

The idea, though, of giving it to Sig, of letting the most murderous man in town profit from the death of Hannah Jacobson and Marcus Stern, turns my stomach.

Meantime, none of the contenders know I have it, which means the killer doesn't know I have it either. Keeping it secret keeps me alive.

There's a small strongbox at the end of the shelf. It contains an item I'll never sell, an eighteenth-century Italian necklace of rubies set in filigreed gold. It was going to be a present for Sophie. I was going to give it to her the night I'd planned to ask her to live with me, the night I knocked on her door and no one answered, the night she was stolen from me.

I don't open the strongbox much anymore for the same reason I took the photo of us off my desk. Seeing it hurts too much. But there's new hope now, a new chance I'll find Sophie and bring her home. I open the box.

The rubies sparkle like fresh blood, the gold's old patina shimmers. Then both blur through tears I thought I'd conquered.

I close the box, take a deep swallow of the scotch to deaden my teary moment, and go back upstairs, where I grab my coat and cap. There's a place I need to go, and a lot of other things I need to do.

In the outer office, Judson's off the phone, but he's not alone. He's talking to Rosie, who's perched on the edge of his desk. Neither of them look too happy. Judson looks like he's expecting the schoolteacher to make him wear a dunce cap and send him to the back of the room. Rosie looks like she's already been sent there.

"Something I should know?" I say.

Rosie slides off the desk, comes near me, and strokes my battered cheek. There's enough sadness in her eyes to make a stone wall cry. "You sure take a beating," she says, "and it never seems to stop."

I take her hand from my cheek, kiss her palm. I mean that kiss, every warm patch of it, but not in the way she wants. "No, it never seems to stop," I say.

Judson gets up from the desk, says, "Um, I'm going for coffee. Anybody want anything?" and walks to the door, escaping the awkward moment.

"Don't go yet, Judson," I say. "I need to talk to you."

"I'll only be a minute, Cantor."

It's Rosie who saves the situation. It seems it's always Rosie who saves any number of situations in my life. Taking her hand back from mine, she says, "No, Judson. You and Cantor have business. I gotta get going anyway. Workin' a double shift. 'Bye, Cantor." And with that, she walks past Judson and out the door.

Judson shuffles back to his desk, leans against it like a guilty schoolboy. "Sorry, Cantor. I screwed up."

"Yeah? How? And what's it got to do with Rosie acting like there's a death in the family?"

"Because she knows."

Judson catches on that I have no idea what he's talking about.

For a guy who always considers his words carefully, I've never seen Judson so tongue-tied. "I was, um…look, I was on the phone when Rosie came in. She heard me digging for information about the boat and Sophie, and when Rosie asked about it, I couldn't cover it up. I can't lie to her, Cantor, not to Rosie. So I blabbed it, told her about the first break in Sophie's case in two years. And soon as the words were out of my mouth, I knew I'd screwed up. I should've let you tell her. I didn't think, Cantor. I just—I didn't think."

Yeah, I should've been the one to tell her, not that it would've been any easier on her to hear it from me. Rosie knows the score with me, about my freedom to take other women to my bed. She handles it because she knows she has my trust and they don't. She also knows that though none of them could ever replace Sophie, she can't either. It didn't matter so much when Sophie was just a memory, a dream receding with each passing month. But the dream has suddenly taken on flesh. There's a chance that Sophie, the living, breathing woman, will become part of my life again. And now Rosie, like Vivienne, knows she's been pushed to the side of the road.

Judson's blab to Rosie is the only indiscretion he's ever made since he started working for me. It might be the only indiscretion he's ever committed in his life. And I figure he'll make up for it by never committing another indiscretion ever again, about anything, even the most trivial, like telling me the odds he gets from his bookie.

I put a friendly hand on his shoulder. "Don't beat yourself up about it," I say. "You've got something else to worry about right now. It seems there's a leak in your gang of contacts."

He snaps out of his hangdog mood, his eyes open wide, curious and alarmed behind his glasses.

"I just came from a meeting with Mom Sheinbaum and Sig Loreale," I say. The color drains from Judson's hollow cheeks at the mere mention of crime's royal twosome. "Seems someone you talked to about the freighter also talked to Sig, or one of his minions. Anyway, it got back to him. It's okay that he knows. It might even prove helpful, but—"

"Yeah," Judson jumps in, "nobody should be privy to our business but us. I'll find the leak, Cantor. And I'll plug it."

"Good. And by the way, in case anybody calls and asks about the Dürer—Loreale, Hagen, Mom, *anybody*—just keep telling them you have no new information."

"Got it." Then, "Huh?" Judson's a smart kid, my own personal genius, and he catches on fast. A smile full of curiosity creeps across his face.

I say, "It's downstairs."

He's grinning now, not only at the news, but at the trust I've just shared with him again. "So where was it? Who had it?"

"Hannah Jacobson had it. It never left her apartment. She prepared a hiding place for it until she could have it secured."

"Wow. She was one smart old girl."

"And a great lady," I say. "She died defending the last vestige of her husband and children." That idea hangs between us, the sadness of it threatening to devour everything else Judson and I need to do. "I have to go," I say, breaking the dark spell. "I'll check back later."

It's time for me to take care of a loose end that's been tickling me in all the wrong places. I have to confront Vivienne, find out one way or the other if she's a killer. It's best if I skip calling her, just show up at her office before she can concoct a story, or even beat it out of town.

The phone rings on my way out. I leave Judson to handle it, but before I'm out the door, he calls, "Cantor! It's Drogan on his ship-to-shore. Says it's urgent."

Drogan's not the dramatic type. If he says something's urgent, he's not kidding. So I go back to Judson's desk and take the phone. "Yeah, Red, what's up?"

"Listen, you gotta come to my boat, Cantor, right now. Somethin'—somethin' you gotta see."

"What's it all about? You get a line on that freighter?"

"I'll tell you when you get here."

"You at your dock in Brooklyn?"

"Nuh-uh. Remember that abandoned barge dock by Little West Street? I'm tied up over there."

"On my way."

It's nearly five o'clock when I park my Buick at the end of Little West Street, near Manhattan's southern tip. The autumn sun's getting low over the Hudson, sending golden ripples along the river and out onto New York Bay. The area's quiet, almost deserted. Automobile traffic's been passing this old dockside neighborhood by since the new Battery Tunnel to Brooklyn opened this past May. Trucks now carry freight to or from the Manhattan and Brooklyn docks at twice the speed and half the cost of tow barges. Barge life is drying up, the old salts who live on their tugs a passing breed.

"Red?" I call out as I step aboard his tug.

"Come below, Cantor."

I go down the few steps to the cabin, where a dark and deadly tableau is spread in front of me. In the sharp light and shadow of late afternoon, a bulky guy in a gray coat and fedora holds a .38 revolver to Drogan's head. A second bulky guy in a similar getup holds another .38 to the head of Jimmy Shea. Shea's tied to Red's old wooden chair, a gag across his mouth, his head drooping, his face black-and-blue, his eyes swollen shut. They sure gave the guy a good working over.

I don't like anything about this scene except the fear on Shea's face. Now the scum knows what it's like to be on the receiving end. I'm tempted to have a good laugh, but I don't dare. The guy with the gun to Drogan's head might think I'm being a smart aleck and respond by pulling the trigger.

The guy with the gun on Shea says, "Gold?"

"Yeah, I'm Cantor Gold. What's going on here?"

There's a muffled pop, the savage whisper of a silenced gun, and Jimmy's head has a hole in the temple, blood spraying.

The shooter looks straight at me, the whites of his eyes gray and steely in the shadow of his hat. "Compliments of Mr. Loreale," he says. "Shea won't do business with cops no more."

The other guy lowers his gun from Drogan's head, then both thugs push past me, thump up the stairs, and get off the boat.

It takes me a minute to find my breath, let my eyes blink, get my heart beating again. By the time my nerve ends are back in place, Red's already pouring two glasses of whiskey, his hands shaking.

We each down the whiskey, a decent bourbon. It steadies us.

Red says, "Those guys tracked me through that sonovabitch harbor master, who radioed me to come in to Pier A. That's where those guys dragged Shea aboard, put guns to our heads, and ordered me to steam over here and call you." Red pours us each another drink. He downs his fast.

I sip mine slowly, thinking, figuring something out. "Sig wanted me to see this, Red. He could've had Jimmy knocked off quietly, gotten word to me later, but he wanted me to see this."

"Yeah, I figured. But why?"

"Because he has a sense of humor after all. A criminal sense of humor." And now I laugh, a slightly crazed chuckle that builds into a more than slightly crazed guffaw that fills me with an almost drunken pleasure. I'm laughing the laugh of outlaws, enjoying the right we give ourselves to do things upright citizens are too scared to do. I say to Red, "Even though it's Sig who had Jimmy killed, it's *me* he's giving the honor of actually getting rid of him. Fire up the engine, Red, and sail us out to sea!"

❖

Out beyond New York Harbor, south of Long Island's beaches and east of the New Jersey coast, Drogan parks us in a lonely spot in the Atlantic Ocean that sits over the Hudson Canyon, an undersea trough that plunges nearly a mile down from the ocean floor. In the last light of a red sunset at the tug's stern, I tie Jimmy's body to a rusty old anchor Drogan kept around for scrap, then hoist him and the anchor overboard. Jimmy hits the water with a big splash, which would've made him happy. Then he sinks fast, which wouldn't.

Chapter Fifteen

It's nearly eight o'clock by the time I'm home and in the shower. The hot water washes away the grime of sea spray and the soot from the smokestack of Drogan's tug, but it can't wash away the dirty truth that I'm part of yet another death. Sure, Jimmy's death was personally satisfying, but it was murder nonetheless, and murder is always dirty.

And the hot water can't stop the shivers coming over me when I think Lieutenant Huber might be right about death squads following me around. Maybe I should start wearing a black hood and carry a sickle.

Huber. I wonder what Sig's got in mind for the guy. Shea's treachery with Huber ended in Jimmy's death, but a mobster's killing is just day-to-day business in this town. The cops even think you're doing them a favor. But killing a cop is another story entirely. It's dangerous. It crosses a line, sets the blue boys on a rampage through the underworld, busting up rackets and rounding up citizens whether they had anything to do with the killing or not. Sig's too smart for such a destructive move; then again, he could have it done so quietly and efficiently, the cops might not realize Huber's missing until his grandchild gets married and he doesn't show up for the wedding.

After the shower, a double Chivas and a leftover chicken leg take care of basic survival. A change into a dark green silk suit, clean white shirt, and dark green and black tie freshens my mood. My .38 under my arm and extra rounds in my pocket stiffen my resolve.

The overcoat and tweed cap I wore all day are grimy from the Shea killing and its briny aftermath, so I slip into a black coat and cap instead, then shut the living room light on my way out the door.

❖

"Is Miss Trent in, George?"

"I will inform her you're here."

I walk past him and into the vestibule. "No, don't tell her I'm here," I say. "Just tell me where she is."

"I'm sorry, you know I can't do that."

"Sure you can. It's not hard."

With a deep breath indicating his solemn commitment to duty and rectitude, he says, "I cannot and will not betray the wishes of my employer, and her wish is that I inform her of all visitors. You are aware of that, I'm sure."

"Yeah, I'm aware of it, but if you tell her I'm at the front door, she may hightail it out the back, and then I'd have to chase her all over town. And after the hellish day I've had, a hectic chase isn't appealing, even if it's chasing one of the prettiest skirts in town. Now, tell me where she is, George." I haven't pulled my gun or laid a hand on the guy, but a theatrical touch of thuggery in my voice and manner scares him enough.

His face pale as porridge, he says, "She—Miss Trent is in the library."

Giving him a smile and a friendly pat on the arm, I say, "Thank you, George. See? I knew you could do it if you tried." That stings him, and rather than suffer further insult to his butler's pride, he pointedly forgoes taking my coat and cap, turns on his heel, and walks away.

I really like the guy.

I take my cap off, start to hang it on the elephant tusk coatrack, then back away as if the thing is about to gore me. It reminds me of Vivienne's mother's crackup at seeing her husband torn apart in the jungle, a horror that caused her already fragile mind to crumble. It reminds me of the violence of the up-from-the-gutter Trents, ridding themselves of rivals, with more recent generations dignifying their bloodlust through the aristocratic sport of killing game. Those elephant tusks remind me that madness and violence might be part of Vivienne.

The library is across the hall from the living room. When I walk in, Vivienne's working at her desk, a great big black-walnut affair with fancy brass fittings and a brass desk set with an oversized ashtray and lighter. Floor-to-ceiling shelves of old books wrap the library in a leathery aura of lineage. A bunch of open books strewn across a big library table give the room a scholarly air, while a radio playing on a bookshelf behind Vivienne's desk—a saxophone's purring a lovelorn tune—struggles to give the blue-blooded room a touch of common humanity.

Shocked to see me without forewarning by George, Vivienne stands up fast, her well-bred elegance nicely turned out in a slender gray suit that silhouettes her shapely body, the severely cut jacket open, revealing a black cashmere sweater and a ladylike strand of pearls. "What are you doing here?" she says. "What have you done to George?"

"I haven't done anything to George. I'm here to get some straight answers from you."

I wish she wasn't fingering her pearls and looking at me the way she's looking at me, like a little girl who's wondering if you're still mad at her, only sexier. The saxophone crooning behind her enhances the seductive effect, throwing me a little off balance. I'm relieved when she asks, "Would you like a drink?"

"Sure. Chiv—"

"Chivas. Neat. Yes, I know."

I toss my coat and cap on the couch while Vivienne pours drinks from a well-stocked liquor cart near the desk. The couch, like everything in here, has a well-lived-in feel of patrician good taste, the burgundy velvet upholstery shimmering softly in the lamplight.

I came here determined to press the case with Vivienne, probe every corner and angle of her to get to the truth of her possible involvement with the Jacobson and Stern killings. But when she hands me my drink and looks at me with a touch of sadness, and then awkwardly looks away, my determination cracks. Not completely, not even a lot, but the fissures are there, and feelings I don't want seep through. I'm not in love with this woman, and never could be—only Sophie claims that part of me—but the passion we shared was a helluva lot more than just sex. Vivienne not only inflamed my body, but her beauty, her lust—for me, for art, for everything in her aristocratic grasp—and those traces of the slums that spice her bloodline inflamed my soul. And maybe so did the thread of craziness, the madness that infects her mother, and maybe Vivienne.

She takes her drink back to the safety of the desk and sits down. I remain standing. It helps bolster my determination to stick to what I came here to do.

The whiskey helps fortify Vivienne, makes her less awkward in my company, though only a little. Looking up at me from the desk, she can't hold the glance and looks away again. "Which straight answers do you want, Cantor?"

"Well, let's start with an easy one," I say. "You called me today, asked me to call you back. So what's on your mind?"

Another sip of her drink, another fingering of her pearls, another glance up at me, and another awkward look away. She's asking me to be kind to her. I want to be. But kindness won't help me find out if she's a murderer.

But neither will badgering her. So I just stay quiet, sip the scotch, and wait.

I don't have to wait long. After another swallow of her drink, followed by a deep breath she lets out slowly, even timidly, while looking down at her desk and idly fingering papers, she says, "I wanted to tell you—that is, I wanted to say that what happened between us last night shouldn't alter our...our professional relationship."

"Uh-huh. So it was a business call."

"Yes, that's right. A business call." Safe behind the big desk, she eventually gives in to an urge to really look at me. "What happened to your face? You look like you were at the losing end of a boxing match."

After a last swallow of scotch, I say, "Something like that," tossing it off as lightly as I can, hiding my ordeal last night at Jimmy Shea's place. I don't want to talk about Jimmy Shea. I'd feel a little queasy talking about someone whose body I recently dumped into the Atlantic, so I move the conversation back to where I want it. "Here's another question for you, Vivienne. Why weren't you at Hannah Jacobson's funeral? You'd worked with her for months, grew fond of her, or so you said, and yet you were nowhere to be seen at her funeral. At least, I didn't see you. Did anyone else?"

She's caught the edge in my voice, looks at me now with an awareness she's being interrogated. "What are you hinting at, Cantor?"

I wouldn't mind another drink but figure I'd better not. I need to stay on top of this game, keep my senses sharp, so I just put my glass down on the library table. But I do it hard, let the thump of the glass unnerve Vivienne a little bit, let her know that hiding behind her desk or her social position won't stop me from pressing her for the truth. "I'm not hinting at anything," I say, "I'm just wondering. Maybe you had reasons to keep out of sight at Mrs. Jacobson's funeral. Maybe you'd like to share those reasons."

Women like Vivienne, who've grown up with the world bending to their every whim, don't take well to being challenged or having their motives questioned, and I've just committed the unpardonable sin of doing both, which causes Vivienne's well-schooled sense of regal superiority to kick in. Standing up from the desk, slowly, almost imperiously, she has no problem looking at me now. In fact, she looks at me as if I'm just another Parkhurst Trent hireling, easily dismissed. "That's not what you're asking, Cantor. You're asking if I had anything to do with Mrs. Jacobson's death. Or even her brother's death. Don't deny it. I see it on your face. Behind all those cuts and bruises is hard suspicion. Suspicion of me."

Denying it would be a losing game. She's caught me. "All right, then give me a reason not to be suspicious."

"Well, because…because…" There's a slight loosening of Vivienne's aristocratic spine, a hint of anxiety threatening her regal composure. She gives up fumbling for words she can't find and comes out from behind the desk instead, stands right in front of me, her hands clenched at her sides as if she's forcing herself not to reach for me, or hit me. "Because do you really think that the woman who shared your bed last night, the woman who… gave you her body and—" She's not crying but she's very near it, choking on words too humiliating to say. Catching her breath, she's finally able to speak again, throwing out a question that comes at me like a pointing finger. "Do you think that woman could ever kill anybody?"

"Yes."

The little word hits her like a slap, her eyes opening wide with the shock of it. There's rage in her eyes, a smoldering rage that the more she fights to control, the more it seeps from her and prowls the room, an animal breathing fire.

But something else is in her eyes: hurt. It fuels her rage. Vivienne's clenched hands spring from her sides, pound me in a fury of pain. She's crying for real now and keeps coming at me, lands several blows before I grab her hands. She fights to pull away, and I'm surprised at her strength, then realize I shouldn't be; if she's really the crack shot Hagen and Vern hinted at, she'd need all that strength to control the sharp recoil of a hunting weapon, the kind of gun powerful enough to fire from a distance and accurately send a bullet through my car window, and blast Marcus Stern's head to smithereens.

With every pull, with every twist, Vivienne's athletic strength runs through my arms, pushes my muscles, convincing me she'd be strong enough to cut up Hannah Jacobson and be the sharpshooter who aimed a high-caliber weapon with enough control to kill Marcus Stern in heavy traffic.

Her crying ebbs, the rage draining out of her, but the hurt in her eyes lingers. "How could you, Cantor?"

"How? Easy," I say, "because the struggle for Hannah Jacobson's life didn't happen near the door. It happened in the living room, meaning she let her killer in, probably knew her killer, maybe even liked her killer, which is a scary idea any way you look at it. Well, she certainly knew you, didn't she, Vivienne. And I know you wanted the Dürer, maybe needed it to secure your position at the museum, so if Mrs. Jacobson wasn't going to hand it over, or maybe even gave you a story that she didn't have it, you had good reason to want her dead. Maybe it drove you crazy that you didn't get it from Mrs. J and that her brother didn't have it either. And from what I hear from Hagen about your abilities with a gun—"

But she's not really listening to me. She's just staring at me through tears trickling down her face, mumbling through choked sobs, "Cantor, how could you? You, you were my first. Did you know that? Do you know how long I've been hiding? Hiding my... my desire for you? I know that phone call last night was about Sophie. I know what she means to you. But to just leave, without a word, just walk out like I was never there..."

Women in tears don't usually leave me speechless. I can be a cad, and I know it, my patter inflected with a sincerity I don't feel, my escape plans well rehearsed. But I'm speechless now, as if my tongue's been cut out with the sharp blade of truth, a blade Vivienne wielded with precision.

I let go of Vivienne's hands, prepared to let her start pounding me again, but her hands just go to her face to wipe her tears as she walks away from me.

The saxophone's finished its number and a commercial jingle comes on the radio, some guy singing the smile-enhancing praises of Pepsodent toothpaste. Three or four lines of its grating cheeriness is all either of us can take, and Vivienne finally turns it off. The sudden silence is a relief, makes the room feel larger, the emotions filling it less cramped.

Vivienne picks up the glass she left on the desk and finishes her drink. It steadies her, absorbs some of the pain of her humiliating confession to me. After pulling a cigarette from a pack on the desk and lighting it with the big brass lighter, a deep drag settles her enough for her to face me again. "So you think I'm a murderer."

I guess she heard me after all.

I light a smoke from my own pack, let it do its calming work before I ask her the damning question. "Are you?"

Her brittle little laugh shreds the wisp of smoke curling along her cheek. "If I were, I'd hardly tell you. Still, maybe I should be flattered you think of me as something more than either a dull and dusty art scholar or a quick one-night stand."

"I don't think of you as either of those things."

"Just a murderer."

"Yeah, maybe."

"And all because Max Hagen told you I'm good with a rifle?"

"That, and it seems the killer was a woman."

That catches her. She escapes into another long pull on her smoke, then says, "I see. Well, what about Stern's wife and daughter? Do you know their greedy little story? I'm sure they're set to inherit a bundle from Stern, and they might've made a handsome profit from the Dürer if the family inherited it from Hannah Jacobson."

"Sure, the wife's greedy," I say, "but until Mrs. Jacobson's death, she'd never heard of Dürer. She had no idea the watercolor ever existed. And the daughter tells me she adored her father and her aunt. Wouldn't hurt a hair on their heads. So it looks like you're it, Vivienne, the only woman still in the picture."

The hurt and humiliation which ground her down earlier are gone. She's the aristocratic Vivienne Parkhurst Trent again as she comes back around to the front of the desk, leans against it, and takes a last pull on her cigarette before stubbing it out in the ashtray. Lamplight glimmers on her strand of pearls and on the serenely confident smile that used to intoxicate me, and if I let it, still could. "Is that what that bobby-socks brat told you? That she loved her daddy and her aunt? And did she cry and bat her dewy young eyelashes at you? Cantor, is there a female alive whose line you don't fall for? Besides mine, that is."

I'm not sure which of those shockers to handle first: the icy one about Francine Stern, or the hot coal Vivienne tossed in my lap about not falling for her.

Necessity insists I take care of the first. And anyway, it's safer. "What gives you the idea Francine didn't love her father or Hannah Jacobson?"

Crossing her arms, Vivienne's in control of the room, the story, and my attention. She's enjoying every minute of it. "I have no doubt that colleague of yours, the young Mr. Zane, dug around in the family secrets after Hannah Jacobson died and the Dürer watercolor disappeared. He's very good at such things, from what I understand."

"Yeah, damn good."

"So I'm sure he learned that Miss Francine Stern was one hell of a wild child."

"If you mean the little episode that got her driver's license lifted and Daddy had to buy it back, pay off the fines, yeah, Judson found out all about that. But how would you know about it? And why would you care?"

"About Francine Stern? I don't care a whit. Or at least I didn't before the Dürer was stolen and people started getting killed. But I had the goods on Miss Stern even before Hannah Jacobson died."

My eyebrows crawl up. No need to add words to it. Vivienne's got me in the headlights.

"Don't be naïve, Cantor," she says with an edgy laugh meant to dig at me, pay me back for pushing her to the side of the road.

"Then educate me," I say.

She starts with a *Sure, why not?* shrug, then says, "Look, whenever the museum enters into business with private citizens, even people as worthy and wonderful as Hannah Jacobson—and she *was* worthy and wonderful, Cantor—we do a thorough investigation."

"You hire a shamus?"

"We don't need to. Believe me, all those old-money stuffed shirts on the Board of Trustees have connections that rival J. Edgar Hoover's. They can get details on matters that would otherwise be kept very quiet, even out of the reach of the talented Mr. Zane. We can get information not just on the person we might do business with, but everyone associated with them. We have to be careful. You never know who's trying to sell a phony sculpture or—"

"A smuggled painting?" I can't help jumping on the joke.

Vivienne gives me a sly smile, sashays over to the liquor cart, and pours us each a fresh drink. Handing me a scotch, she says, still smiling, "Yes, or a stolen painting. Of course, we're quite, um, *selective* in our investigations."

"Uh-huh. If the stolen painting is one you want, the investigation just provides tidbits you can use for bargaining power. Now I know why you're always such a tough *hondler*."

"A what?"

"*Hondler.* A bargainer. A dealmaker. You should get out of your neighborhood more often, Vivienne."

She starts to say something, but whatever she had in mind she ditches in favor of another shrug.

I say, "All right, tell me what you've got on Francine Stern. Why should I believe she didn't love her father or her aunt?"

"Well"—she takes her time getting into the telling, enjoying making me wait, enjoying taking control away from me—"that little driver's license incident? It wasn't so little. Seems Francine had a knock-down drag-out fight with her father about her allowance."

"Don't all pretty young debs? Didn't you?"

She answers with no answer at all, just a raised eyebrow dismissing any suggestion that the Sterns and the Parkhurst Trents could ever be in the same league. She goes on with her story, the interruption nothing more than a nuisance to be swatted away. "Young Francine wanted more money, Daddy insisted on holding the line. To get back at him for keeping her on a short financial leash, sweet little Francine drove Daddy's car along the street and purposely crashed it into every car parked on the block. But there was a man in one of the cars, getting ready to drive away. Francine's temper tantrum crippled him."

That last bit tears at me, and Vivienne sees it, sees my eyes narrow, my mouth crease, the knifelike scar above my lip no doubt twisting into a jagged shape from my shock at the story and my suspicion of its truth. And that's when Vivienne says, "And during that whole episode, darling daughter Francine Stern screams that she wished her father was dead."

I'm looking at Vivienne. She's looking at me. My stare is meant to probe for something, anything, that would tell me she's lying. Vivienne's stare dares me to deny her story.

But I can't, not yet, not until I know why Vivienne would have such a tale and Judson didn't. "How could something like that be kept quiet, Vivienne? There'd be a police report."

"There was no police report, at least, not for very long. Certain parties made certain phone calls to certain other parties and the report was destroyed." She's having the time of her life putting it over on me, savoring my ignorance of worlds I'm not privy to. "And here's something else you probably didn't know," she says. "Your Professor Marcus Stern was important enough to those parties, in circles very high up, to get the incident hushed up. Actually, it was his chemical and plastics factory which made him important. Let's just say these certain parties, here and in Washington, would do anything to protect Marcus Stern and his chemicals from scandal."

I need more than a stiff drink now. I need a change of story. "Where did you hear this, Vivienne? How do you know it's true and not someone's vicious little fable?"

The trim gray suit Vivienne's wearing, its severe cut suggesting a woman of authority, is perfect for the woman who stands before me now, her posture easy but commanding, her smile soft but arrogant, the light in her eyes glowing with privilege. "Keep this in mind, Cantor: If you want to know things about who keeps the trains running on time, or the sewers unclogged, or the streets swept, or who's being paid off to do it, you dig around City Hall. The politicians and their flunkies keep things running in the city. If you want to know where the money flows, whose pockets are lined with all those payoffs, or who died stealing it, you ask your pals in the underworld. They run the money. But if you want to know everything else, you ask the stuffed-shirt men and lace-gloved women in my world, the people who were first off the boat, who've been here longest, whose money is oldest and most deeply embedded in everything, everywhere. We run the world."

The library suddenly feels very cold, everything in it, including Vivienne, giving me a chill. The only way I'm going to warm up is to get out of here, get away from this vault of hidden power and secrets, get that whole new story. "Let's go," I say.

"Go? Go where?"

CHAPTER SIXTEEN

A young uniformed night-shift cop has taken over protective patrol of the Stern house. With no postfuneral gathering to go to, no social event going on inside, getting past him is going to be tricky.

Or so I thought.

Vivienne's out of the car before me, and after a few words, a smile, and a handshake with the cop, she waves me along and I accompany her up the front stairs.

I ask her, "What magic words did you say to him?"

"I sent regards to his father. Don't look so shocked, Cantor. Even Wall Street financiers with Mayflower pedigrees are sometimes disappointed in their children, and believe me, that young man's father was sorely disappointed when his son decided to join the police force."

So Wall Street and I actually have something in common; I might disown any kid of mine who became a cop, too.

After we ring the doorbell, the door opens and the widow Katherine Stern is even less happy to see me on her doorstep than George was to see me on Vivienne's. Sneering at me from above the flouncy collar of a floor-length robe decorated with palm fronds and bought with more money than taste, she's unsteady on her feet, a glass of what's likely her preferred libation of straight bourbon whiskey in one hand, a cigarette in the other. She nearly drops the glass as she tosses her hair away from her face, the blond waves brassy in the light of the vestibule. Recovering, she gives me a glassy stare, then gives the stare to Vivienne, then gives it back to me. "Well, don't you have your nerve," she says, very much in her cups but not fall-down drunk, though she's on her way. "I thought I got rid of you earlier, and now you show up at—What is it? Almost eleven o'clock? And with a trollop?"

Vivienne takes no offense at the trollop jab. She doesn't have to. Katherine Stern's insult reached no higher than the soles of Vivienne's shoes. Smiling with the cool friendliness of someone more important than you are and who deigns to give you a few moments of their time, Vivienne says, "I'm Vivienne Parkhurst Trent, curator of European Renaissance paintings and drawings at the most important museum in the city. If you're at all interested in finding out what happened to the Dürer watercolor, or who killed your husband and sister-in-law, you will let us in, Mrs. Stern."

I'm not sure which of those possibilities did the trick, but after a few seconds' boozy thought, the widow steps aside, letting me and Vivienne into the house. She doesn't offer to take our coats.

When we're all in the vestibule, I say, "Where's Francine?"

Katherine Stern may not be the world's best mother, but she's still a mother, full of all those maternal instincts to protect her young at the slightest hint of trouble. Those instincts are aroused now, clawing through her liquored-up fog, ready to pounce. "Why do you want my daughter?"

"We need to talk to her," I say.

"S'ppose you let me be the judge of that," she says. "First you gotta tell me what you want to talk to her about."

"Don't you think Francine's old enough to decide for herself?"

Mrs. Stern starts to answer back, but Vivienne doesn't let her. "I don't think you understand, Mrs. Stern. We are not giving you a choice. Cantor has a gun, and believe me, she will not hesitate to use it. Do I make myself clear? Now, where is that—where is your daughter?"

Too tipsy to push back, but fully understanding her situation, Mrs. Stern steadies herself as much as she's able and pulls herself up to her full height in a last woozy effort at dignity. "All right, all right, you don't have to get huffy, threaten me like you own the place." She gives me the once over, eyes me through her whiskey haze with the same chilly attitude she gave me this morning. A day's worth of bourbon hasn't warmed her soul at all. The woman's made of ice and stone, which are probably the only props keeping her on her feet. "All you want is to talk to Francine?"

"Just talk," I say.

"Okay, but that's all it better be. I don't care if you do have a gun. This is a house of mourning. I've lost my dear husband"—I'm not sure if she's choking on the whiskey or the word *dear*—"and Francine's lost her father. We are both very upset. You make one nasty move against my daughter and I'll scratch your eyes out, understand?" I bet she would, too.

"I'll say it once more, Mrs. Stern, we're just here to talk."

"Do you...do you really have a gun?"

I open my coat, unbutton my suit jacket, pull it aside, and show her the iron in the rig.

The threat under my arm makes its case. Mrs. Stern takes another gulp of bourbon to escape the threat, then says, "Well then, Francine's upstairs in the den." Cigarette smoke trails her as she turns and walks from the vestibule. Vivienne and I follow her through the living room and up a stairway carpeted in an all-over Chinese poppy motif. Poor Vivienne, walking behind Mrs. Stern. I'm sure the clashing colors and busy patterns of the palm-frond robe and the Chinese carpet are making her curatorial eyes cross. Even worse, Mrs. Stern is slugging down more bourbon along the way, turning her climb up the stairs into a dicey balancing act. If it fails, she'll come tumbling backward into Vivienne and then me, sending us all rolling down the stairs, breaking our necks.

The laughter of a crowd drifts toward us on the second floor landing. The laughter comes from down the hall where Francine is watching television, lounging on a tweedy brown couch in the dimly lit den, catching the last few minutes of the *Cavalcade of Stars* as we walk in. A lamp on a side table throws a pool of light near the couch, the television screen sends a silvery glow across the reclining Francine. On the television, that hefty side of beef of a young comic named Gleason, gray faced and cramped on the small screen in its big mahogany console, must've just said something funny, setting off all that laughter from the studio audience. Then music comes on and two entirely too clean-cut guys and a girl-next-door kinda blonde sing the drugstore sponsor's jingle, which sends Francine off the couch to turn off the set. With the silvery glow from the television gone, light from the single lamp is the only illumination in the room. The soft light and surrounding shadows treat Francine's youth and Vivienne's beauty kindly. They don't extend the same courtesy to Katherine Stern. The shadows just carve her age and hardness even deeper.

Francine's still in the same black flared skirt, white blouse, and open button-down black sweater she wore when I was here this morning after her father's funeral, only now the blouse isn't buttoned to the neck. The top three or four buttons are open, making for a whole different impression than the girl who gave me a peck on the check on my way out the door.

Seeing me, Francine throws me a big smile while she quickly runs her hands through her short blond hair to unmuss it, ignoring her mother and sliding a fast sidelong glance at Vivienne. "Cantor, what a surprise! What are you doing here? Though, um, I'm happy to see you. Are you happy to see me?" She sits on the couch again, pats the area beside her. "Come sit by me," she says.

"No, thanks, not tonight, Francine." I keep it polite but sidestep Francine's flirty-girl routine. "This isn't a social call. We need to talk to you."

"What about?"

Mrs. Stern chimes in, "Yes, what about?" Her speech is slurring a little more now, giving her trouble with consonants she can't quite peel off the roof of her mouth.

Francine snaps, "You're dropping your ashes, Mom."

A humiliated Mrs. Stern mutters, "Oh!" and quickly stubs her cigarette out in an ashtray on the coffee table, nearly tripping over it, which annoys Francine even more.

"Mom, why don't you just sit down? No, not here on the couch. Over there in the club chair." Francine doesn't even help her mother, who finally settles into the chair without spilling a drop of her drink. Well, they say God and liquor-store owners love a drunk.

But the painful family drama between the pickled Katherine Stern and her devil-doll daughter nearly skins me, though it seems to just bore Vivienne. There's no expression on that aristocratic face at all, not even disgust.

Lucky me, stuck in a room with a shriveling widow who's losing herself in whiskey, a society dame who might be crazy enough to kill and is certainly proving cold-hearted enough to do it, and a wild child whose hatred of her mother is clearer by the minute, who might have hated her father just as much, and who may have her own violent soul.

The wild child pats the sofa again. "If you want to talk to me, Cantor, you'll have to sit next to me." The kid's smile is sweet as peaches and cream, which scares the hell outta me. But I need Francine's cooperation, and to clinch it I'll have to sit down next to her on the couch.

Light from the lamp on the side table flows across the couch to Francine, usefully illuminating her face. She won't be able to hide from me, can't hide her first, true reactions to my questions. But the light's finding other parts of her, too, like the bit of soft cleavage exposed by her open blouse.

Vivienne, standing against the back of the couch, notices me noticing what's displayed by Francine's open blouse. The small but acid smile Vivienne gives me threatens to strip the flesh from my bones.

Clearing my throat, and my head, I say, "Francine, there are a few things I need to know."

This kid's reading my dark side like a book, or maybe she's just seen too many movies, swanning toward me like a B-picture femme fatale, lamplight sparkling in her green eyes and catching a far too adorable sheen of moisture above her lip. Either way, after a quick glance at her mother, who's busy taking another drink, Francine slides my coat open and puts her hand on my leg. "Whatever you want, Cantor."

What I want is to keep control of this conversation, and I can't with the girl's hand on my leg, where its warmth is giving me the shivers. I lift her hand but keep it in mine with just enough tenderness to convince Francine not to bolt, to stay with me and answer my questions.

I say, "Do you know anything about handling a gun?"

Mrs. Stern, drunk but not dead, pounces on that with the remaining shreds of her maternal dignity. "How dare you!"

But Francine just laughs at the question, or maybe at her mother. "Settle down, Mom. I don't mind if Cantor knows I'm good with a gun. I bet she's good with a gun, too. Aren't you, Cantor? Maybe we could go out shooting together sometime. There's a riflery club in the neighborhood with a target-practice range. I could show you just how good I am."

I don't think that last line has anything to do with shooting a rifle. And neither, evidently, does Vivienne, who grabs hold of both the conversation and Francine. Leaning over the back of the couch, taking Francine's chin in her hand, and turning the kid's face up to her, Vivienne says, "Since Cantor wasn't polite enough to introduce us, and your mother's in no shape to even remember my name, it's up to me to do the honors. I'm Vivienne Parkhurst Trent, and I want to know just how you came by your expertise with firearms."

Up to now, except for that first sidelong glance when we walked in, Francine's ignored Vivienne as if she's not here. But she's lost that game now, caught in the grip of the older, more self-assured woman who's trained for a lifetime in the art of getting her way.

Katherine Stern's suddenly on her feet, more or less. "Take your hands off my little girl!"

The patrician Miss Vivienne Parkhurst Trent is not about to be bossed around by the drunken command of the boorishly nouveau riche Katherine Stern. Vivienne's grip on the kid doesn't let up. Mrs. Stern, defeated simply by being ignored, sinks back into the chair.

Francine, as sharp as her mother is dull witted, knows she has no way out. "It was something to do at school," she says with a shrug.

Vivienne loosens her grip, nods for the girl to keep talking, and as Francine talks, Vivienne lets go of her. "A hoity-toity girl in my English lit class kept bragging about going off every weekend to her family's country place to hunt and shoot." Vivienne smiles a little at that, a smile full of nostalgia, but with enough chill under it to ice my marrow. As far as I'm concerned, she's not off the hook for the Jacobson and Stern killings, even as Francine spills about her own prowess with guns. "That snobby girl loved to lord it over everybody," the kid says. "Especially me. She kept spouting about how the lower orders and mongrel races were too clumsy to master the finesse of marksmanship. So I took up the sport." She says this with such determined defiance it could make even a brute think twice about tackling her. "I got as good at shooting things as she was," she says. "I even beat her in competitions. She absolutely hated it that with the right gun, I can bag a squirrel at fifty feet. A moving squirrel." The glow in her eyes is terrifying.

Mrs. Stern struggles to sit up in her chair again, finally gets there by a desperate act of will. The day's worth of whiskey is taking its harsh toll on her body, and tying her tongue in knots. "You're my li—little girl and I love you, Francy. But your father and—your father and I hated all that gun business of yours," she says. "He hated it 'cause he was weak. And I hate it 'cause you scare me."

"And you disgust me, Mom," is Francine's sneery answer, making my skin shrivel on my bones.

But the kid's just given me my way into the big, ugly question. "Did your father disgust you, too, Francine?"

"What? No!" She's the innocent again, the Daddy's Girl whose smile opens the hearts and empties the pockets of fathers in living rooms across America. "How could you even think such a thing, Cantor? My father was the strongest, sweetest, most—"

Vivienne cuts off Francine's loving litany with a sharp, "Cut the crap, girlie." The kid's Daddy's Girl act must've triggered a surge of the Trent gutter-blood in Vivienne's veins. She presses Francine with the blunt force of a stevedore. "We know all about your little escapade with Daddy's car, and the unfortunate man you crippled while screaming that you wished your father was dead. So don't give us any sob stories about dear sweet Daddykins. You're a cold-blooded little monster. Even your mother's afraid of you."

Francine jumps up from the couch as if something bit her. "Who the hell are you to talk to me like that? Cantor, what is she doing here? Why are you letting her talk to me like that?"

I stand up, too, get face to face with the enraged wild child. "Because she's got you pegged, Francine."

"No, she doesn't. She can't. She's making things up. Just ask the police. There's no record of anything like that. You'll see. You'll see!"

Vivienne's the calmest person in the room, the Parkhurst blue-blood dignity back in command as she comes around to the front of the couch and sits down with the easy confidence of the always privileged. Two minutes ago she was the foul-mouthed slum-queen Trent. Now she's the aristocratic Parkhurst again. I don't know if this flip in personality is just one of her skills, trotted out when required, or that streak of her mother's madness. I just know it gives me the creeps.

In a cool, steady voice through an in-charge smile, she says, "Yes, Miss Stern, we know about that, too. Your father was an important man, important enough to have powerful people rid the police department of damaging paperwork and bury any scandal. But there are people in the world even more important than your father. And common things"—Vivienne's accent on the word common is unmistakable—"like police paperwork, or lack of it, aren't enough to keep secrets from their ears. So stop lying to us.

You're nothing but a dangerous good-for-nothing brat. In fact, we think you killed your father and your aunt Hannah."

Francine doesn't look at her accuser, but at me, her face hard with equal parts hate and fear. Her rage runs so deep, it gags her, gets stuck in her throat. "How—how—how could you think—why would I—?"

"You tell me," I say. "Your aunt told you about the Dürer watercolor. Maybe you thought you could make a fast buck, get past the purse strings your father held too tight for your taste."

But it's Mrs. Stern who answers. "Oh yeah, that Dürer picture," she says with tipsy difficulty. "A guy called me 'bout that today. Guy named Hogan, no—"

"Hagen?" Vivienne and I say it nearly in unison.

"Yeah, that's it," Mrs. Stern says. "Hagen." The now empty bourbon glass falls from her hand to the floor. She kicks it away like she's angry at it, then says, "This Hagen guy says he can get me lotsa money for this Dürer picture. That is, if it comes my way. Francy, did you steal that picture from your aunt Hannah?"

I keep quiet, not about to let on that the Dürer was never stolen, and that it's safe and sound in my vault. Let's see who takes the bait.

It's Vivienne. "Yes, Francine, that's something we'd all like to know."

The kid's working hard to keep her temper and not give us fuel for Vivienne's suspicions. "No, I did *not* steal the picture. I did not steal anything, and I did not kill anybody. Cantor, please, you've got to believe me! And…and besides"—her faulty teenage self-control is slipping, not with anger, but with nearly hysterical glee—"how could I kill my father? I was in the car with my mother on the way back from the funeral! We left before you. We were way ahead of you on the road back home. Mom! Wake up. Tell them. Tell them I was in the car with you when Daddy was killed!"

Mrs. Stern is nearly out for the count, her head down, her tongue dangling. With the last of her juice, she mumbles, "Course you were in the car, Francy. That rabbi was waitin' for us…"

Which brings it all back to Vivienne. I give her a smile. It makes her wince.

The insertion of Hagen into the Stern story complicates things, though. I don't know where Vivienne fits in. Maybe she's gotten into cahoots with Hagen, or maybe she doesn't fit in there at all.

There's only one way to sort this out.

Vivienne's surprised when I extend a hand to her, the gesture an invitation to help her up from the couch. But before Vivienne even has the chance to accept my hand or tell me to go to hell, Francine's tugging at my elbow. "What do you want to take her hand for, Cantor? She's mean. She's been nasty to me. Please, Cantor, please take my hand instead."

The movie-magazine pleading in Francine's eyes is as scary as her pride in her skill with guns. She's turning out to be the sort of kid you handle with care, the kind of care you take picking out glass shards from your flesh. "Francine, you want me to find whoever killed your father and your aunt, don't you? You want them brought to justice, yes?"

"I guess so."

"And do you trust me to do it?" I even give her a smile. Out of the corner of my eye, I notice Vivienne cringe.

Francine reaches up to me and plants another of her girlish pecks on my cheek.

That does it for Vivienne. She takes my hand and rises from the couch, plants herself next to me.

Then I give her another surprise. "Vivienne, I assume you know the way to Hagen's country place?"

"Well, yes, of course."

"Good. You drive."

CHAPTER SEVENTEEN

During the day, the drive along Route 9 is one of the prettiest in the upstate countryside, especially at this time of year, when autumn shows off its flashy colors in high style. At night, though, Route 9 is just dark. The Buick's headlights are no match for the primeval blackness of a backwoods night, the car's high beams only able to pick out a few red and gold leaves and terrify the occasional raccoon as Vivienne drives us north.

I've let her do the driving because she knows the way to Hagen's, and—as she pointed out to Katherine Stern—I'm the one with the gun, which is my insurance against Vivienne diverting us to Timbuktu.

She's tried to make conversation during the drive, tossed me questions I've either sidestepped or haven't bothered to answer, questions like *What do you expect to find at Max's place?* and *You think he knows more about the Dürer than he's told us?* and, my favorite, *Do you really think I'm a murderer?*

I've answered every question the same way, when I've answered her at all: *I'll let you know when we get there.*

By the time we're about an hour and a half out of the city, Vivienne finally gives up grilling me, but with each silent mile the tension in the car grows thicker, colder. The air cracks when Vivienne suddenly says, "You're a louse, Cantor."

"I've been called worse," I say.

She doesn't let up. "You really are low. The way you walked out on me last night was rotten. The way you treat your cabbie friend—Rosie, right?—is rotten, too. You think of yourself as so courtly, but you're just a louse, Cantor. Frankly, I don't know what Sophie ever saw in you."

That comes at me hard, sharp as a knife to the gut, and not just because I don't want to hear Sophie's name through the hate of Vivienne's hurt feelings, but because Vivienne is horribly, monstrously, and perfectly right.

I was always mystified by what Sophie saw in me, always wondered why she put up with the dangerous, unreliable existence that's my life. She said she loved me, and maybe that was all it took for her to throw her life in with mine, but she deserved better. She deserved peace and security, and I gave her neither.

But maybe I'll have a second chance. I give myself over to imagining it, imagine mornings with the sun coming up over the city streets and Sophie asleep against me, snug and safe in our bed, my arm around her, the palm of my hand enjoying the warmth of her body, her hand unexpectedly taking mine, moving it up to her breast...

"We're here," Vivienne says, breaking my reverie. I'm back in the dark night, where I'm not holding Sophie but untangling the tentacles of murder that have threatened to choke me since Hannah Jacobson died.

Hagen's place is at the end of a long avenue of trees that serves as a driveway. The house, or what I can see of it in the nighttime murk, is one of those gentlemanly rustic places newly rich city boys like to buy from landed locals whose pedigreed lineage has lived past their money. Lights are on downstairs, with music and male laughter filtering through the windows.

"Sounds like a party," I say when we're out of the car.

"Max likes parties."

"Yeah, he's just a real good-time guy."

"He likes what he likes, same as anyone." Vivienne's shrug is either meant to defend Hagen or be dismissive of me. Probably both.

As we near the front door, Vivienne takes a compact from her handbag, opens it, and in the light drifting from a nearby window, she applies fresh lipstick and fluffs her hair.

Even in this meager light, Vivienne's face, her lips freshly red, is as sensual as a royal portrait—the one of the king's mistress, not his wife. "You're beautiful," I say in that dry way meant to state the obvious. "I don't need convincing."

She shuts the compact with a loud snap, a stand-in, I guess, for slapping my face. "Who says it's for you? It's been a long drive and I just like to freshen up, look my best."

"I doubt anyone in this house would notice," I say.

"How do you know? How do you know who else is in the house besides Max and Vern?"

I ring the doorbell and say with a laugh, "Vivienne, do you really think any of Max and Vern's friends are in your market?"

A smile pulls at the corners of her mouth. She tries to stop it, tries to stop herself from enjoying a joke with me, but the joke and the smile win.

I like seeing her smile again. I like seeing that elegance of hers, part high-hat, part gutter, take its place beside me, until I remember she probably committed cold-blooded murder. Twice.

The front door opens. Hagen is silhouetted against the light, the rim of a highball glass glinting in his hand. "Well, I'm surprised—no, *shocked* to see you two," he says. "What on earth are you doing here in the middle of the night? Wait, do you have a new line on the Dürer?"

"Down boy," I say, "we have other things to talk about. The Dürer is only one of them."

"I see. Well, come in then. My guests will be calling it a night shortly and retiring to their rooms. Vern can see to their comfort in the meantime."

I follow Vivienne through the door. Music and chatter, some of it the melodious, slightly high-pitched sort of male voice I hear at certain friendly nightspots, drifts from what I suppose is the living room. With a smile and a nod toward the party, I ask Hagen, "Hunting buddies?" He ignores the question.

Hagen's decked out in a well-tailored tuxedo, as formal as a night at the opera. I expected him to be tweedy. And since it's nearly two in the morning, I figured even his pajamas would be tweedy. I might have to rethink the whole concept of proper country attire—that is, if I ever decide to live in the country, which I don't really see in my future. I wouldn't live anyplace where I'd have to drive to buy my whiskey.

Hagen leads us across a Tudor-style main hall tricked out in brown leather club chairs and dark, heavy furniture. It wouldn't surprise me to see pretty pageboys in red tunics announce our arrival. Instead, Hagen leads us away from the music and laughter coming from the living room and through a door which opens into a den.

Unlike the study in his Park Avenue apartment, which crawls with a carefully cultivated taste in old books and antique maps, the walls of this room hold paintings of hunting scenes, most from the eighteenth and nineteenth centuries: lots of guys in red jackets and black caps riding horses at breakneck speed across the English landscape, with castles and country houses in the distance.

Hagen evidently leaves his profession back in New York and treats the house purely as a vacation spot because there's no desk in the room. There's just two facing sofas separated by a burled maple coffee table of a consciously rustic design, side tables at either end of the sofas with a telephone on one of the tables, a burled maple liquor cabinet, a stone fireplace with the expected picture-perfect fire, and two dark walnut gun racks, one at each end of the room. One rack holds an assortment of fancy rifles, the other an assortment of equally fancy pistols.

Also unlike the Park Avenue study, this one's intimate, with a freer feeling, even a little homey. The green velvet overstuffed couches and chairs are comfortably tatty, as if time spent in them is relaxed and easy. There's even a few framed photos around the room, all of them pictures of Hagen and Vern in various states of vacationing: waving from a swimming pool, waving from horseback, waving from wooden deck chairs, and one overly cheery picture of the two of them in flap-eared caps and heavy jackets, carrying their rifles and waving next to a couple of dead deer hanging by their hind legs, presumably that day's prey.

Hagen, always mindful of the social niceties, helps Vivienne off with her coat and places it carefully over a club chair. He says, "May I offer you a drink?"

Vivienne asks for a cognac, I tell him to make mine Chivas. He pours both from the liquor cabinet. After handing us our drinks, Hagen refreshes his highball with gin over ice.

Smiling an oozy smile, his brushstroke mustache spreading across his lip like a diva in repose, he seats himself at one end of a couch. Vivienne, not smiling, sits at the other end. I remove my coat and cap, toss them on the opposite couch, and sit down, forming the third point of our uneasy triangle.

Hagen says, "All right, Gold, you said the Dürer is among the things you want to talk about. Let's start with that, shall we? Since it's the only item I'm really interested in."

"Nice place you've got here, Hagen," I say after a pull on the scotch. "It must've cost you a pretty penny, not to mention the upkeep. You must do all right."

He takes a cigarette from a pearly box on the coffee table and a small gold lighter from his pocket. Before he lights his smoke, he offers a cigarette to Vivienne, who takes one from the box. Lighting her smoke, then his, he's a master at tasteful flaunting. "I work hard for my money, Gold," he says through an exhale, "if that's what you mean."

"Yeah, that's what I mean," I say. I light a smoke of my own, take a deep pull, and let Hagen fidget while I busy myself with putting my pack of Chesterfields and my lighter back in the inside pocket of my suit jacket. Hagen might be the master of this country castle, but I've got a lot riding on this trip to the sticks, so I'll be damned if I let him be master of this conversation. After a long exhale, but before Hagen has a chance take a drag on his own smoke, I say, "Tell you the truth, I had no idea your auction commissions at Pauling-Barnett brought in this kind of cash."

"They can, if you handle the higher-end items," he says with a tart mix of snobby pride and equally snobby annoyance. "I handle nothing but the very best, and you know that."

"Well, it certainly has paid off handsomely."

"Indeed."

"I assume you pay Vern's expenses, too?"

"Now look here, Gold, what does this line of questioning have to do with the missing Dürer?" His annoyance is no longer snobby. It's just raw.

"I'm just trying to figure how you make your scratch, Hagen, trying to figure how your loyalties to Pauling-Barnett jive with going behind their backs. And mine. And maybe Vivienne's, too."

Hagen's doing his best to look like he doesn't know what I'm talking about, or at least not specifically what I'm talking about. "I beg your pardon?" he says, as much a probe as a question. I guess his side-deal shenanigans regarding the Dürer—first with me, then with Katherine Stern—aren't the first time he's gone catting around behind his employer and clients.

Hagen keeps his eyes on me, his stare like an ice pick trying to dig out what I know or what I don't, but it's Vivienne who blows his secret. "We know," she says, her tone soft as silk, her red lips around a smile bright and cold as winter moonlight. "We know about your call to Katherine Stern, Max. We know about your offer to buy the Dürer from her, if she ever gets her hands on it. I can understand you not telling Cantor, but not telling me? Really, Max? After all the business we've done together? All the museum business I've steered your way?"

"My dear Vivienne," he says, his voice thick with false benevolence as if speaking to a hopelessly ignorant child, "surely you don't expect me to share everything? You certainly don't share the museum's secrets with me."

It never fails to fascinate me, the way Vivienne's chin tilts up, the way her eyes narrow as she assumes that regal bearing she trots out when the common folk—even rich common folk like Hagen—becomes presumptuous. "I don't have to share," she says with a chill in it. "I'm not pursuing the Dürer to make money."

"Well, how fortunate for you," Hagen says. "Some of us need to make our way in the world, and we rather enjoy it, too. Wouldn't you agree, Gold?"

"Sure," I say. "It's a regular barrel of laughs. Why, in just the last few days my life's been graced with two grisly killings, cops with guns and handcuffs coming at me from one side, and gangsters with more guns coming at me from the other. I don't remember the last time I've had this much fun."

Hagen's looking at me as if I've introduced a vulgar odor into the room. Vivienne's looking at me with a surprising hint of fear. It must've been my bit about cops and gangsters that upset them. The Jacobson and Stern killings certainly haven't shaken these two cold and selfish paragons of the art game. "Listen, Hagen," I say, "when I visited Mrs. Stern after her husband's funeral, she'd never heard of Albrecht Dürer and had no idea she'd married into a family that owned one of his watercolors. And by the time I visited her again tonight, she was swimming in a bottle of bourbon, barely able to tell me her name, never mind give me any useful information. But maybe when you spoke to her this afternoon, before she got lost in her heavy drinking, she was sober enough to know what's what. So my question is this: What did she say when you made her an offer for the Dürer?"

Glad to be talking about things more comfortable and familiar to him than my world of predatory cops and bloodthirsty gangsters, the irritation is gone from Hagen's face, replaced by his usual air of high culture. "She said she'd think about it. But of course, until the picture is found," he adds with a showy wave of his well-manicured hand, "it's all moot."

"Uh-huh. Did she seem frightened? Like maybe her life was next in line after the deaths of her sister-in-law and her husband?"

"No. Why? Oh!"

"Oh, what?" I say.

"You're right, Gold, she certainly should have been frightened, unless, of course, *she* killed them! It wouldn't be the first time a wife did away with her husband to collect an inheritance."

I toss that away. "Nope. Won't work. Katherine Stern was with her daughter in the limousine on their way home from the cemetery, far ahead of me when her husband was killed in my car."

"Oh, I see. Yes, of course."

Vivienne, finishing her cognac, says, "And besides, Cantor seems to think I killed Hannah Jacobson and Marcus Stern." She says it as if it amuses her and takes a long, haughty drag on her smoke.

A light glints in Hagen's eyes, flickers brighter, then settles into an easy glow fueled by cunning. "Well, there's an idea," he says.

Vivienne's surprise snuffs her amusement. She stubs out her cigarette in an ashtray on the coffee table with a fast, nervous rat-a-tat tapping, her red polished fingers flashing in the firelight. "Don't joke, Max."

"But I'm not joking," he says. "It makes perfect sense." Hagen's pleasure in this scenario has all the charm of a circling vulture, smiling as if he can't wait to feast on Vivienne's bountiful carcass. The smug cheeriness in his voice makes me wonder how long he's wanted to take her down. "And you could do it, too, Vivienne. You're a first-rate huntress, an excellent shot, and strong, too. I've seen you bag a running buck from a hundred feet and then skin him with ease. No doubt about it, my dear, you're athletic enough to have cut up poor Mrs. Jacobson, and you've got the skill to pick off Marcus Stern." Hagen's smile is a thin crease of knifelike sparkle, and then he digs that knife even deeper, twisting it into Vivienne's very soul. "Oh, and let's not forget there's violence in that tawdry Trent family of yours."

The guy's overblown sense of triumph annoys me, and I'm caught off guard by how much it annoys me, considering he's strengthened my case to nab Vivienne as the killer. Maybe that's what annoys me. Maybe I wanted to be proven wrong.

Hagen stands up from the couch with the puffed-up seriousness of a mind too easily satisfied. "Well, Gold, I must admit, you've done it. You've solved the case. Very clever of you to recognize Miss Parkhurst Trent as a cold-blooded killer. Perhaps we should call the authorities?"

But Vivienne's not down for the count. She might be nervous, she might be facing the electric chair, but she stands up and gives Hagen a stare that pins him to the wall. "Wouldn't that be oh so convenient for you, Max. With me out of the way, you'd get rid of the competition for the Dürer—that is, if Cantor ever finds it."

I'm about to stub out my smoke to hide my enjoyment of the verbal shoving match going on between Vivienne and Hagen, when I hear a gentle male voice say, "Finds what?" It's Vern. He's walking into the den, and the whole world turns upside down.

CHAPTER EIGHTEEN

I nearly trip over the coffee table. Vivienne asks if I'm all right.

"Yeah, fine," I say, more a mumble than a certainty as Vern sashays over to me. He puts one hand on his hip, fingers the lapel of my suit jacket with his other hand, says, "Well hello again, Cantor Gold. Why the shocked expression? I'd think a fashionable sort like you would appreciate my style," and lifts the veil of his hat. It's a wide-brimmed black Victorian number, perfect for a woman attending a funeral.

Vern, as svelte and elegant in his black cocktail dress and black elbow-length gloves as he was in his trim tuxedo last night, slinks gracefully on high-heeled pumps over to Hagen while I stand there, numb, the brutal acts of the recent days and nights slipping through my mind and circling around this cross dressing, red-lipsticked vision of a femme fatale who's taken over the room. "Darling," he says to Hagen, though the pronoun *he* doesn't really fit the bill for Vern tonight, "where are you? The party is winding down and everyone wants to say good night before they go upstairs." With an affectionate stroke of Hagen's cheek, his pale green nail-polished fingertips brushing across Hagen's lips, Vern coos, "And I want to go upstairs, too."

With no prudish guests or closed-minded clients in the next room who could barge in and discover Hagen's secret, ruin his reputation and his career, Hagen's more at ease with Vern tonight than he was in his Park Avenue study. He's free to return his lover's affection, which he does through the tenderness in his eyes and a doting smile.

Their romance is touching, I'm even envious of their happiness, but it shatters my open-and-shut case against Vivienne as the killer, throws all the broken pieces around the room. I don't understand how to fit all the broken pieces back together. I don't understand who belongs where in the splintered puzzle: Vivienne's the dame with the motive, but Vern's the dame with the hat.

Hagen gently disentangles himself from Vern. "Vern's right," he says, and reaches for the telephone on the side table. "I really must see to my guests, and then get to bed. Vern and I have an early start in the morning. We're preparing the hunt breakfast, you know, so we need to wind this up and call the authorities, let them take Vivienne away." He starts to dial.

Two hands, Vivienne's and mine, move fast and at the same time, but hers comes down on the phone first, stopping Hagen from dialing.

The surprise on Vivienne's face as she throws me a quick glance is equal to the surprise and confusion on Hagen's face and the plain old confusion on Vern's, whose hand is back on his hip, diva style. He asks Hagen, "Why do you want the authorities to take Vivienne away?"

"Because she's a killer. Did you know she murdered two people?"

"Really?"

"Yes, really. She knifed a poor old woman and shot the woman's brother."

"Oh my," Vern says so casually you'd think Hagen said nothing more alarming than maybe Vivienne swiped a couple of sandwiches from a lunchroom.

Graceful as a swan aware of his own beauty, Vern bends to take a cigarette from the box on the coffee table. He rises, supple and slinky, slips the cigarette between his lips, and waits for Hagen to light it, which Hagen dutifully does with the gold lighter from his pocket.

Still holding the phone's receiver in his other hand, Hagen says to me, "Listen, Gold, I want this business over with. I can understand Vivienne preventing me from calling the police—I'm sure she'd rather not go to jail. But I don't understand your motive at all."

"No, I guess you wouldn't. But maybe Vern does."

Pretty Vern eyes me like he woke up from a pleasant dream only to find a monster standing at the foot of the bed. He lowers the hat veil, hiding, I guess, from the monster that scared him, as he sashays across the room and leans against the pistol rack, lithe as a ballet dancer. "Why, I have no idea what you're talking about."

Hagen chimes in, "And neither do I."

Vivienne says, "But I do," and sits down again on the sofa with renewed poise and a small but satisfied smile. "Or at least I'm beginning to, and it certainly gets me off the hook."

But I kill her ease. "You're not off the hook yet, dearie. You're still my best bet. You've got a motive I can put my finger on. All Vern has is a veiled hat."

Hagen, finally catching on, his eyebrows rising, his mustache spreading over a sneer, slams the phone down and snaps at me. "Just a minute, Gold. You can't be serious. Are you really suggesting Vern killed two people? Why would he?"

"Oh, I don't know," I say with a smart-alecky shrug. "Why wouldn't he? Hannah Jacobson and Marcus Stern were killed for the Dürer watercolor. Maybe Vern wanted it for you, Hagen. Maybe you even sent him to get it."

Seems like an odd time for Hagen to enjoy a laugh, even a small one, but he's laughing all right, a rolling chuckle lathered in ridicule. "Preposterous! I'd never send Vern on such an errand. He wouldn't know the difference between a Dürer and a picture in a coloring book."

"He wouldn't have to," I say. "He'd just—"

An incensed Vern cuts me off. "How do you know I wouldn't know the difference?" The veil's up again on Vern's hat, revealing his face. There's enough pain in it to bring even a stony brute to tears. "Why do you always think I'm stupid, Max?"

Hagen extends a hand to Vern as he walks over to him, tries to soothe him, says, "No, I don't think any—"

"Sure you do, Max! You treat me like a toy, a dumb toy you like to pet and play with. And you don't like it if I don't always play along, when sometimes I'm even more...more..." He bleats a rough laugh, plants his cigarette in the corner of his mouth, thug-like, says, "When I'm more *manly* than you. That's right, like when we're out hunting, and I'm the better shot."

Hagen, pale and gray faced, sees his world falling apart before his eyes. He opens his mouth, tries to speak, tries to say the words that will put his fairy-tale world back together again, but Vern's not done demolishing it. "Look at you, Max, you who usually have so many words, all the right words, smooth and elegant words you use with your snobby clients when you push me out of sight. Well, I've got some words of my own. Here, I'll toss them at you." He throws his arm back like a baseball pitcher, a bizarre sight in his cocktail dress and gloves, then flings his arm forward as he tosses out each word in a frenzy. "*I! Love! You!* You hear that? I love you, Max. I'd do anything for you."

I jump at my moment, grab hold of Vern's blind hysteria and squeeze it. "Even kill?"

Hagen shouts, "Don't answer that, Vern. Don't say anything else until we contact my attorney, understand?"

But Vern's anger and pain have spiraled out of Hagen's reach. "Still telling me what to do, Max? Still trying to silence me? Well, that's over. From now on, you'll show a little appreciation for the things I do, things like trying to get that Dürer picture for you. You wanted it so much," he says, his last grip on rationality giving way to convulsive tears that shake him all the way down to his high-heeled pumps. "I—I saw how much you wanted it, my love. You nearly swooned whenever you talked about it, and you know how much I hate it when you're frustrated or upset, so I decided to get it for you. Because I adore you, Max. But that old lady wouldn't give it up. She kept lying, kept saying she didn't have it. Her lies drove me wild, so I shut her up, slashed her mouth. And when she tried to fight me, I cut the rest of her."

All Hagen can do is beg, "Vern, stop, please."

"What's the matter, Max? Don't you want to know how much I love you? Don't you want to know how hard I tried to get that picture from that old bat and then from her brother? But he was stubborn, too. So the next day, I went to his sister's funeral. I figured I'd scare him into giving it up. I was going to show him the rifle I'd brought along, flash it around for him, maybe shoot a bird or a squirrel to show him I mean business, you know, just for a little theatrical incentive." The memory makes him laugh. His shrill, mad giggle makes me cringe, and it makes Hagen cry silent, tormented tears, which Vern doesn't even notice. He just races on. "But I never got the chance to talk to him, because I saw him go off with someone, and now I know it was with you, Gold. You spoiled everything! I couldn't let that happen. I couldn't let you team up with Stern and get your hands on that Dürer picture. If my Max couldn't have it, no one would." Vern wipes his runny nose on his arm with all the grace of a stevedore, the delicate fabric of his elbow-length glove forgotten. "So I followed your car—it's a beauty, all shiny and new, easy to spot—and then pulled over when the traffic in your lane got thick. Lucky break for me. With traffic crawling to a standstill, and your pretty car shining in the sun, all I had to do was wait for my moment, and blam!" His arms are raised, shooting his imaginary rifle. "I always was the better shot, Max," he says with a cheery smile that chills me.

Hagen hasn't said a word. He probably can't. He'd probably choke on whatever words came out of his mouth. His tears are doing his talking for him.

Vivienne says, "You could use a drink, Max," and gets up from the couch. She pours him a stiff gin, hands it to him, and then walks to the other end of the room, tossing me a sly smile along the way. She's officially off the hook now, and she's not about to let me forget it.

It's time to end this thing. It's time for me to thrust the real killer into Lieutenant Huber's bony, vicious face.

"Listen, Vern," I say, friendly as a barroom buddy, "why don't you come along with me? You can tell me all about your little victory on the drive back to the city." I extend a hand, a courtly gesture to lure the mad diva.

Vern, caught up in the fantasy, reaches to take my hand, but Hagen interferes, slaps my hand away and thrusts his arm across Vern's chest, blocking him. "No. Vern's not going anywhere. Not until I contact my attorney."

"Sorry, Hagen," I say, "you can call a lawyer later, but right now I need to get the cops off my back, and the only way I can do that is to feed them raw meat, the real killer of Hannah Jacobson and Marcus Stern."

"I won't let you take him, Gold."

"I'm not giving you a choice, Hagen." I pull my gun.

Hagen, to my surprise, finds his courage and blocks my way. Well, maybe I'm not so surprised. He's doing what you're supposed to do when you love someone down to their marrow: protect them. It's what I failed to do for Sophie. "What are you going to do, Gold?" Hagen says. "Shoot me?"

"If I have to."

Now it's Vern who shouts, "No!" He has a pistol in his hand. He must've grabbed it from the rack while I was chit-chatting with Hagen. He's pointing the gun past Hagen's head, directly at me, and at this close range, he doesn't have to be a crack shot. All he has to do is pull the trigger to blow my brains out.

A loud *bang* slams across the room, a whine zings past my ear. Blood gushes from Vern's forehead, spattering across Hagen's shocked face, dripping onto his starched white shirt and the shiny lapels of his tuxedo as Vern goes down.

When I turn around, I see an empty spot in the gun rack behind Vivienne and a rifle, aimed across the room, in her grip. Her head is still cocked, her eye still primed along the gun sight. She slowly lowers the rifle.

But she raises it up again when Hagen grabs Vern's gun and aims it at her, his bloody face ugly with rage.

Vivienne is calm as a sunny day in winter. All she says is, "Don't Max. Just don't."

CHAPTER NINETEEN

In the game of life, New York crooks the wheel. It gives a few people everything, a lot of people nothing, and everyone else gets squeezed between the boot at the top and the snapping jaws at the bottom. But it's that grinding friction, that live-or-die danger, which sparks our air and ignites the great talents, and even greater dreams, of the city's striving hordes. It's what gives us the best of everything, and beats us up with the worst.

A bit of the best, a cup of Doris's coffee at the counter of Pete's luncheonette, helps revive me after a crummy, sleepless night. I'm tired and punchy and find myself idly staring at the ripples my breath makes across the surface of the coffee. Gets me thinking, yeah, the city is like that, its breath rippling across the whole damn state, inflating the lungs of the greedy, the needy, and the upstate Law. That's why Vivienne will get away with, well, maybe not murder, but a killing, no questions asked.

I'm sure I'll need a second cup of coffee, maybe even a third, and just as sure I'll spike the cup with another hefty drop of scotch from the flask in my jacket pocket. The coffee keeps me awake, but the scotch makes the events of my no-sleep night bearable, though I'll probably never get comfortable with the memory of Max Hagen on his knees, wailing over the body of his beloved Vern. Hagen's cry, raw and guttural, like the suffering of something primeval, is still drilling through my ears.

And Hagen's misery wasn't the worst of it. The rest of the goings-on at his country house may not have been as dramatic, but in the honor department, it was a whole lot shabbier. At Vivienne's direction, which actually was more forceful than shabby, Hagen's mortified party guests made themselves scarce, throwing coats over tuxedos and gowns and leaving the house so fast you'd think someone yelled fire. I can't blame 'em, really. The Law, when it finally arrived, would've taken their statements and then tossed them in the clink or the psycho ward, stuff I've been dodging since I put on my first suit.

After the party guests were gone, Vivienne made a couple of long distance calls back to the city, and after twenty minutes or so, during which time Vivienne and I said nothing, but drank a lot, the local cops arrived. They were accompanied by the mayor of whatever little town has jurisdiction over Hagen's rural property. The mayor, a short, ruddy guy in a pinstriped brown suit with lapels that hadn't been cut that wide since 1935, had a few words with Vivienne, and another few words with the lead cop. Hannah Jacobson's name was thrown around, and Marcus Stern's, too, and mine, and two others I didn't recognize, but they weren't the sort of names I would've heard in my old Coney Island neighborhood. They were more in line with Vivienne's crowd. The little mayor then declared Vern's killing justifiable. I was hardly in a position to argue.

Ten minutes after that, the boys from a funeral parlor arrived, carted Vern away, and except for the last milling around of the mayor and the cops, and Hagen collapsing on the couch, that was that. Vivienne was never seriously questioned. She'll never be questioned at all. There will be no inquest. Vivienne Parkhurst Trent, and whoever she phoned, whoever's fancy names she tossed into the hayseed mayor's ear, rule the world.

But I suppose Vern got what he deserved; justice done, another killer meeting his own violent end. Same story, I tell myself, about Jimmy Shea. And now Lieutenant Huber's off my back, too. Seems he got a phone call from the precinct captain who got a call from the police commissioner who got a call from New York's mayor who got a call from I don't know who, but Vivienne probably does. Evidently everyone along the chain is happy to let the upstate cops take credit for closing the book on a big-city double homicide. Everyone except Huber, who I have no doubt will keep shadowing me like a bad dream.

So justice, if not the Law, got its pound of flesh. Hell, the Law would've fried Vern anyway. Jimmy Shea, too, if it ever got the goods on him.

But it's tainted justice. Too cunning. Too hidden. Sure, I don't trust the Law, but solid citizens do, and they have the right to make sure justice is done in daylight.

Fat chance. The idea's so funny, I gotta laugh, nearly spit up my coffee.

I pour another dollop of Chivas into my cup. I doubt the whiskey will quiet Hagen's keening cry in my bones or sort out my feelings about Vivienne's jeweled hand on New York's rigged wheel, but the booze might help me figure out what to do about the Dürer watercolor still hidden in my office vault. I've got five choices, none of them sweet. The first one involves Vivienne. If I give it to Vivienne's museum, I won't learn anything about the freighter that took Sophie, but a lot of people will see the Dürer, maybe be as captivated as I am by its beauty. After all the ugliness that's followed that picture around, all the blood spilled over it, it might be a graceful ending to its story. The spirit of Hannah Jacobson might even approve.

Or I could give it to Francine and Katherine Stern, who are Mrs. Jacobson's family after all. That would satisfy the legal angle, but the idea of sending it into that witches' brew turns my stomach.

I could make a deal with Hagen. He may be grieving, but I bet he'd still be receptive to a big-money deal. I've never been queasy about lining my pockets with the help of the bereaved.

And then there's Sig Loreale. I could hand it over to Sig, who may be a monster but he's a monster who's as good as his word. He'd use his considerable resources to find the freighter that stole Sophie from me. But giving the Dürer to Sig feels like blood money for having Jimmy Shea killed on my behalf, a killing he's made me complicit in. On the other hand, if I don't give Sig the Dürer, chances are good he'll have me killed, too.

Or I could do nothing at all. No one knows I have it. I could just hold on to it, enjoy it for myself, or maybe sell it to an out-of-town or out-of-the-country buyer on the sly, cut Hagen out altogether. The idea has a lot of appeal; big money is just a phone call away.

"*Now* what's the matter, Cantor?" It's the cigarette voice of Doris, who's ready with another pour of coffee. "Yesterday you sat here lookin' like someone just killed your dog. Today you look like the dog that got killed. What's up with you?"

I give her a shrug, say, "I'm trying to figure life out, Doris."

She pours the coffee, then looks me straight in the eye. "What's to figure? I already told you. Everything in this life is about love or money. Cantor, what's goin' on? You look like you just seen a ghost."

I get up from my stool at the counter, head to the back of the luncheonette.

I drop a nickel into the pay phone on the wall, dial a number. When the other end picks up, I say, "Hello, Sig."

About the Author

Ann Aptaker has earned a reputation as respected curator and exhibition designer during her career in museums and galleries. She has curated and organized exhibitions across the cultural spectrum, from fine art to popular culture. Her work has garnered favorable reviews in the *New York Times*, *Art in America*, *American Art Review*, and other publications. In addition to her curatorial assignments, Ann is an art writer and Adjunct Professor of Art and Art History at New York Institute of Technology.

Ann's debut novel, *Criminal Gold*, Book One in the Cantor Gold crime series, received outstanding reviews and was honored as a Goldie Award finalist in the Debut Author category.

Follow Ann's Facebook page, Ann Aptaker, Author, and on Twitter, @AnnAptaker

Books Available from Bold Strokes Books

Deadly Medicine by Jaime Maddox. Dr. Ward Thrasher's life is in turmoil. Her partner Jess has left her, and her job puts her in the path of a murderous physician who has Jess in his sights. (978-1-62639-4-247)

New Beginnings by KC Richardson. Can the connection and attraction between Jordan Roberts and Kirsten Murphy be enough for Jordan to trust Kirsten with her heart? (978-1-62639-4-506)

Officer Down by Erin Dutton. Can two women who've made careers out of being there for others in crisis find the strength to need each other? (978-1-62639-4-230)

Reasonable Doubt by Carsen Taite. Just when Sarah and Ellery think they've left dangerous careers behind, a new case sets them—and their hearts—on a collision course. (978-1-62639-4-421)

Tarnished Gold by Ann Aptaker. Cantor Gold must outsmart the Law, outrun New York's dockside gangsters, outplay a shady art dealer, his lover, and a beautiful curator, and stay out of a killer's gun sights. (978-1-62639-4-261)

The Renegade by Amy Dunne. Post-apocalyptic survivors Alex and Evelyn secretly find love while held captive by a deranged cult, but when their relationship is discovered, they must fight for their freedom—or die trying. (978-1-62639-4-278)

Thrall by Barbara Ann Wright. Four women in a warrior society must work together to lift an insidious curse while caught between their own desires, the will of their peoples, and an ancient evil. (978-1-62639-4-377)

White Horse in Winter by Franci McMahon. Love between two women collides with the inner poison of a closeted horse trainer in the green hills of Vermont. (978-1-62639-4-292)

The Chameleon by Andrea Bramhall. Two old friends must work through a web of lies and deceit to find themselves again, but in the search they discover far more than they ever went looking for. (978-1-62639-363-9)

Side Effects by VK Powell. Detective Jordan Bishop and Dr. Neela Sahjani must decide if it's easier to trust someone with your heart or your life as they face threatening protestors, corrupt politicians, and their increasing attraction. (978-1-62639-364-6)

Autumn Spring by Shelley Thrasher. Can Bree and Linda, two women in the autumn of their lives, put their hearts first and find the love they've never dared seize? (978-1-62639-365-3)

Warm November by Kathleen Knowles. What do you do if the one woman you want is the only one you can't have? (978-1-62639-366-0)

In Every Cloud by Tina Michele. When she finally leaves her shattered life behind, is Bree strong enough to salvage the remaining pieces of her heart and find the place where it truly fits? (978-1-62639-413-1)

Rise of the Gorgon by Tanai Walker. When independent Internet journalist Elle Pharell goes to Kuwait to investigate a veteran's mysterious suicide, she hires Cassandra Hunt, an interpreter with a covert agenda. (978-1-62639-367-7)

Crossed by Meredith Doench. Agent Luce Hansen returns home to catch a killer and risks everything to revisit the unsolved murder of her first girlfriend and confront the demons of her youth. (978-1-62639-361-5)

Making a Comeback by Julie Blair. Music and love take center stage when jazz pianist Liz Randall tries to make a comeback with the help of her reclusive, blind neighbor, Jac Winters. (978-1-62639-357-8)

Soul Unique by Gun Brooke. Self-proclaimed cynic Greer Landon falls for Hayden Rowe's paintings and the young woman shortly after, but will Hayden, who lives with Asperger syndrome, trust her and reciprocate her feelings? (978-1-62639-358-5)

The Price of Honor by Radclyffe. Honor and duty are not always black and white—and when self-styled patriots take up arms against the government, the price of honor may be a life. (978-1-62639-359-2)

Mounting Evidence by Karis Walsh. Lieutenant Abigail Hargrove and her mounted police unit need to solve a murder and protect wetland biologist Kira Lovell during the Washington State Fair. (978-1-62639-343-1)

Threads of the Heart by Jeannie Levig. Maggie and Addison Rae-McInnis share a love and a life, but are the threads that bind them together strong enough to withstand Addison's restlessness and the seductive Victoria Fontaine? (978-1-62639-410-0)

Sheltered Love by MJ Williamz. Boone Fairway and Grey Dawson—two women touched by abuse—overcome their pasts to find happiness in each other. (978-1-62639-362-2)

Asher's Out by Elizabeth Wheeler. Asher Price's candid photographs capture the truth, but when his success requires exposing an enemy, Asher discovers his only shot at happiness involves revealing secrets of his own. (978-1-62639-411-7)

The Ground Beneath by Missouri Vaun. An improbable barter deal involving a hope chest and dinners for a month places lovely

Jessica Walker distractingly in the way of Sam Casey's bachelor lifestyle. (978-1-62639-606-7)

Hardwired by C.P. Rowlands. Award-winning teacher Clary Stone, and Leefe Ellis, manager of the homeless shelter for small children, stand together in a part of Clary's hometown that she never knew existed. (978-1-62639-351-6)

No Good Reason by Cari Hunter. A violent kidnapping in a Peak District village pushes Detective Sanne Jensen and lifelong friend Dr. Meg Fielding closer, just as it threatens to tear everything apart. (978-1-62639-352-3)

Romance by the Book by Jo Victor. If Cam didn't keep disrupting her life, maybe Alex could uncover the secret of a century-old love story, and solve the greatest mystery of all—her own heart. (978-1-62639-353-0)

Death's Doorway by Crin Claxton. Helping the dead can be deadly: Tony may be listening to the dead, but she needs to learn to listen to the living. (978-1-62639-354-7)

Searching for Celia by Elizabeth Ridley. As American spy novelist Dayle Salvesen investigates the mysterious disappearance of her ex-lover, Celia, in London, she begins questioning how well she knew Celia—and how well she knows herself. (978-1-62639-356-1)

The 45th Parallel by Lisa Girolami. Burying her mother isn't the worst thing that can happen to Val Montague when she returns to the woodsy but peculiar town of Hemlock, Oregon. (978-1-62639-342-4)

A Royal Romance by Jenny Frame. In a country where class still divides, can love topple the last social taboo and allow Queen

Georgina and Beatrice Elliot, a working class girl, their happy ever after? (978-1-62639-360-8)

Bouncing by Jaime Maddox. Basketball Coach Alex Dalton has been bouncing from woman to woman, because no one ever held her interest, until she meets her new assistant, Britain Dodge. (978-1-62639-344-8)

Same Time Next Week by Emily Smith. A chance encounter between Alex Harris and the beautiful Michelle Masters leads to a whirlwind friendship, and causes Alex to question everything she's ever known—including her own marriage. (978-1-62639-345-5)

All Things Rise by Missouri Vaun. Cole rescues a striking pilot who crash-lands near her family's farm, setting in motion a chain of events that will forever alter the course of her life. (978-1-62639-346-2)

Riding Passion by D. Jackson Leigh. Mount up for the ride through a sizzling anthology of chance encounters, buried desires, romantic surprises, and blazing passion. (978-1-62639-349-3)

Love's Bounty by Yolanda Wallace. Lobster boat captain Jake Myers stopped living the day she cheated death, but meeting greenhorn Shy Silva stirs her back to life. (978-1-62639-334-9)

Just Three Words by Melissa Brayden. Sometimes the one you want is the one you least suspect. Accountant Samantha Ennis has her ordered life disrupted when heartbreaker Hunter Blair moves into her trendy Soho loft. (978-1-62639-335-6)

Lay Down the Law by Carsen Taite. Attorney Peyton Davis returns to her Texas roots to take on big oil and the Mexican Mafia, but will her investigation thwart her chance at true love? (978-1-62639-336-3)

Playing in Shadow by Lesley Davis. Survivor's guilt threatens to keep Bryce trapped in her nightmare world unless Scarlet's love can pull her out of the darkness back into the light. (978-1-62639-337-0)

Soul Selecta by Gill McKnight. Soul mates are hell to work with. (978-1-62639-338-7)

The Revelation of Beatrice Darby by Jean Copeland. Adolescence is complicated, but Beatrice Darby is about to discover how impossible it can seem to a lesbian coming of age in conservative 1950s New England. (978-1-62639-339-4)

Twice Lucky by Mardi Alexander. For firefighter Mackenzie James and Dr. Sarah Macarthur, there's suddenly a whole lot more in life to understand, to consider, to risk…someone will need to fight for her life. (978-1-62639-325-7)

Shadow Hunt by L.L. Raand. With young to raise and her Pack under attack, Sylvan, Alpha of the wolf Weres, takes on her greatest challenge when she determines to uncover the faceless enemies known as the Shadow Lords. A Midnight Hunters novel. (978-1-62639-326-4)

Heart of the Game by Rachel Spangler. A baseball writer falls for a single mom, but can she ever love anything as much as she loves the game? (978-1-62639-327-1)

Getting Lost by Michelle Grubb. Twenty-eight days, thirteen European countries, a tour manager fighting attraction, and an accused murderer: Stella and Phoebe's journey of a lifetime begins here. (978-1-62639-328-8)

Prayer of the Handmaiden by Merry Shannon. Celibate priestess Kadrian must defend the kingdom of Ithyria from a dangerous enemy and ultimately choose between her duty to the Goddess and the love of her childhood sweetheart, Erinda. (978-1-62639-329-5)

The Witch of Stalingrad by Justine Saracen. A Soviet "night witch" pilot and American journalist meet on the Eastern Front in WW II and struggle through carnage, conflicting politics, and the deadly Russian winter. (978-1-62639-330-1)

Pedal to the Metal by Jesse J. Thoma. When unreformed thief Dubs Williams is released from prison to help Max Winters bust a car theft ring, Max learns that to catch a thief, get in bed with one. (978-1-62639-239-7)

Dragon Horse War by D. Jackson Leigh. A priestess of peace and a fiery warrior must defeat a vicious uprising that entwines their destinies and ultimately their hearts. (978-1-62639-240-3)

For the Love of Cake by Erin Dutton. When everything is on the line, and one taste can break a heart, will pastry chefs Maya and Shannon take a chance on reality? (978-1-62639-241-0)

Betting on Love by Alyssa Linn Palmer. A quiet country-girl-at-heart and a live-life-to-the-fullest biker take a risk at offering each other their hearts. (978-1-62639-242-7)

The Deadening by Yvonne Heidt. The lines between good and evil, right and wrong, have always been blurry for Shade. When Raven's actions force her to choose, which side will she come out on? (978-1-62639-243-4)